CW01024906

Silly Beggars

by

S Ben Hawksworth

Grosvenor House
Publishing Limited

All rights reserved
Copyright © S Ben Hawksworth, 2024

The right of S Ben Hawksworth to be identified as the author of this
work has been asserted in accordance with Section 78
of the Copyright, Designs and Patents Act 1988

The book cover is copyright to S Ben Hawksworth
Book cover design by Brian Jones

This book is published by
Grosvenor House Publishing Ltd
Link House
140 The Broadway, Tolworth, Surrey, KT6 7HT.
www.grosvenorhousepublishing.co.uk

This book is sold subject to the conditions that it shall not, by way of
trade or otherwise, be lent, resold, hired out or otherwise circulated
without the author's or publisher's prior consent in any form of
binding or cover other than that in which it is published and
without a similar condition including this condition being
imposed on the subsequent purchaser.

This book is a work of fiction. Any resemblance to
people or events, past or present, is purely coincidental.

A CIP record for this book
is available from the British Library

ISBN 978-1-80381-904-4

All royalties earned by the author will be donated to
Alzheimer's Research UK – alzheimersresearchuk.org

In memory of my wife Lynne.
Alzheimer's took her but not my memories of her love.

When your mind began to slowly fade
And you drifted in to your own reality,
My logic had to argue that you were deluded.
Everyone knew you can't go back to happier times,
To talk with your father,
To ask where your mother was,
To live in a distant loving home,
To which you longed to return each evening.
Everyone knew but you.
Your reality was different, but every bit as real as ours.
I fought to bring you back
And in so doing I became your nemesis.
My arguments were seen as cruel
And my attentiveness deemed insincere and unwanted.
I see you now as you look out from behind your eyes.
Eyes that once sparkled with joy and love
But faded eyes that now show mere disdain for me.
You don't remember the man who was your lover for fifty years
You now only see the man who became the target of your anger.
For all this, I am sorry,
Sorry I acted in the way I did,
Sorry that you have no feelings for me
But most importantly,
Sorry that you can't understand that I still love you.

CHAPTER ONE

The image created by TV commercials of suburban families at breakfast is generally one of domestic bliss. Dad, clean-cut and handsome, smiles benevolently upon his beautiful wife, who has apparently spent hours applying make-up and selecting an appropriate outfit. Their audacious flirting goes largely unnoticed by their ideal family unit of one daughter, pretty and polite, and one son, a little on the unkempt side with a tendency to be ever so slightly naughty but in an endearing way. Convivial music plays while the room is bathed in sunlight, reflected by the golden cereal in their bowls.

The Sullivan household did not match this image on that November morning. The kitchen was not bathed in glorious warming sunlight, and a glance from the kitchen window showed a back garden that was grey rather than golden. Clive might be described as the head of the family, although it was a title he would never presume to seek and one which his wife would contest, and he sat finishing off his honey on toast while trying to read through the morning mail with his sticky fingers before suddenly looking up and declaring, "The old bugger's dead!"

It had been one of those thinking-out-loud moments, and one Clive immediately knew he would regret. Maureen looked sharply over the top of her morning paper and with a dramatic show of disapproval said, "Clive. The children!"

He followed her gaze around the breakfast table where the 'children' had been singularly unimpressed by his utterance. Nichole sipped her fruit tea and continued to read through the article she was to discuss at her tutorial at the university that morning while Sebastian was engrossed in conversation on his mobile phone, negotiating the price of a car he had for sale. Clearly neither 'child' had been shocked by his language.

Clive resumed reading the letter that had arrived with the usual plethora of unwanted junk mail that morning while the family got on with their separate breakfast routines. Maureen was reading her paper while drinking a black coffee and nibbling at something that appeared to have the consistency of cardboard and which she covered with her own expensive continental preserve. As ever, she was immaculately made-up with not a hair out of place and dressed in a smart business suit upon which not one crumb of her breakfast cardboard would ever dare to fall. Clive looked at his wife; she had put considerable effort into keeping her good looks, and in a way he was glad because he felt she had done so to please him, and he still found her very attractive. It would be true to say that Maureen had weathered well, a fact she was keen to point out to Clive to whom she would frequently say, "I can still fit into my wedding dress, and that's more than you can say."

He had never harboured any desire to try on her dress but knew that any attempt to enter into such a pedantic argument would be futile. He had to concede that he would have considerable difficulty in getting into his own wedding outfit these days; indeed, he would have difficulty with most of his clothes from that day, with the possible exception of his handkerchief.

He wasn't fat, but his youthful athleticism had long since disappeared, and his interest in rugby had degenerated from his being a half-decent player to someone who now just talked a good game. It would take only a tertiary glance to recognise that he didn't share Maureen's preoccupation with always

2

having to appear at one's best. His clothes were comfortable while her outfits were designed to impress; his found their way to the floor in his bedroom each night while hers were examined minutely, brushed and hung in one of her immaculately organised wardrobes. Her outfits were elegant, his were shabby chic but without the chic; she made clothes look good on her while, even when dressed up, he succeeded in making all his outfits look as if they had been tailor-made for someone else.

Sebastian shared his mother's love of clothes, and he dressed to impress. It was no exaggeration to say that he could pay more for one shirt than Clive would spend on a suit, and this expensive taste extended to his entire wardrobe despite the fact that his personal finances had never stretched to such extravagance. He endeavoured to cultivate the appearance of a young trader from the floor of the stock exchange but despite all his expensive clothes and grooming, only succeeded in looking like a junior car salesman, which is exactly what he was. He worked for a major car franchise outlet in town but made no secret of the fact that this was a temporary situation while he continued to carry out his own private deals so he could set himself up in business. This ambition was thwarted because he had little business sense and was inherently lazy. Sebastian laboured under the illusion that the world owed him a living and that it should have delivered yesterday. Thus he continued to make losses in most of his private dealings. His current investment, which was preoccupying him over breakfast, was no exception, and Clive suspected that once again there was little likelihood of Sebastian paying his board this month.

Nichole was completely unlike her brother. She dressed casually, took life pretty much as it came and showed little interest in material things. These qualities, combined with the fact that she had inherited her mother's good looks, made her very popular with her fellow students at the university. Clive was also aware that she could twist him around her little finger, and it was this that had persuaded him to buy her the puppy she had always wanted. The purchase, which was made after one of Clive's more congenial sessions at the pub, was not received well by Maureen, who viewed the prospect of a hairy muck-magnet in her home in a less than positive light. Initially, Clive had tried to pass the dog off as a home security feature, but its placid nature and love of anyone who visited the house meant that his lack of deterrence value was soon apparent and his original name of Tyson was quickly replaced by a less aggressive one of Arkwright. It was only because he refused to go into Maureen's room that persuaded her to let him stay. He would approach the doorway but then whimper and make it quite clear he wasn't going in. Thus it was that Arkwright's presence was suffered by Maureen, and he took up his role, not so much as guard as plate and dish cleaner. It was his eagerness to carry out this function which caused him to sit patiently looking up at the kitchen table, waiting for his breakfast.

"Which old bugger's dead?" enquired Nichole, looking up from her journal.

Maureen gave Clive one of her looks that would have seriously injured a man who had not developed a degree of immunity from repeated exposure to those piercing glares.

"It's Norman Hargreaves, the guy I used to work for in Hull."

"In the days when you had a real job," interjected Maureen pointedly, without lifting her eyes from her paper.

"I do have a real job. I may not be a captain of industry and earning a big salary, but my job is important to me."

Maureen briskly folded her paper before declaring, "Well, one of us has to earn decent money to give us a reasonable standard of living after you opted out of the responsibility."

The embers of a long-standing argument were threatening to re-ignite, but in his role as peacekeeper, Clive chose to try to divert the conversation away from his employment status and resumed his discussion with Nichole.

"It seems that Norman died recently. It doesn't give any details, but I have been invited to attend the reading of his will up in Hull next week. The solicitors suggest that I may hear something to my advantage."

On hearing this last phrase, Sebastian's interest was aroused, and he assailed his father with a barrage of questions.

"So you think you might have inherited a few quid? He must have been worth a bob or two. Did he have children or other relatives? Weren't you always a friend of his?"

Clive winced at the ill-concealed avarice displayed by the salvo of questions, and he took a perverse delight in responding. "He was just my employer in the paint business that went bust shortly after I left, and he had dozens of relatives, most of whom seemed to work for him in the company, so don't give up your day job."

Sebastian was obviously disappointed at this response, and with a despondent shrug he returned to his trade paper to make his fortune in some other way.

"That old skinflint wouldn't leave you a penny," added Maureen. "You spent twenty-odd years working for him and keeping the business going, despite the efforts of his own family to screw the whole thing up, and what did he do for you? Nothing; he didn't try and persuade you to stay on when you had your breakdown. No, just waved you off into unemployment and penury."

Clive was one of the most affable individuals one could imagine, but Maureen knew exactly how to hit his response button.

"For the umpteenth time, Maureen, I did not have a breakdown. I simply wanted a change of career, a new path to follow in my life, and Norman appreciated that. He didn't understand my motives, but he didn't try to stop me. Can't you understand that there has to be more to life than earning a big salary?"

"Well, thank goodness one of us grasped the need to bring home the money to put food on the table each month. While you were giving it all up and swanning around in your new hippie lifestyle, I had to get out there and earn enough to support the children and keep a roof over our heads."

Clive was once again amazed at his wife's interpretation of the events surrounding his employment history but recognised that he couldn't win and refused to be drawn further. Instead, he carried out a mental audit of the family home. When he had left the factory, they had a very comfortable home, paid for thanks to a small inheritance from his parents, so what were the big sacrifices that Maureen felt they had needed to make? True, he had lost his company car, but then he had never liked driving and now felt more comfortable taking his bike to work. Maureen had viewed the loss of the car in a markedly different way; having two cars parked on the drive made more of a statement than having one and a bicycle in the garage. Having Sebastian's succession of old heaps on the front over the years had done little to help the image deficit. It was also true that they no longer took two family holidays a year, but latterly they had been little more than a source of irritation to all of them as they never wanted to go to the same places anyway. Maureen had always preferred somewhere fashionable so she could lord it over her friends in the golf club with her tales of the 'sweetest little place' on the Costa-something that was as yet undiscovered by the riff-raff. Sebastian would go anywhere with cheap booze and a tolerance of underage drinking, and Nichole wanted to go somewhere quiet where she didn't have to watch her brother getting drunk. Clive just wanted to stay at home and watch his tomatoes grow and catch up with his reading.

It wasn't as if Maureen had missed her regular holidays as her business involved her in making frequent trips to explore markets in other countries, and this invariably meant staying in some comfortable hotel in an attractive location. As she was quick to point out, you can't represent a high-class cosmetic company and stay in some dingy little hotel on an industrial estate on the outskirts of town somewhere. They had never been short of money, and certainly Maureen's cosmetic company had been doing very well, for which he was very grateful, not so much because it brought money in but because it enabled her to go out.

Maureen looked up at the kitchen clock, washed down the last of a small plateful of assorted vitamin pills and dietary supplements and announced in a less than subtle fashion, "Well, one of us has to get off to work." She then rose elegantly, brushed a non-existent speck from her suit and went through to the hall, where she spent 10 minutes checking her hair and retouching her make-up before leaving.

Clive listened as her car left the drive and felt a calmness descend. Sebastian grabbed his phone, and his trade paper, and a last mouthful of coffee. He could be heard in the hall for a few minutes as he checked his appearance in the mirror before shouting, "Ciao, folks," and leaving the house. His car started up noisily, and off he went with the loud music almost concealing the sound of the dilapidated engine.

"What time's your tutorial today, Nicky?" He used his pet name for her when her mother wasn't around, as she always insisted upon the children having their proper forenames. It had taken weeks to select names of the right calibre, in keeping with Maureen's social aspirations. For some reason, Sebastian was always exactly that, partly because Clive didn't like the sound of Seb and partly because his son had always been a child who liked his full name.

"It's down for 10, but Lusty George is never on time, so I'll get there about a quarter past."

"Why Lusty? Is there something I should be worried about here?"

"No. He's a sweetie, but he gets so involved in his subject. When he reads poetry out loud, he really lives it. Some of the guys think he's a bit of a letch, but he's not at all. I don't see how anyone could read out the love poems of John Donne without wanting to be transported by them, to live them, not just spout the words."

Clive envied his daughter being able to study literature and, in particular, having the opportunity to discuss poetry with like-minded people. Poetry was his greatest love, but he had gone straight from school, where poetry had never been popular among his classmates, to the paint depot, where there were even fewer chances to share views on such cultural matters. To most of the workforce, poetry was a posh name for dirty limericks, which they were pleased to share at every opportunity. While many of these were funny in a Chaucerian way, they could hardly be passed off as a high art form.

"Are you on duty today, Dad?"

"Yes, it should be just a half day from ten until three, but Larry has been missing one or two handovers recently, so I could be a bit later. You know what it's like in Kitchener House at the best of times; it only takes one of the group to throw a bit of a wobbly and timetables are forgotten."

"Yeh; I remember the times we have been waiting at home and you haven't got back until hours later than expected. Even if you phoned up to explain the delay, Mum still went ballistic.

She always seemed to be waiting to go off to one of her important social meetings, social-climbing meetings more like!"

Clive busied himself loading the dishwasher; he didn't want to start criticising his wife with his daughter. Some misplaced sense of loyalty forced him to stay clear of the subject, so he tried to look preoccupied with a couple of marks on one of the glasses he was loading into the machine, but Nicky was not to be put off.

"Why do you put up with it, Dad, the bullying, the constant attempts to belittle everything you do? You work damned hard, and all you get is criticism for not bringing in the same kind of money as you got at the paint depot. You had the courage to say 'stuff your pension' and all she can do is tell her friends that you were in a very responsible executive position until you had your 'breakdown' and opted out. She actually finds it more acceptable to tell everyone that you had a breakdown rather than tell the truth that you wanted a change. It's like you must want to earn shedloads of money or you must be mad."

"Nicky, Nicky," he protested. "Your mum just wants what she thinks is best for you. She wants you and Sebastian to have a comfortable life."

"Look around you, Dad. We live in a five-bedroom house in a very desirable part of town, not exactly a hovel. You bring in a reasonable wage, albeit a fraction of what you deserve. Money is available to bail Sebastian out of most of his bad investments, and I have everything I need. Mum's business more than supports her extravagant lifestyle. There are a lot of people who would relish this degree of 'penury'. When the day arrives that Sebastian is sent up chimneys to clean them and I have to go on the game, then you can feel guilty about not bringing in obscene amounts of money!"

"I'd sell my own body to make up the shortfall before I'd let you do that."

"Thanks, Dad, a grand gesture, but that would barely earn enough small change to buy a morning paper."

The tension had been broken, and having given her father a noisy kiss on the cheek, Nicky picked up her journals and stuffed them into her bag.

"See you later, Dad, must go – academia awaits."

"I thought that was a kind of nut?"

"If you were half as daft as you'd like people to believe, then you would be wearing gloves on your feet."

Nichole picked up her bag, kissed him again and breezed out of the kitchen. Without stopping to check herself in the hall mirror, she was out and on her walk to the university.

Clive poured himself another cup of tea, poured it down the sink as it was cold and got himself a carton of orange from the fridge,

He liked his chats with Nicky and felt a bit cheated that it had been wasted discussing his marriage. He almost chuckled at the recollection of Nicky's reference to his having effectively said, "Stuff your pension." Both he and Nicky shared a love of Philip Larkin's poetry, and he recognised the line from 'Toads'. With a mock dramatic swagger, he lifted his orange juice to the sky and toasted.

"Here's to you, Philip – Bard of Humber."

He furtively glanced out of the window across the back garden to the similarly large houses beyond and was relieved to see no one had been watching. He was particularly fond of Larkin's poem, which dealt with the fact that few people were prepared to say stuff your pension because 'that's the stuff that dreams are made on,' but he had never seen himself as someone making such a heroic gesture, and he felt an almost guilty pride that Nicky should see him in such a light.

"Right then, Arkwright old chap, time for your superhero to go and do battle with the members of Kitchener House. Granny Pru will be over in a couple of hours to see you."

Maureen's mother, Pru, came in most days to spend some time with Arkwright, which he particularly liked because of her habit of making herself a pot of tea and getting out the biscuit barrel, most of the contents of which ended up in the dog.

It was a contented Clive who packed away the rest of the breakfast things before sauntering into the hall where he picked up his shoulder bag, and then, remembering his mail, went back to the kitchen, grabbed the solicitor's letter and crammed it into his bag.

It had been a rather chilly late autumn morning, but by now the sun was just starting to warm the air, even though the lawn was still covered by a frosty dew. Clive pushed his squeaking bike out of the garage and leant on it for a while, looking at the garden. It was going to be a nice day, and with a bit of luck he would get away from work on time and be able to rake up the last few remaining leaves on the lawn before it got too dark.

CHAPTER TWO

Clive knocked dutifully on the door of Kitchener House and waited for a response that he knew was unlikely to materialise. The company that ran the sheltered housing had a clear policy which dictated that every effort should be made to treat the residents as one would treat any other independent householders. He knew that the residents would probably still be in their bedrooms if not still in bed, and he had a key to let himself in if the evening staff had been diligent enough to remember to lock it. There was no sound of activity inside, so he tried the door which he found to be unlocked and let himself in. The kitchen showed signs that someone had made a half-hearted attempt to clear up after supper. Clive guessed that Larry had been on duty the previous evening. At numerous staff and residents meetings it had been stressed that it was up to the staff to encourage and support the residents to keep the house tidy at all times. It had been particularly stressed that at the end of their shift, staff should ensure that the house was left in a reasonable state for their colleagues who took over from them. Most of the residential units had staff on duty all the time, so it was possible to discuss lapses at handover time, but the Kitchener House members were often left without staff for a short time. This was largely because they were considered able to do more for themselves, but staff shortages sometimes meant deploying extra staff to houses where the residents needed a higher level of support. The main consequence of this was that the staff duty roster for Kitchener was more like a statement of desired outcomes rather than a declaration of serious intent. This was not helped by the degree of incompetence displayed by June, the supervisor who drew up the rosters. Clive had soon realised that he could have done a much better job himself but was content just to muddle through; he wasn't going to be seduced back onto the management path.

Clive went around drawing back the curtains downstairs, making just enough noise to inform the residents that a new day was beginning. His subtlety was wasted on the assorted residents, so he had to resort to knocking on each door in turn, starting with Len's room.

"Morning, Len," he called through the door. "Another lovely day. It's your day to set out the breakfast things."

"Ah, reet, mister Clive. I'll sithee soon, put kettle on, will tha?"

"OK, Len, don't forget your shower this morning. See you in a few minutes."

This conversation had prompted Minnie to stir from her room, and she greeted Clive with a cheery,

"Hello, lovie, I keep reminding him about his showers. He'd be caked in muck before he thought to take one himself. I had a bath last night, and I shall be having a good wash after breakfast."

Minnie was a sprightly soul, now in her seventies, who had spent most of her life in institutions of one sort or another, and she was very good with routines. She was by far the easiest of the three residents of the house to work with and, in fact, when things stuck to her routines, she was as capable as many of the staff. She mothered the men in the house mercilessly, but if anything happened to upset her routine, she would flap about asking what the world was coming to. So far today was going as planned, so a carefree Minnie headed downstairs to get on with her day.

Clive went over to prepare to rouse the last of the trio.

"Conrad," he called loudly through the door. "Time to get up, breakfast soon."

There was a noise of movement within the room before the occupant called out, "I'd love a cup of tea."

"Surprise, surprise," muttered Clive to himself, before calling through the closed door, "See you downstairs soon."

By the time he got downstairs, Minnie had set out the table for breakfast and was busily tidying up the kitchen. Clive wandered over, put the kettle on, and watched in amazement as Minnie got on with her work. The whole idea of the sheltered housing project was that the staff were there to encourage the residents to do more and more for themselves, but the reality in Kitchener House was that Minnie did just about everything, while the other two residents were more than willing to let her. By the time Len came down, the cereal bowls had been taken out and put in their correct places on the table. In a deliberate attempt to annoy Minnie, he made to sit in the chair by the cooker, but Minnie was having none of it and guided him to his proper place, taking the opportunity to straighten his collar at the same time.

"Eeh, what's tha doin, woman?" he protested. "Tha's not me mother, tha knows."

"If I was, I'd have done a damn sight better job of bringing you up, you scruffy devil."

There was no animosity in the banter; it was just part of their daily routine.

"Nearly 60 years old, and you can't even dress smart," she continued. "You look like you've been dragged through a hedge backwards, and you've made a poor job of showering again. Look at the muck there."

"Give o'er, woman. I knows fine how to ev a shower, and I'm dressed fer work not tea wi' the queen."

"When you've finished your shower, the cubicle's barely damp," she quipped. "I'll bet there's bits of your body that haven't been touched by soap and water in years. Did nobody ever show you how to have a shower?"

"Nay, and I'm in no mind to tek lessons from thee, so tha can keep thi 'ands to thisen."

Before Minnie had chance to reply they were joined by Conrad, who was met by a warm smile from Minnie, who took a further opportunity to get at Len by remarking, "Why can't you be more like our Conrad? Look at the darling boy, not a hair out of place, smartly dressed, and doesn't he smell just lovely?"

Conrad was indeed perfectly turned out for breakfast and his general appearance, if slightly dated, could have graced the window of any high-class gents outfitters. He wore a perfectly fitting three-piece suit with tasteful pale blue shirt and matching tie, and his shoes were polished to a high shine. Clive often felt that only the absence of spats and a small, waxed moustache prevented him from looking every inch a latter-day Hercule Poirot.

Conrad took his usual seat at the table, and Minnie proceeded to fuss over him.

"And what would you like this morning, love?" she asked while resting a protective arm on his shoulder.

"I'd love a cup of tea," he announced after some thought.

"Certainly, my love, and I'll get your wheat flakes out. Plenty of vitamin W in wheat flakes."

Once again, Minnie was showing her less than perfect grasp of nutritional issues. She had heard so much about these vitamin things and the fact that they were often called after letters in the alphabet, so it was but a small jump of logic to assume that the original letter of the food indicated its vitamin content. Occasionally she got it right and would point out that vitamin C was in cauliflower and vitamin B was in banana, but most of her routine nutritional advice was somewhat flawed, and it could become complicated. Potatoes contained vitamin P, but mashed potatoes contained lots of vitamin M, while roast potatoes were a rich source of vitamin R. If pressed, and often without being pressed, she would go on to say exactly why one needed a particular vitamin in one's diet. Vitamin F, to be found in fish, helps to ward off the flu, and the large stores of vitamin E in eggs give some defence against earache; the logic was simple, even if the deductions made were less than accurate.

Minnie set a small bowl of flakes in front of him and proceeded to pour him a cup of black coffee. Conrad carefully took a sip of his coffee and smiled politely at her to show his approval.

While Minnie enjoyed her friendly run-ins with Len, there was no hiding the fact that Conrad was the favourite of her 'boys'.

In due course, Len got up from the table, folded his paper into his jacket pocket, declaring, "Well, some on us hev work to go to. T' plants don't grow thiselves."

As he left, he leaned towards Minnie,. "Si thi later, Mother," he said, puckering his lips in feigned anticipation of a goodbye kiss.

"You daft lump!" she said with a little giggle. "Get off to work."

Throughout this, Conrad had been quietly finishing his breakfast, and when Len had gone, Minnie was able to concentrate her attention on him.

"Anything else, love?" she queried, holding the coffee pot towards his cup.

Conrad smiled and lifted his cup slightly so it could be topped up, and then he carefully placed his breakfast dish in the dishwasher before sitting back at the table to finish his coffee.

Clive had seen this little performance most mornings when he'd happened to be on duty; Minnie, the over-attentive mother figure and Conrad, the perfectly behaved 'son'. She did all she could to anticipate his every need, and he repaid her with his appreciative smiles and by presenting himself as a smart, well-groomed figure that she took as testimony to the work she put in. The truth was that his behaviour was set before they met, but Minnie still felt proud of 'her' protégé.

While Len and Minnie had been born with some degree of learning difficulties, compounded at least in Len's case by indifferent parenting skills, Conrad's life had taken a tragic turn after a traffic accident that had left a very different person. On the surface, he appeared to be a well-functioning individual, extremely smartly dressed, even if his style was more than a little dated, but he needed his routines and people around him who understood his needs. Clive often felt that Len and Minnie could be left without any support except for someone to keep an eye on their finances. They would no doubt have bumbled along, their domestic bliss heightened by their good-hearted bickering with Minnie doing all the work. Conrad was different, and Minnie had come to understand his little ways so that she could avoid any disruptions to their comfortable way of life. She had learned to avoid the little triggers that could so easily upset him. Above all, she knew that he needed his sleep; he tended to wake at a reasonable time each morning, but any attempt to rouse him before that time, given that it was almost impossible to wake him anyway, would generally result in one of his little turns that involved thrashing around and thwarting all efforts to get him up. With Conrad, it was very much a case of letting sleeping dogs lie.

Clive spent some time during the morning helping Conrad to polish his shoes but, while Conrad was particularly good at putting on shoes, and while he would never wear a pair without a perfect shine, he could see little point in doing the polishing himself. That was a job that Minnie usually did with some enthusiasm, and by the end of the shoe-cleaning session, it was obvious that Conrad had contributed little, but he looked at his shoes with pride before announcing, "I'd love a cup of tea."

The session had not been a resounding success, but Clive decided he deserved a break himself. He switched on the kettle and then sat down at the table to check through the house diary. The diary was a large loose-leaf file containing a record of staff duty hours as well as a method of keeping track of any activities arranged for the residents. Clive thumbed through to the current date, and he felt a moment of slight panic as he noted the entry: *6.00 Conrad to PW*. It was his writing and his abbreviation. He recalled that he had arranged for Conrad to go out on his regular social outing to the Prince William pub. Clive checked the column to see which staff would be on duty. It should be Larry starting at six; this was not good news as Larry was the least reliable of the staff on the team. Conrad would be looking forward to his hour at the pub, and he would be very disappointed if he couldn't go. It looked like Clive would not be getting away early to sweep up the leaves on his lawn.

He quickly phoned Pru to check the arrangements for Arkwright. The phone rang for a while before a breathless Pru answered, "Hello, Pru's dog-sitting service."

"Hi Pru, Clive here. You sound out of breath. Are you OK.?"

"Clive darling! Of course I'm fine. I was just enjoying a session of passionate love-making with your milkman."

"We don't have a milkman, Pru."

"Then I've just made a lucky passer-by very happy."

"You are a very naughty lady, Pru. Anyway, I may be a little late tonight; Nicky should be back by half past four, but I wondered if you would be able to stay with Arkwright a little longer until she gets back?"

"Anything for you, darling. Anyway, it will give me the opportunity to check out that nice man who delivers your organic vegetables."

"Old Arthur? He's nearly 80; be gentle with him, Pru. Must go. May see you later if you're still in when I get back. Bye."

"I'll look forward to it, darling. Bye."

Pru was not your average mother-in-law. She was already divorced when Clive and Maureen married, and she had had a number of gentlemen friends since then, a fact that Maureen found decidedly distasteful. Pru made no secret of the fact that she liked the company of men, and Maureen made it equally obvious that she thought her mother should be 'past all that', which only served to encourage Pru to flaunt her relationships. Her lurid and frequently completely fictitious accounts of her evenings with her latest gentleman were designed to wind up Maureen, and Clive took a perverse delight in watching his wife's prudish squirming.

Clive wrote his name in the diary to show he was going to take Conrad out that evening, and he put it back on the shelf. He was about to embark on what he knew was probably a futile attempt to get Conrad to prepare a sandwich for lunch when there was a knock on the door. Minnie bustled through to see who it was, and Clive heard her ushering someone in.

"Go straight through, Doctor; would you like a cup of tea?"

Clive looked up to see his colleague Sally being subjected to Minnie's very best mothering skills. Everyone knew Sally as Doc, but for Minnie after many years involvement with a number of medical agencies, this had to be 'Doctor'. Sally, alias Doc, Livingstone had been a workmate for some years, but her and Clive had rarely worked on the same team, so he was surprised to see her.

"Nice to see you, Doc. What brings you in to Kitchener?"

"Please call me Sally," she asked with a sweet smile. "After all, we've known each other for years. The simple answer to your question is that I am going to take over some of Larry's hours. Evidently, he's been having a few problems at home and needs a bit more time to get it sorted, so he's going to be working less hours. I gather he has been a little erratic in his time-keeping of late, and with Sue spending an increasing amount of time co-opted to Nightingale House, you've been a bit short-staffed."

"It's true that I seem to spend a lot of time here. My wife reminds me all the time. Sue is great when she's here, but they've had such problems at Nightingale that they keep switching her over to cover there. I had noticed that Larry was a bit unpredictable, but I never guessed that he was having problems. It's strange that we are in one of the so-called caring professions but I had no idea."

"Yes. You work with someone for years and then find that you know nothing about their life beyond work," commented Sally before continuing, "I was on June's team here for two years before I found out that in the evenings she was a stripper."

"Mousy June? A stripper?" he asked incredulously.

"Yes, three nights a week at the King's Head. Evidently she does this belting routine with a Burmese python. Brings the house down."

"Mousy June?"

"Yes, been doing it for years. She started doing it to support her habit when it got out of control."

"What habit?"

"Bread sniffing. She was a five-loaves-a-day woman at one point, always to be found lingering in the bakery section at Tesco's, couldn't get enough of their French stuff, and it was when she was seduced into sampling the croissants that she realised that she had to do something about it."

Belatedly, Clive realised that he was being taken for a ride.

"You're having me on, you devil."

"No, it's all true," she said, trying to suppress a giggle. "Trust me, I'm a doctor."

She remembered the boundless gullibility that Clive had shown in the past and indeed saw this as a very endearing quality. She loved to see just how outlandish her stories had to become before Clive realised, and he rarely let her down.

"So I'm taking over some of Larry's hours – honestly!" she added. "So could you update me on the clients here? I hate the term 'client', don't you? It sounds so impersonal."

"Yes, but whatever title the company policy decides upon has a tendency to sound that way; in the past, we've had 'residents' and 'occupants'. Some of the older staff found it hard to stop using the term 'patients', but I just like to think of my little gang as the family in Kitchener House."

"I see you've got Minnie, we're old friends, and Conrad, who else?"

"There's just Len, but he's out working at the moment at the nursery."

"Len? I don't remember him… Oh yes, Yorkshire Len. How is he getting on?"

"Well, he turns up at the nursery most days, but it was misleading to suggest that he works there. He just sits with a mug of tea most of the day, sharing all his North Country wisdom with anyone in earshot."

"So where in Yorkshire was Len born? I've never been able to pinpoint his accent."

"Croydon."

"Croydon? Come off it," she replied with a knowing smile.

"No, honestly, born in Croydon."

Sally could tell that Clive was telling the truth; apart from anything else, he lacked the guile to fool her, so she changed her area of questioning.

"Oh, I see. He was born in Croydon but moved up north at an early age when the family broke up?"

"It's true that he was taken into care when he was quite young, but he has never been to Yorkshire in his life as far as we can make out. In fact he spent most of his life in London and has never lived further north than here in Leicestershire."

"But he has a broad Yorkshire accent."

"Well, it is Yorkshire-ish, but if you listen carefully, you will notice that he has no particular local dialect; he picked it up using distance learning."

"I don't remember that particular Open University unit," she scoffed. "Larn thisen, Tyke."

"Nothing so highbrow for our Len. He did his initial work with the University of *Emmerdale* and rounded off his studies in Aidensfield. But if you listen carefully, you also get the odd bit of influence from over the border with his *Coronation Street* studies."

"So he has based his image entirely on television programmes set in the north! No wonder I couldn't pin him down to a particular area. I suppose if he had watched more of *Neighbours*, he might have been Aussie Len, heaven forbid!"

Clive spent some time updating Sally about the residents of Kitchener House before Minnie started setting the table for her and Conrad's lunch. Clive made coffee for himself and Sally, and they took their drinks through to the lounge. Clive tried to give the members of the household space to get on with their meals on their own as far as possible and usually took in a packet of biscuits or a sandwich for himself if he was expecting to be away from home for a while.

"I wish I'd known that you were going to turn up, Sally," he said, sipping his coffee. "The fact is that I'd arranged for Conrad to go to the pub this evening, and I've had to re-jig my domestic arrangements to make sure I can go with him. He would have been so upset if he hadn't been able to go."

"No problems then," she said with a smile. "I can go with you and then come back with Conrad. It will be a good opportunity to see him in a different context. I can walk back with him while you get off home."

Clive hadn't the heart to tell her that he had half hoped that she would take Conrad, thus freeing him to get away early, but her obvious enthusiasm for the outing made it impossible for him to disappoint her.

CHAPTER THREE

The Prince William was the sort of establishment that was proud to call itself a local pub. The truth was that it was tucked out of the way in a small estate of houses, with little or no passing trade, so it was only the locals who bothered to seek it out. Clive had found it by way of a slight detour on his way home from work one day and had discovered it to be the ideal place to take a succession of residents. The locals had readily accepted all the people that Clive had taken along and had behaved sympathetically on the rare occasion that there had been any sort of problem.

Clive casually pushed his bike round to the back of the pub and put it in the yard before joining Sally and Conrad and walking into the bar. The weather was decidedly cold by now, so Clive was pleased to see the welcoming glow of the fire, and he eagerly went over to warm himself. Meanwhile, Conrad made his way to the bar and announced, "I'd love a cup of tea."

"Certainly, Conrad," replied the landlord as he made his way to pull a pint of bitter, which he placed before the eager Conrad. "There you are, sir, enjoy."

Conrad carefully picked up his pint, took a small sip and carried it over to his usual seat by the fire. Clive went over to the bar with Sally.

"Evening, Bill, the usual?" enquired the landlord of Clive.

"Yes, please, Bill. And what are you having, Sally?"

"Hearing problems, I think. Didn't he just call you Bill?"

"Oh yes, we've got a lot of Bills in here," replied Clive in a deliberately casual way.

"I'll have an orange juice, please," said Sally, turning to the landlord with a quizzical look on her face. "And why exactly do you call him Bill?"

"It goes back some years now. We had a guy who dropped in for a quiet half most nights on his way home, and when he started he used to tell his wife that he had been to the Prince William, but it turned out she didn't want any of her friends to know that he had been to the pub so she persuaded him to declare that he'd called in to see Bill. It sort of caught on. After a while we had lots of locals with the name."

"But surely you get confused?"

"We got around that by having different forenames. I'm Beer Bill because I serve the beer, see? The guy in the overall there is Gas Bill because he works for the Gas Board. The chap with the whisky is Council Bill, who works at the town hall. They are talking to Old Bill."

"Because he's in the police?"

"No. Because he's old. Oh, and there's the chap who brings eggs in from his chickens on the allotment. Duck Bill."

"So why not Chicken Bill?"

"Chickens don't have bills."

Sally was half convinced that she was being had on, but she persevered,

"So is anyone in this pub actually called Bill?"

The landlord thought for a moment and then said, "No. Oh yes, wait a minute, there's Jock."

"And he's Scottish?"

"No Welsh; he got fed up being called Taff."

Sally inwardly conceded defeat and took her orange juice over to join Conrad and Clive.

"So what is your full name then, Bill?" she asked Clive.

"Caring Bill," he replied sheepishly, much to Sally's amusement.

Throughout this Conrad had been sipping his beer. Each time, he would pick up his glass, take a small mouthful, put his glass down on the table and then beam with obvious delight. Periodically, he would lift his glass to the small group of Bills at the bar, and they would dutifully respond in imitation. Conrad was in his element.

"You were saying that we hardly know the people we work with," said Sally, "so what do you do in real life and whatever persuaded you to come into this bizarre line of work?"

"As my wife would readily point out, I used to have a real job. I was in paint for nearly 30 years."

"Sounds messy."

"I must admit that I felt my life was a bit of a mess. Sure, it paid well, but I suppose that deep down, I just wasn't suited to it."

"Oh. Yes," interrupted Sally, "I remember talking to your wife at that staff barbecue, and she said you'd had problems."

Clive rolled his eyes upwards despairingly. "That woman! Just to put the record straight, Sally, I never at any point had any sort of breakdown. Maureen just assumed that anyone who was prepared to move away from a very well-paid job like that had to be suffering from a mental health problem."

"So you walked away from a well-paid job and came here to work for an organisation that is run by a management team with all the administrative skills of a group of poorly trained dung beetles who pay you the equivalent of a bowl of rice a day. Sounds a perfectly rational thing to do."

"I knew you'd understand," he said with a knowing smile.

Clive noticed that Conrad's glass was almost empty. He pointed at it and said, "Fancy another?"

"I'd love a cup of tea," said Conrad, handing him the emptied glass.

As he stood by the bar waiting for Conrad's next pint to be pulled, he looked over at Sally who was engaging Conrad in small talk while the latter nodded politely and smiled at her. At first sight, they would have appeared an ill-matched couple, the dapper Conrad sitting smartly in his seat with his young, casually dressed friend by his side. It suddenly struck Clive that Sally always seemed to be relaxed; she never appeared to be anything other than herself with no attempt to impress others by pretending to be something she wasn't. This uncomplicated sincerity made her very easy to get on with, and Clive had always enjoyed her company. She was one of those genuinely attractive people who made others feel appreciated, and at that moment Conrad was enjoying every minute of the attention he was getting. A stranger observing the couple would never have guessed the severity of Conrad's communication difficulties. Over the years, Clive had noted that Conrad obviously understood a lot of what was being said to him, but in all the time he had known him he had only ever heard him produce the one sentence. Sometimes the intonation would vary a little, but still all one ever heard from Conrad was, "I'd love a cup of tea."

Clive put Conrad's 'tea' in front of him, much to his obvious delight.

"I'd forgotten all about that barbecue," said Clive in an attempt to get back to their conversation. "It was the last time Maureen ever turned up at any function linked with my work. I recall that your husband Steve was there as well; I think that between us we got through more than our fair share of that cheap red that Mousy June had brought in from France."

"Yes, but tell me, do you ever hear from your old colleagues in the paint world?"

Sally seemed keen not to dwell on the barbecue. Clive considered that perhaps she and Steve had had a difference of opinion after the barbecue, just as he and Maureen had experienced. In their case, the difference being that Maureen had suggested that Clive was in a less than sober state and might consider alternative accommodation that night. To be more precise, she had said that he was as drunk as a skunk and he'd have to sleep in the shed. Clive had remonstrated as best he could, saying that her suggestion was ridiculous, that a man couldn't be treated in such a way in his own house, and then he had slunk off to the shed. Clive was certainly not going to drag up any similar memories for Sally so he forgot about the matter and answered her question.

"I rarely get back to Hull these days," he started, but then he remembered the letter he had received that morning. "As a matter of fact, I did receive this today," he said, rummaging in his bag and drawing out the solicitor's letter, which he took from its envelope and handed to her.

"What do you make of that?" he asked.

Sally took the letter and gave him a quizzical look as she noted that the letter was still a bit sticky.

"Sorry about that. Honey," he added by way of explanation.

"That's OK. Darling," she replied teasingly.

Sally read the letter while Clive chatted to Conrad, who continued to obtain great delight from his evening out with friends and his beers, the second of which was half empty by now.

Sally handed the letter back to Clive.

"Sounds interesting. So was that your former employer that has died?"

"Yes. Norman. Mind you, I'd been working for him for 20 years before he suggested I called him by his forename. Most of the staff used to call him 'sir', even some of his senior staff, and most of them were relatives!"

"He doesn't sound to be a particularly likeable sort of guy, your Norman."

"He was fine. He had worked hard to set the business up and then to keep it going. He was plagued by relatives that seemed to find their way into senior positions in the firm, most of whom would have made Mousy June look efficient. In the end, Norman got fed up with the lot of them, but he had no children of his own, and I think he had hoped to leave the business to the assorted relatives he employed."

"It states in the letter that you are invited to hear the reading of the will and that you might hear 'something to your advantage', but if he was leaving the company to his family, it doesn't look like you will receive any life-changing legacy. But if you do get a bob or two, you will remember your friends, won't you?" she said, smiling and gently laying her hand on his arm.

Clive smiled back. "Don't get your hopes up. Shortly after I left the company, the factory was closed down, much to the annoyance of lots of his family who felt they lost their jobs and inheritance at a stroke. But if I do inherit a fortune, don't worry, I'd whisk you away from all this and treat you to a wild weekend savouring the exotic delights of Withernsea."

"Withernsea, how romantic. You sure know how to spoil a girl."

"I know. I spent many happy holidays in Withernsea, a bit like Benidorm but without the culture."

"Or climate, I suppose?"

"True, but it does have a lighthouse that's a credit to the area; it's been standing for over a hundred years, but the sea hasn't made a mark on it. Building it in the middle of the town a quarter of a mile from the beach does go some way to explaining its resilience."

Sally thought he might be trying to have her on, but recognising his inability to lie, she just took the fact, however improbable, as being the truth that it certainly was.

"You will be going to the reading, won't you?"

"I hadn't thought about it. Hull is a long way to go just to face a roomful of Norman's relatives with the prospect of hearing that I've been left some meaningless memento of my life in paint. I think I'll cry off."

"When is the reading anyway?"

Clive browsed over the letter. "The twenty-ninth at three in the afternoon, that's next Thursday."

"You must go, Clive. It isn't every day that you are called in to a solicitor's office for a will reading. There might even be a glass of dry sherry in it for you. That's the favourite tipple of solicitors, isn't it?"

"It may be, but I've just remembered that I've arranged to take Conrad on a train outing that day."

At the mention of 'train outing', Conrad looked up from his beer, smiled more broadly and nodded before exclaiming, in his own inimitable way, "I'd love a cup of tea."

"You see," continued Clive. "He's got his heart set on it. He just loves going on the train, and so I thought I might take him up to York."

"Does it have to be York? Why don't you take him up to Hull?"

To many people, this might have seemed a poor exchange, but Clive knew that for Conrad it was the journey that was important. On a previous trip to London, Conrad had been generally unimpressed by the major tourist sites but had thoroughly enjoyed the train journey both ways and the time spent on the open-top bus tour round the city. Clive could well remember the journey around the city in the rain, with only himself and Conrad braving the elements upstairs. Clive looked to Conrad, who by now appeared to be listening keenly to the conversation.

"What do you think, Conrad? Would you like to go to Hull on the train next week?" asked Clive, who knew that this might be seen as a question devised to get the required answer, but at the same time knowing that Conrad would have travelled anywhere on a train. To Conrad, it was the journey that was to be enjoyed, and the destination was largely irrelevant. Clive felt that this was confirmed by Conrad's appreciative nods and his usual announcement about the desirability of a cup of tea.

"Sorted!" announced Sally, leaning over and squeezing Conrad's arm gently. "You'll love the trip to Hull, and you'll see the river and the bridge."

"Hang on though," said Clive, "I'm not sure that the solicitor will be too pleased if I bring a guest to the party, and Conrad wouldn't want to spend time hanging about waiting in some kind of outer office. Goodness knows how long these things go on; it's not exactly a routine event for me."

"I could come with you. After all, Mousy June is always going on about ensuring adequate cover on visits. We could catch the train here in the morning, nip in to Hull, and I could take Conrad to see the sights, I assume there are sights, while you do your legal stuff. We could catch the return train and be back here by eight or thereabouts."

Sally's plan met with Conrad's obvious approval, and it did sound very simple. Only time would show that her timetable was more than a little optimistic. Clive felt that he had been pressured into this whole plan, but somehow he didn't care. Maureen routinely ordered his life for him, and he complied begrudgingly, but while Sally was every bit as persuasive, he ended up doing what she decreed, and he felt good about it. He liked people organising his life for him; making decisions for himself was too reminiscent of his executive days.

Conrad had by now finished his second pint and was showing signs of being ready to leave. His nights out, or what Mousy June referred to as his 'advanced social training sessions', had to follow the same pattern. Conrad met his friends, had two pints, which he never rushed, and then it was time to go. His last routine was to take his empty glass to the bar where any of the regulars present would wish him a cordial goodnight. With a contented smile, Conrad would be ready to set off home. Clive had tried, after prior consultation with the landlord, to encourage Conrad to carry his own money and to pay for his drinks, but it all seemed too much for him. Similarly, the staff at Kitchener House had tried to encourage him to walk the short distance to the pub on his own, but Conrad couldn't cope. He was quite prepared to go out with discreet supervision, but if he sensed he was on his own, he would become very agitated and unable to cope.

Outside the pub that evening, Sally continued to gently firm up the plans for the day in Hull.

"I'll put a memo into June's office stating that we are taking Conrad out on the 29th. I'll fill it with all the usual jargon she likes and emphasise the fact that we will be leaving Len and Minnie during the day so that they can 'exercise a greater degree of autonomy'. The truth is that they can organise the day-to-day running of the place better than we can."

"Yes, but don't tell anyone. If it weren't for our friend Conrad here, we would have nothing to do most days."

Clive picked up his bike as Sally set off back with Conrad.

"Bye, Caring Bill," she giggled.

"Bye, Doc."

"I'd love a cup of tea."

CHAPTER FOUR

Clive pushed his squeaking bike into the garage as quietly as he could. It was far from late, but he knew he was later than expected, and he intended to make a quiet entrance and not give Maureen the satisfaction of making a comment. A glance at the space where Maureen's car should have been made it clear that she was still out. Arkwright rushed to meet him as he entered the kitchen; at least the dog was generally pleased to see him.

"Good evening, darling," called out Pru as she made her way in from the lounge with a glass of wine in her hand. "And what sort of day have you had, my sweet?"

"Hi Pru, pretty ordinary. How about you and Arkwright?"

"We've been fine. I made a casserole with that beef that Maureen had left out, and I put a splash of wine in, so I thought I'd treat myself to a glass."

"You are a darling, Pru, but you shouldn't have put yourself out. I'd intended to throw something together when I got in."

"But that would have been four hours ago if you'd managed to get home on time."

Pru realised that this minor rebuke was not what Clive wanted and added," Sorry, darling, I didn't mean to sound like Maureen. You get more than your fair share of moaning from her. She can return at whatever time she likes, without explanation, but still gives you a roasting if you are a bit delayed."

"That's because she earns a lot of money, and I bring in a pittance, but thanks again for the meal. It smells great."

Pru was far from being the archetypal mother-in-law, and if truth were known, she had a lot more time for him than she had for her daughter. She was quite like Maureen in appearance and shared her daughter's commitment to dressing well at all times, if not her preoccupation with having impeccable make-up. Maureen's foundation had an almost sculpted texture in an attempt to iron out or fill up any wrinkles. Similarly, her lipstick was applied with laser precision, and her eye shadow was always a perfect match for her outfit of the day. If she had appeared on *Desert Island Discs*, her luxury item would be a revolver; she would have had to kill herself if she couldn't have access to a full range of cosmetics and her frequent beautician's appointments. Pru didn't go in for excessive paintwork but always looked smart and remained an attractive woman, as was evidenced by her string of gentlemen friends.

"I think I'll grab myself a glass of wine; fancy another, Pru?"

"Go on then, darling," she replied. "Now that I'm off duty."

As Clive was pouring himself a generous glass of wine, Nicky breezed in.

"Hi Gran, still sober? I must be earlier home than I thought."

Nicky kissed Pru before gratefully accepting the glass of wine that Clive had just poured for himself. Clive looked at the empty wine bottle, shrugged, and went off to open another.

He rooted through the selection of wines in the larder and chose a bottle that he knew was one of Pru's favourites. Opening the bottle carefully, he poured himself a drink before taking the bottle through and putting it on the table. He knew that with his two favourite women engrossed in their chat, he was surplus to requirements, so he excused himself and went through to the lounge to lose himself for an hour in his favourite book of the collected works of Larkin.

Pru took little persuading to stay for dinner, which was just as well because Maureen failed to turn up, and Sebastian, having obviously stopped off on the way home for a business drink with some of his car dealer colleagues, ate very little before going up to bed. After finishing what turned out to be an enjoyable meal, Pru and Clive stacked the dishwasher while Nicky generally tidied up before going to her room.

"Thanks again, Pru," said Clive, "I think we'd better be getting you home now."

"I can see myself home; it's only a five-minute walk."

"It's dark out there, and the street lighting is not good."

"For goodness sake, darling, I'm not going to be ravaged by some strange man."

"I know, Pru, but there are some very sensitive old men in the area, and it's their safety I'm thinking of."

Pru took no convincing. She enjoyed her walks home with Clive, so she put on her coat and they set off arm-in-arm on the short walk to her house. For a while they walked in silence, which was broken by Pru declaring, "It's not natural, you know, you and Maureen and your separate bedrooms."

Clive made no immediate response, partly because he didn't know how best to answer but largely because he didn't want to start on that particular subject with Pru again. She was, after all, his mother-in-law. But Pru was not to be put off, and she continued with her observations.

"Sex is important, you know. Marriage vows are not vows of celibacy. Good grief, if I felt I had to do without my fair share, I'd go mad. When Maureen's dad was around, we had a very healthy sex life. Sex is good for you."

This last sentence was uttered at some volume, just as their paths crossed with an elderly woman walking her dog. Clive silently hoped that it wasn't anyone who would have recognised him, and he tried to calm Pru down a bit.

"Pru, please! I've told you before there isn't a problem. Separate beds don't mean there isn't scope for a relationship.

Maureen and I get on fine, but she has a demanding job with irregular hours. Our relationship works better this way." His hushed voice and his very proper vocabulary indicated the great embarrassment that the whole topic caused him, which contrasted markedly with her complete openness.

"You can't have 'a relationship' by appointment. It's not something that can be restricted to dates mutually agreed in your diaries. Where's the scope for romance? For passion, the snatched moments together? Sex should be orgasmic rather than organised."

"Please don't worry about us. Things are fine, honestly."

They continued their walk in a tense silence. At the door to her house, Clive waited until she had gone in and switched the light on, and then he kissed her on the cheek, thanked her for helping the family out again and wished her goodnight. As he turned to go, she gently put her hand on his arm and said, "I'm sorry, Clive, but I do worry about you."

"I know, Pru. Goodnight."

As he walked home, the very memory of their conversation caused him a further flush of embarrassment. Surely his mother-in-law shouldn't feel the need to give him advice on his sex life; it was somehow wrong. But deep down he knew there was a lot in her argument that struck an uncomfortable note somewhere. It didn't take a genius to notice that his marriage was somewhat unconventional, and an observer might be forgiven for assuming that Maureen didn't care for him. She did tend to find fault in him and, even in company, didn't always show him the respect he deserved, but Clive had long since convinced himself that this was just a hard veneer she had developed in her attempts to cope in the world of business. People didn't see the other side of her, the feminine side, the caring side that had been evident in abundance when he had first met her. She still shared intimate moments with him, just not as often. Clive recognised that she had never been what one might describe as a passionate woman, and he conceded that he would probably win few prizes as a lover himself. He had once bought a rather expensive book that promised to 'rekindle the fire' in a couple's sex life. It had not been an unqualified success. Clive had quickly conceded that even to attempt some of the positions would have necessitated having a medic standing by, and Maureen was reluctant to contemplate anything that would mess her hair up. Their love-making was better described as polite rather than passionate, dignified rather than dramatic, but he knew she cared for him.

When he got home, he noticed Maureen's car in the driveway, but when he let himself in he realised she had gone to bed. He opened the back door to let Arkwright out for his routine sniff around the garden and followed him out onto the patio. While Arkwright explored the frosted flowerbeds, Clive started to reflect on what had been a very full day. He had never thought of Norman as being the sort of person to just up and die, but he realised that, of course it happened to everyone. He remembered his former life at the paintworks. It occurred to him that he had rarely been back to Hull, but then Hull was a place you had to want to go to specifically because you didn't really go through Hull on the way to anywhere else.

So, old Norman was dead. Clive tried to work out just how old his former boss would have been, but he had to concede that he could only narrow it down to somewhere between 80 and 95, and he wasn't even sure of those figures. Clive tried to remember his early days at the factory. Norman had seemed old to him then, but anyone over 30 can seem ancient to a school leaver. Clive gave up on his calculations, not least because he knew he had considerable difficulty estimating anyone's age. All he knew was that Norman had had a good innings. While most of his employees had seen him as a miserable old devil, Clive had seen a different side of his former boss; a wicked sense of humour that often caused him to play tricks on those around him. Clive smiled as he suddenly recalled that the solicitors had suggested he might get good news at the reading of the will. He wondered just what useless piece of paint shop memorabilia Norman had put aside for him.

Thought of the will reading prompted him to recall the planned outing with Conrad and Sally. Conrad was rarely any bother on such days out, but it would be good to have Sally with him to share some of the responsibility; anyway, he liked her company. She had an enthusiasm for life that was infectious and always seemed to be smiling.

The following morning, Clive was the first one downstairs as usual, and he set about preparing the various breakfasts that the family would be expecting. Clive enjoyed this responsibility and did it whenever his shifts permitted. Maureen came in and gave him a light kiss on the cheek.

"Sorry I missed you last night," she said. "We just had one hell of a day preparing our presentation for the Accrington convention, so I just had to grab an early night."

"No problem, I had an interesting evening with Nichole and your mum."

"So I see," she said, glancing towards the two empty wine bottles on the draining board. "Sorry I missed it."

"It was the usual evening with Pru. She sank a few glasses, danced frantically until she dropped and then I took her home in the wheelbarrow."

"Sounds like Mum," she said with a smile. "I really think she has just about got over her shyness."

Clive placed her breakfast cardboard in front of her and watched, with no sense of relish, as she adorned it with a smear of her low-fat spread and her special preserve before biting into it. Not for the first time, he marvelled at the fact that she could eat her high-fibre diet biscuits without a single morsel dropping onto the table, but if he had tried to eat one, he knew he would be ankle-deep in crumbs in no time. He had taken the trouble to take out her regular selection of assorted vitamin pills and food supplements and placed them on a small plate on the table. Maureen's nibbles on her cardboard were interspersed with a selection of pills of various colours. This almost religious ritual was carried out every morning, supported by her unshakable belief, despite a complete lack of scientific evidence, that they were essential to stop her ageing overnight.

"Is it the Accrington do this weekend?" he asked, trying to take an interest in her work.

"Yes, we're driving up on Friday morning to get our display set up. It's a big event in the trade, and we have to get it absolutely right."

Clive was at a loss as to how to sustain his apparent interest, and he had to suppress a laugh when it occurred to him that it was not the most obvious place to be associated with cosmetics; he could think of none of the major cosmetics firms that would boast of being, 'of London, Paris, New York and Accrington'. Nicky's arrival was a welcome distraction.

"Morning," she said in her usual cheery tone. "Gran was on form last night, wasn't she? I'm sure she becomes more energetic by the day."

"She may be going through a phase with her hormones; puberty probably," suggested Clive.

"She seems to want to party her life away, and good luck to her," commented Nicky with more than a trace of admiration in her voice.

Maureen gave a mildly disapproving look, but she was secretly quite pleased that her mother was keeping so well as it augured well for her own later years.

"I just wish she would show a little more maturity in her social life," commented Maureen. "All those men!"

"You make it sound like Gran has cupboards full of them standing by her bed, just in case she fancies a little something during the night. She's just had a few men friends over the years, and personally I hope I'm up for it when I'm her age."

Clive began to feel a little uncomfortable. It wasn't just the fact that it seemed wrong for a girl to discuss her grandmother's love life in such terms or even that she should openly express admiration for her; it was the inference of the misapprehension held by so many young people that sex after 30 was some kind of special achievement. He felt he ought to comment somehow but knew he would only become even more embarrassed, so he changed the subject.

"Your mum's away this weekend at her convention, and I'm working a split shift on Saturday, so meals might be a little haphazard, but I'll do a roast on Sunday."

"No problem, Dad. I'm out with Stan on Saturday, so we'll grab something in town," replied Nicky before turning to Maureen and adding, "I suppose you're taking the lovely Josslyn with you, Mum."

"Of course, I couldn't do without his designer skills at such events, and we've got to get it right in Accrington."

Nicky and her dad shared a sly glance and smiled at each other at the sound of the venue, but fortunately Maureen didn't notice. Josslyn, or 'the lovely Josslyn' as Nicky habitually referred to him, was Maureen's PA who also doubled as her design consultant. Josslyn had visited the house a few times, often to pick up Maureen before they went on one of their many trade conventions or promotional events. Clive made no secret of the fact that he found it hard to get on with him. During the awkward silences that often occurred while Maureen was doing her final lengthy make-up checks on departure days, Clive had tried to engage the younger man in polite conversation, but they had so little in common. Clive would be in his usual very casual clothes, while the lovely Josslyn would be attired in the sort of outfit one would usually only ever expect to see in a glossy fashion magazine. He was always perfectly groomed and wore the kind of eau de toilette that had the strength to kill small rodents at five paces. He also wore make-up and didn't so much walk as parade around wherever he went. Clive couldn't help the feeling that Josslyn had the sort of walk that would have somehow better lent itself to women's underwear. In short, he was not the kind of young man who would ever have frequented the bar of the Prince William, and if he ever had he would probably have been allocated the title of Pretty Bill. The fact remained that Maureen obviously relied on him to arrange their many excursions and to generally carry out the work that had made her business such a success, and he got on well with Arkwright, so he couldn't be all bad.

The relative quiet of breakfast was broken by Sebastian's noisy entrance.

"Morning all. You are looking at a business genius. Guess who was top of last month's sales statistics?"

The answer seemed to be implied by his description of himself, so the family dutifully congratulated him on his latest achievement.

"Well done, darling, I see you've inherited my grasp of business sense," commented Maureen.

"Yes, well done, brother dear," added Nicky. "Drinks on you at the club?"

"Good show, Sebastian," added Clive before asking, "So how many cars did you sell last month?"

"Three," replied his son. "Well, two and a half actually on the list."

"Two and a half?" queried Nicky. "So which half did you have left, the front or back?"

"It's not as simple as that," replied Sebastian, somewhat annoyed that his sales prowess was being ridiculed a little. "We are credited with a sale when we complete a deal and the company has calculated its profit."

"And?" prompted Nicky.

"Well, on one sale there wasn't a clear profit showing. I cleared a total profit of nearly three grand on the other two sales."

"And the other half sale?"

"Well, you have to look at the trade-in price of the old car and the price on the new one with warranty issues, finance deals, etcetera, and balance all that against the need to create space on the forecourt."

"So how much do you expect it to be when it's all done and dusted," continued Nicky, who was as tenacious as a terrier with a bone.

"It should be about six hundred pounds."

"A six-hundred-pound profit isn't too bad," added Clive by way of consolation.

"Not so much a profit as a shortfall," declared Sebastian sheepishly before adding, "But I've got the half point because it was a sale, and we've created an extra space on the forecourt."

"But what about the car you took in part exchange? Isn't that cluttering up the forecourt?" suggested Nicky with more than a sense of glee in her voice.

"No, it had to be scrapped," replied Sebastian, conscious of the fact that the triumphal nature of his earlier announcement had probably been ill-advised. Clive made a mental note not to expect any board from Sebastian for a while.

CHAPTER FIVE

It was a particularly quiet morning at Kitchener House. By the time Clive had arrived, Len had gone to work, leaving Minnie to prepare lunch for them all. Len generally took a few sandwiches or bought a pasty for his lunch, but Minnie was doing corned beef hash today, so he had decided he was going to come home instead. Clive busied himself with some of the paperwork required by Mousy June and her cohorts while keeping a general eye on the domestic scene that was being played out in front of him. As usual, Minnie did most of the work, but periodically she would give Conrad something to do.

"There you are, Conrad love," she said, putting four carrots and a scraper in front of him.

"Carrots, packed with vitamin C, good for you." Minnie had vague memories of the wartime character Doctor Carrot and the advice to eat fresh vegetables for their vitamin content. She continued preparing some onions and then returned to Conrad, who had been sitting motionless with the scraper still in his hand where she had placed it.

"That's the way, love, you're doing well," she encouraged him, paying scant regard to the fact that he had done virtually nothing.

"Let me finish them off for you, love," she continued, taking the carrots and quickly preparing them before putting them into a pan of water on the stove. "Now what shall we have?" she asked as she ploughed on with her monologue. "I know. You like your peas, don't you? You need your peas, plenty of vitamin P in peas."

Conrad and Minnie were the perfect couple; she liked to do everything for him, and he was more than pleased to let her.

Pretty soon the kitchen was filled with the glorious smell of Minnie's corned beef hash, and after clearing away, she turned to Conrad and announced, "Now we've got that on the go, what would you like?"

"I'd love a cup of tea," replied Conrad.

Minnie bustled away for a few minutes before bringing over a tray with three mugs of coffee and a plate of biscuits and placing it on the table. "There you are, boys," she announced with pride. "This should keep us going for a while."

Clive was pleased to be included in their little bit of domestic bliss, but he had reservations about the coffee. Minnie made a robust cup of coffee, strong enough to stand a spoon up in and with enough caffeine to keep the average elephant awake for a couple of days. Making the excuse that it was a little hot, he poured some of it down the sink before surreptitiously adding a little extra water from the kettle. Minnie didn't notice as she and Conrad drank their coffees and nibbled a biscuit each.

"Our Len shouldn't be long," she announced, glancing at the clock. "And I suppose he'll be tired out after his morning; mind you, he can tire himself out just thinking about work, and he never bothers to even think about it much."

Minnie was interrupted by the sound of the doorbell. She straightened her pinny and went to see who it was.

"Hello, Doctor, you should have just come straight through," she announced.

As ever, Sally had respected the fact that, while it was her place of work, it was home for Minnie and her boys.

"Hi Sally," said Clive. "I wasn't expecting to see you until tea time handover. Is there a problem?"

"No, not at all. I was just passing, and so I thought I'd come in and chat through the plans for our day out next week. It's more or less sorted. I happened to see Mousey June in the supermarket this morning, probably on her way to the bread aisle, and told her that we were planning a romantic trip to Hull together. I could tell that she was insanely jealous, what with the secret passion she harbours for your body, but she said it was OK as long as I put in the risk assessment form. By the way, what is it she knows about you? Exactly what sort of risk am I taking with you in Hull?"

"Here in the deep south of Leicestershire, I'm just mild-mannered Clive, but when I get back to my ancestral stomping grounds in Hull, it's like unleashing a wild animal. At least, I think that's how I remember it; it's been a while since I've been back."

"Well, we shall see next week, animal. I'll have to be on my guard."

Clive felt at ease with Sally. He knew she teased him and made a point of exploiting his natural gullibility, but she was fun.

"I checked the train times," she continued, "and it looks like we need to be at the station for just after nine; that way we avoid the morning rush. It will involve the odd change along the way, but it all adds to the fun. I thought that I could pick you up, and then we would go and get Conrad before going on to the station."

"Parking is a devil at the station, so I thought we'd take a taxi."

"No need to bother. I'll take Steve's car, and I've got a friend quite near the station where we can leave it. It will be a lot easier, and we don't have the bother of trying to grab a taxi in the evening. We should be back about half past nine. I'll book the tickets over the weekend, put in the outing planning form on Monday and look forward to a wild day in Hull."

Their conversation was interrupted by Len's early return from the nursery and his dramatic announcement, "I'm fair riggweltered. Yon new gaffer's 'ad us worked into a reet old lather. Tha'd think we were slaves."

"What's up now, Len?" enquired Clive. "Have they been making you make your own tea?"

"It's all reet fer thee, tha's paid good money to sit abaht doin' nowt, but yon new gaffer expects us to work ar fingers to t'bone fer pennies, an' now 'e sez we mun work 'arder or no wages."

Len was obviously very upset by this apparent change to his working conditions. He had been a long-standing member of the workforce at the nursery, which had been established some years previously to provide sheltered employment for the residents of a number of assorted hostels and supervised housing schemes such as Kitchener House. The main reason for the establishment of the nursery had never originally been to make any profit, but the company running the scheme had come under increasing pressure to run 'viable economic units', much to the disgust of the likes of Len. Clive would readily concede that Len was far from being a hard worker, but he would carry out routine tasks, albeit at his own pace, and in return he had a roof over his head and what he called his beer money. The recent attempts to make the nursery pay its way were part of a series of management efforts, variously described as 'efficiency measures', 'rationalisation strategies', and any one of a number of similar examples of corporate jargon.

"It's not reet," continued Len. "T'gaffer even 'ad me pullin' one o' those gert big trolleys. I'm a seeds an' cuttins man; I works at me bench. Ah's not a bloody donkey. Beggin' yer pardon, Doctor."

"Now, now, love," said Minnie in an attempt to calm him down. "Don't worry about it. Sit down and have a cup of coffee. I'll be setting the table for your dinner soon. Your favourite, remember? Corned beef hash; top up on your vitamin C."

Len was still fuming slightly when Clive and Sally left the trio and walked through to the lounge.

"He's a lazy old devil," declared Clive, "but he's got a point. The nursery was set up as a training unit and to give some of the clients a place to use those skills in a meaningful way."

"Yes, and now the whole organisation is driven by the need to make profit. I've been with the company nearly six years, and I've noticed how budgets have been tightened. To begin with it wasn't too difficult to get money for special events for the clients, but now you have to justify every penny. The only increase in expenditure seems to be with admin and paperwork."

"Too right. Conrad hasn't had a day out for months, and then when it is decided that he can have a bit of money for his outing, it can take hours to fill in the paperwork. I'm sure it's a deliberate disincentive; by the time you've done all the paperwork, you're too tired to go on the trip! And to top it all, it is Conrad's money anyway; apart from his usual state benefits, he has a hefty sum in the bank from his compensation award."

"I'd forgotten his accident," commented Sally. "Something to do with a motorbike smash, wasn't it?"

"Yes, you wouldn't believe it now, but he was a bit of a rebel in his youth. Big bike, leather jacket, bad attitude, violent, the lot. In fact, it was his refusal to be governed by authority that contributed to his problem. He always refused to wear a crash helmet, so when he came off and bounced along the road he suffered major brain damage."

Sally winced at the thought of the accident before asking, "And had he been speeding prior to the crash?"

"That's another cruel point; he was almost stationary when some guy came up from behind in a builder's lorry and smashed straight into him. Poor old Conrad. It was a major incident, and the emergency service people had to close the road for quite a while as they worked on him. Conrad still doesn't like blue flashing lights on emergency vehicles; perhaps it's one of his last memories."

"Poor soul."

"Yes. He was in a coma for months, and it wasn't thought he would make it. His family had long given up on him, so there wasn't even anybody there at his bedside, but he pulled through. It took years of work on him to get to the Conrad we know and love today. The compensation claim took even longer. In the end, the owners of the building firm accepted responsibility. It turns out that the lorry was unfit for the road on several counts, and the driver had been driving far too long after completing a night shift; it was an open and shut case but it still took years to sort out. In the end, Conrad got the money, but he's not aware of what he has, and I'm absolutely sure that Conrad the rebel would rather have driven his bike off a cliff at speed and have finished it there and then."

"Well, he'll have a bloody good day out in Hull," asserted Sally in a deliberate attempt to add a positive note to the conversation.

By the time Minnie's corned beef hash had done its job, Len was feeling a lot more positive about life, but it still took a bit of gentle persuasion from Sally to persuade him to return to work for the afternoon session. In the end, he agreed to give it one more chance after she suggested walking him back to the nursery on her way home and assuring him that she would be back in the evening to see how things had gone.

Clive walked to the shops in the afternoon with Conrad. It was hard to imagine what Conrad would have been like if his life hadn't been so cruelly altered. No doubt he would have mellowed, as most of his contemporaries probably had, but instead he had become this dapper, unassuming figure who walked silently with the friend who looked after him. In the supermarket, Conrad took little interest in the shopping process but seemed happy to wander around after Clive, pushing the small trolley when he was reminded of the necessity to do so, but quite content to let Clive do anything that appeared like work. Clive dutifully tried to involve Conrad in choosing items, but it was obvious he had little interest in the process. The only part of the shopping experience that seemed to be of any interest to Conrad was when they approached the area designated for cigarettes. At this point, he would stop and stare in fascination at the array of assorted tobacco products. For months, Clive had assumed that it was merely an obsession with the assortment of colours, but then he began to suspect that, while Conrad didn't smoke now, it was likely that the youthful Conrad had done so, and so there was still some vestigial memory of the allure of tobacco. Whatever the cause, it took a while to persuade him to move on to complete the rest of his non-shopping experience.

The small supermarket was one they used regularly as a lot of the other shoppers had seen Conrad frequently and so tacitly accepted him. In Clive's experience, most members of the public treated his 'different' friends very well, if anything they tended to be a little too helpful, but there had been occasions when there had been a lack of empathy shown. Conrad was blissfully unaware of the odd sideward glance he was given or the snatch of a conversation that was overheard, but Clive still noted these signs of a lack of acceptance that both disappointed and annoyed him.

Sally arrived at Kitchener House that evening just as the trio were finishing their meal and Clive was writing a few brief notes in the diary about the day's happenings.

"Good grief, you're prompt," said Clive. "You shouldn't have rushed to get back; you seem to have spent half your day here already."

"I just couldn't bear to be away from you a moment longer. Well, to be brutally honest, I get a bit bored at home sometimes and anyway, you've had to work over a lot of your shifts with Larry's problems and all. I thought you might appreciate the chance to get off home on time for once."

"Thanks, that's kind, but you needn't worry too much about exact times. I'm flexible, and I'm sure you'd do the same for me."

Clive enjoyed spending time with Sally, and he felt tempted to stop on and chat with her for a while, but she obviously wanted to give him the opportunity to get away on time so he felt he ought to.

CHAPTER SIX

It was not an atypical weekend; Josslyn took Maureen off to enjoy the delights of Accrington, Nicky spent much of the time with her boyfriend Stan, and Sebastian worked both days at the car salerooms in an attempt to boost his figures and to compensate for his last month's shortfall.

Clive quite enjoyed a bit of time on his own to read or potter about in the garden. There was little that could be done in the garden at the moment, so his weekend was largely an opportunity to get down to some serious reading. He still had a couple of short sessions at Kitchener House thanks to the chaotic staff duty roster, but he didn't mind too much as it was rather like visiting old friends, and now there was the added bonus of seeing Sally for a chat when their shifts overlapped. Even with this benefit, Clive did slightly resent working some weekends; true, he often had up to three days off at a time, but these could fall mid-week, and family events had long since proven very difficult to arrange.

Maureen arrived back late on Sunday evening, claiming to have had a hectic couple of days at the convention but looking remarkably refreshed. She made it very clear that, in view of the week of pressing engagements she had in front of her, she was in need of her beauty sleep and must not be disturbed. Mildly disappointed, but far from surprised, Clive made a mental note that her room was definitely out of bounds that night.

The following week was rather an enjoyable one for Clive. Things were going very well at Kitchener House. Minnie obviously enjoyed having Sally around so they could chat about 'women's stuff' and, like some homely grandmother figure,

Minnie could pass on some of her little cooking secrets. If truth were known, with the one exception of her legendary corned beef hash, Minnie was not the most gifted person in the kitchen, and it would have been a service to the culinary world to let most of her secrets go unrecorded, but Sally listened dutifully to it all.

Len was still slightly aggrieved by the attitude of his new 'gaffer', but the two of them were beginning to forge some kind of workable understanding; the new boss made it clear that more work was needed to be done, and Len made it equally clear that he was quite prepared to let him do it.

Conrad was obviously looking forward to his journey to Hull, and he regularly browsed through some of the pamphlets that Sally had brought him from the station when she had booked the tickets. He would bring the brochures and set them in front of Sally or Clive, who would dutifully outline the plan for their big day. Kitchener House benefited from a good deal of extra unpaid staff time that week. For some of the time, they were scheduled to be working alongside each other but the handover periods were also becoming extended as neither was late for duty or eager to go home when they were relieved. Even on his day off on Tuesday, Clive had decided to stroll round to Kitchener House as Arkwright deserved a longer walk, and both he and the residents had got on very well in the past when Clive had driven him round in the car. It was only halfway through this 'stroll' that Clive realised that what was a relatively short journey on his bike had become almost a route march. Arkwright liked his walks, but in moderation and with a great deal of built-in sniffing time, so by the time they got to Kitchener House he was tired out. He was not too tired to bolt down some biscuits that Minnie found for him.

Clive always considered it a shame that none of the residential units were allowed pets because many of the residents loved animals. Arkwright revelled in the attention he received from everyone and made a couple of circuits of the group before settling down for a much-needed sleep.

"I'm not surprised that he's tired," explained Sally after a while. "It's not a breed that was intended for such sustained efforts."

"Breed?" exclaimed Clive, looking down at the snoring scraggy mass on the floor. "He was a rescue dog, and we just assumed he was a mutt."

"A mutt; I very much doubt it. No, there may just possibly have been some slight breeding indiscretion some generations back, but what you have there is an almost purebred miniature watchdog from one of the smaller cantons in Switzerland. I bet there can't be more than a couple of hundred of them in the country now. They've almost died out in their native Switzerland."

Clive saw Arkwright in a different light now and pressed for more information.

"A miniature watchdog, eh?"

"Yes, one of the remarkable classes known as 'pocket' breeds, specifically bred for guarding the smaller chalets in the high Alps. Arkwright is almost certainly a Swiss pocket watchdog."

Sally couldn't suppress a giggle after this last revelation, and belatedly Clive saw that he had been fooled again.

"I should have known," he remarked. "But then I have to trust you because you're a doctor!"

After Arkwright had had time to recuperate, Clive picked up the dog's lead and made ready for the return hike home.

"You can't put the little mite through that again," protested Sally. "I've got the car outside; I can have you home in a couple of minutes."

"No, that's very kind of you, but Arkwright could make a mess of your car," protested Clive.

"No problem, my car looks like a disaster zone inside, and anyway it will give you a chance to show me where I need to pick you up on Thursday."

Clive was in no mood to protest too much because he wasn't exactly looking forward to dragging Arkwright all the way home on foot.

They arrived at Clive's place to find Nicky sweeping up the leaves on the front lawn.

"Great job! Thanks, love," said Clive as he got out of the car. "I've been meaning to get that done. No university today?"

"I did a couple of hours in the library, and I've got an evening session later. You must be the friend from work that Dad has told us so much about," she added as she saw Sally emerge from the car, having had to entice Arkwright from his comfy bed among the papers and general debris on the back seat.

"Hi. Yes, I'm Sally, and you must be Nicky."

"Do you fancy a cup of coffee, or do you have to rush off?" asked Nicky as she loaded the last of the leaves into a large tarpaulin sack.

"Lovely, thanks. I'm sure the Kitchener crowd will be able to manage just fine without me breathing down their necks for a few minutes."

Clive found himself left to carry the large bag of leaves round to the back of the house and to put away the few tools Nicky had been using, so it was some minutes before he arrived in the kitchen. He was just in time to hear Nicky saying, "Yes, isn't he just? If there were prizes for gullibility in the honours list, he would have received his knighthood years ago."

The two women laughed, and Clive was in no doubt as to whom they had been discussing, but he didn't mind being the source of their gentle humour. He knew all too well that he had a habit of seeing the best in people and taking them at their word, but that was just the way he was.

The three sat for a while, chatting and drinking their coffees before Sally excused herself and set off back to work.

"She's nice," commented Nicky. "Have you known her long?"

"She's been with the company for a few years, but we haven't worked together much as we've been on different teams. We have met occasionally at staff meetings and on those awful staff social events, but apart from that our paths have rarely crossed."

"Is she married?"

Clive was mildly surprised at this apparently sudden interest in Sally's marital status, but he replied, "Yes, but I think I've only met him a couple of times. The last time was at the last, and it proved to be the last, staff barbecue at June's place. Nice guy, Steve. He could certainly down the red wine."

"And did he have to spend the night in his shed?" chuckled Nicky, who obviously remembered more of that weekend than Clive cared to.

"I think I had a bit too much sun that day, and as for Steve, I've no idea, but I guess he had a rough time of it because Sally always seems reluctant to talk about it. I think Steve used to do some work in a consultancy capacity as a psychologist or psychiatrist or something in assessing prospective clients for any vacancies in sheltered housing units such as ours."

"She's nice."

"Yes, so you said."

"Genuinely nice and nicely genuine," mused Nicky in a philosophical sort of way. "She's a bit like the big sister I always wanted."

"You've known her two minutes, and you want us to adopt her?"

Nicky smiled and finished the last of her coffee before going off to tidy herself up after her afternoon in the garden and leaving Clive to ponder on the way the two women had obviously hit it off so well. Nicky was right; Sally was, to use a much over-used word, 'nice', and she had a certain unpretentious quality that both he and his daughter obviously found so attractive.

CHAPTER SEVEN

On Thursday morning, Clive answered the door to find Sally waiting on the drive beside a rather smart BMW.

"Morning, sir," she said, half saluting. "Your taxi, as requested."

"What a beauty."

"Why thank you, sir. I do scrub up well, don't I?" she declared with a provocative little pout.

"No. I meant the car," he explained before adding, "But you look good as well."

This was the nearest Clive was likely to come to initiating a charm offensive. Sally certainly looked different; she had obviously dressed for a day out and had even put on some make-up, although such details were generally lost on Clive but he did think she looked particularly good.

"You silver-tongued charmer," she teased him. "You sure know how to make a girl feel good. The truth is that I reckoned even you would dress up for the reading of a will, Conrad is never less than a beacon of sartorial elegance, so I was determined not to stand out as the scruffy one. Come to think of it: when you put on a suit like that, you look pretty damn smart yourself."

Until that moment, Clive had been feeling rather uncomfortable in a suit after years of distinctly more casual attire, but suddenly he felt a lot better and even went to the extent of discreetly pulling his stomach in as he wandered round to the passenger door.

They set off to pick up Conrad, and Clive was impressed by the difference between this and Sally's last car. It was pristine, cleaned inside and out and not a single article of junk or litter anywhere. Even the ashtrays were empty, their metal interiors shining.

"Nice car," he said. "But what was wrong with taking the other one?"

"Oh nothing. I love my old junk bucket; it's very reliable, and you don't have to worry about the scruffy paintwork getting damaged."

"A bit like me," quipped Clive.

"Don't run yourself down; there are plenty of people out there prepared to do that for you. You're not a junk heap; more of a comfortable family saloon. I suspect that you're relatively cheap to run, far from flash, and certainly reliable in a solid sort of way. And, of course, you are at that stage in life where depreciation is not a major concern."

Clive was not at all sure about the last remark, but before he could even start to think of a witty reply, Sally continued.

"I love my little car, but when I want to have a special day out, I take Steve's. We have to be at the station for nine, so I hope Conrad is ready," she added, changing the subject. "But I'm sure he'll be raring to go."

Conrad was indeed ready and waiting. As ever, he was immaculately attired with the added accessory of a small plastic box containing the sandwiches Minnie had prepared for him to eat on the train. She had insisted that her boy was not going out for the day without 'a little something' in case he was peckish. Conrad looked at the shining car in front of the house and was obviously very impressed.

"I'd love a cup of tea," he said as he surveyed his transport for the first stage of his day out.

"Yes, she's a beauty, isn't she?" added Clive, trying not to catch Sally's eye.

Sally just smiled and ushered her fellow travellers into the car. Conrad took pride of place in the back on his own, looking every inch the wealthy tycoon while his staff sat in the front. As they drove off, he waved politely to Minnie, who waited outside, waving back until the car had disappeared around the corner. Clive felt good. The experience of being chauffeured around in such comfort and with such agreeable company led Clive to feel assured that this was going to be a good day.

Sally was right about her friend living near the station. Less than a hundred yards from the station car park, she pulled onto the parking space that had been created in what had been the front garden of a smart terrace house, and while her passengers squeezed out of the car, she went over and rang the doorbell. The door was answered by a smartly dressed young man who greeted Sally warmly.

"Sally, great to see you," he said, kissing her on the cheek. "Still using Steve's car, I see."

"It is a bit more comfortable than mine," she replied before adding, "We should be back by 10 at the latest, depending upon connections, of course, so we won't disturb you tonight when we get back."

"You won't disturb me, I'm catching a train to Swansea this afternoon for a long, and I hope very romantic, weekend, and I've got nobody booked for the space while I'm away."

Sally kissed him, made her apologies for having to rush, and then the three happy day-trippers walked briskly off to the station.

As they had hoped, the train was not too full, and they were able to get seats for the first part of their epic journey that was to take them to Peterborough and Doncaster before the final link in their journey that was to take them into Hull. Clive enjoyed rail travel but would normally have been put out by the need for changing trains. Today was different because he knew that Conrad loved the whole experience of pulling in and out of stations, getting on and off trains and even sitting on platform benches. For once, Clive was disappointed that there were no long delays between trains that might have enabled them to offer Conrad the further experience of spending time in the station cafés at some point. Conrad fairly beamed with delight throughout the whole experience, so it seemed like no time at all before they were on the last stage of the journey, which ran from Doncaster to Hull.

Clive was pleased to see that the train was relatively empty, and he was easily able to find seats on the side of the train that he knew would afford them great views of the Humber as they approached Hull. He ushered Sally into the seats by the window and then sat down beside Conrad, who was engrossed in watching the people on the platform.

"This is one of my favourite journeys," enthused Clive. "I used to travel along this stretch quite frequently when I started at the paint factory because we had dealings with a big engineering unit in Doncaster."

"Have you got your passport with you?" asked Sally, as if suddenly remembering something.

"I think I can get into Hull without a passport, and as a last resort I could always bribe the customs officers."

"No, I'm being serious. Shouldn't you have some form of identification if you are going to the solicitors to hear something 'to your advantage' as they say?"

"Well, they will just have to settle for the fact that I've got the letter they sent me because my old wallet and driving licence are in my jeans pocket. That should be enough identification to pick up any junk I'm due to collect."

"I've never been to Hull," commented Sally. "I nearly went to the university at one point, but I ended up going to Manchester instead because Steve was involved in a research programme there."

"Hull is the kind of place you only go to if you want to go to Hull. As the great man said, it's a place 'where only salesmen and relations come'. You don't pass through it on the way to anywhere else really. It's just Hull and then; well, not much really."

"Except Withernsea," suggested Sally with a grin.

"I thought you said you'd never been."

"I haven't, but when you promised to whisk me away to Withernsea, I had to find out where it was, didn't I?"

"I think I ought to warn you that Withernsea may not prove to be the romantic idyll that you imagine it to be."

As the train journeyed on, Clive was pleased to note that the weather was being kind to them. It was a clear, bright day with no trace of the fog and mist that could so easily have spoilt his view of the Humber at that time of year. He watched the river for some time, and then, half to himself, he said, "The river's level drifting breadth began, where sky and Lincolnshire and water meet."

"'Whitsun Weddings'," declared Sally. "I didn't know you were a poetry geek."

Clive was more than a little surprised that she should recognise the quote, and he was quick to get on to one of his favourite topics. "I have to confess to being a bit of a poetry junky, and Larkin has become a favourite. It was that poem that started me off, probably because I knew the train journey along the Humber bank so well; later I read other pieces that seemed to reflect the Hull I used to remember as a child."

"All in black and white and miserable?"

"True, his work wasn't a lot of laughs, but he just seemed to have a knack of picking out things that resonated with my experiences."

Clive was conscious of a certain pretentiousness creeping into his explanation, so he simply concluded by saying,

"The poems just seem to chat to you like a bloke in a pub, sort of ordinary but special."

"You needn't apologise," Sally said with a smile. "I'm a secret poetry lover as well; it just surprised me to find out that you were. Of course that bit in 'Whitsun Weddings' is really describing the journey out of Hull. The journey we are taking is better reflected in Larkin's poem 'Here' where he talks of the journey into and beyond Hull."

"Yes," interjected Clive enthusiastically. "He describes all this, 'the shining gull-marked mud', and that's what it's like."

"And having gone past Hull, the land ends suddenly 'beyond a beach of shapes and shingle'."

"Sounds like Withernsea," suggested Clive, feeling pleased to be able to tease her a bit.

"You romantic devil," said Sally.

For the rest of the journey into Hull, the two eagerly shared their collected memories of the way Larkin had described the very journey they were now on. Many things had changed in the intervening years, but Larkin's Hull was still there. Clive felt blissfully happy, and he made no secret of the fact to Sally, who, in turn, was happy to discuss their mutual love of poetry. Conrad was just happy to be on a train.

Shortly after their arrival at Paragon station in Hull, the three happy travellers found their way to a small café, and Clive ordered sandwiches and coffee for them all before sitting down to finalise their plans for the day.

"The solicitors are a short walk from here near the Land of Green Ginger," started Clive.

"Land of Green Ginger?" interrupted Sally. "I suppose that's where the Green Ginger fairies live?"

"No, honestly, it's an area in the old part of the city," explained Clive. "And it's not far from Wilberforce House, where the slavery abolitionist lived. It's a museum now, so you and Conrad could pop in there while I check out the will reading."

"Sounds good to me. How about you, Conrad?"

Conrad smiled in approval as he daintily finished his sandwich. He was still carrying the small box of refreshments that Minnie had prepared for him, but he preferred the sandwiches Clive had bought. After their refreshments, the three strolled like tourists down towards the solicitor's office, doing a bit of shopping along the way to while away the time until Clive's appointment.

CHAPTER EIGHT

When they arrived at the solicitor's office, Clive was a bit apprehensive and felt he would much rather go off with his friends than climb the stone steps to the large imposing door on which was fastened an impressive brass plaque announcing this to be the premises of Pearson, Pearson and Wentlock. Clive was not to be put off, so having arranged for the others to meet him back there in an hour, he straightened his tie and ascended the steps. He let himself in to an imposing reception area. He was immediately reminded of the times as a child when he had visited his own father's office; this was a more impressive establishment than the one he remembered from childhood but it had that same air of dated solidity, designed to impress clients. A young woman behind a large desk took his name before taking him through to an impressive conference room. Most of the chairs down each side of the large table were already occupied. At one end of the table, there was a larger empty chair in front of which was a reading slope and a water carafe. The opposite end of the table had no chair set out, but behind where that chair should have been was a large television screen.

Clive found an empty chair and sat down. He looked around the room at the array of seated figures; there were many familiar, if not to say friendly, faces that he recognised from his days in the factory. He nodded politely at one or two of those he knew, and they more or less nodded back. He became aware of the presence of a young woman on his left who seemed even more ill at ease than he was, so he turned to her and quietly said, "This is my first time at one of these events. How about you?"

"Yes," she said nervously, "and I've no idea why I'm here. I hardly knew the man."

"I'm Clive, by the way."

"I'm Maisie. Yes, I remember you; you were one of the bosses."

"Hardly that. I was just a general paper-pusher."

"Mr Hargreaves always valued what you had to say though."

"That's kind, but I was only a small cog in the business. But how do you know so much about it?"

"I used to do the cleaning in his office, and we often had a little chat in the evening when he was working late. He said I was his link with the real world. He could be odd that way."

Their conversation was interrupted by the arrival of an elderly gentleman dressed in a smart three-piece chalk stripe suit, who was followed by the young woman from the outer office.

He took his seat at the head of the table, and the young woman sat in a chair to his side and opened her notebook with an air of secretarial efficiency.

After a few seconds, he cleared his throat dramatically to ensure the attention of the assembled group. This was quite unnecessary, as all eyes were on him from the moment he entered the room.

"Good afternoon, ladies and gentlemen. My name is Winstanley Pearson, and I am acting on behalf of the late Mr Norman Hargreaves. Miss Selhurst here will be keeping a record of the events."

Clive couldn't help but think that the solicitor had a strangely old-fashioned way of speaking; each word was delivered with perfect diction and at a rather slow, deliberate pace, probably reflecting a high-class education at some exclusive school. The general effect was somewhere between a butler and a country vicar.

The solicitor placed a manila file on the reading slope in front of him and opened it in a deliberate fashion.

"I feel duty-bound to inform you that the method of delivery of this 'reading' is somewhat unorthodox and largely against my better judgement. That being said, I can assure you that the will as such is perfectly legal, and a written copy of the said will has been produced and appropriately witnessed in the conventional manner. It was Mr Hargreaves' decision to record his wishes on a film that you will have the opportunity to watch this afternoon. Notwithstanding my misgivings, his wishes have been complied with, so it only remains for me to ask you to watch this film through without interruption. Miss Selhurst, would you start up that contraption, please?"

The young woman dutifully walked over to the large screen and pressed a button on the box by its side. After a while, the sound of a brass band playing 'For Those in Peril on the Sea' came from the speakers within the room. Then the screen was filled with what Clive recognised as an old advertising poster for the paint factory that declared *Hargreaves paint – Hard grafting paint* next to a picture of a tough-looking chap in a flat cap and overalls with his sleeves rolled up, ready for business. It had never been a successful slogan in its day, and the passing of time did it no favours.

After a few seconds, the music and the image faded, and there on the large screen was Norman Hargreaves. Although it had been many years since they had last met, Clive easily recognised his former boss. He had obviously aged somewhat, but he still looked quite fit with no suggestion that this had been a deathbed recording.

"Good afternoon, I see you've all made it today," announced the former Norman. "Well, obviously, I can't actually see you as such because I'm dead, but I know that most of you wouldn't miss out on the chance of getting a few bob out of me, so you'll be there. As I said, by the time you hear this, I will be dead, or I will be suing the hell out of my doctors for gross incompetence over my misdiagnosis. I guess that you are thinking that I don't look ill, but unfortunately my doctors probably know better than you do. The nature of my condition is that I have been given three months, give or take, but the good news for me, if not for some of you, is that I will be in complete possession of all my marbles to the very end."

There was a murmur around the table, which was met by a loud "Hush please" from Mr Pearson.

"The problem I faced," continued the recording, "is what to do with that little bit of money I've managed to put aside in spite of the incompetence displayed by some of those I had the misfortune to employ. This was not an easy decision because I've had to work hard for my money. As some of you know, I wasn't born with a silver spoon in my mouth, and in order to explain what I have left, it will be necessary to have a very quick resume of my business career."

At the mention of something having been 'left', there was some surreptitious nudging and exchanging of glances between some of the assembled audience that was met by a disapproving look from the solicitor.

The late Norman Hargreaves continued, "My dad worked on the docks when he could get work, and my mother had to bring us up on whatever money he brought in. During the war, Dad managed to acquire a number of commodities that were in short supply. He was adamant that he was not a black marketeer, rather an entrepreneur, but it was a difficult distinction to make at times. After the war, there was a bit of money to be made out of war surplus, and I joined Dad in a bit of buying and selling. That went well, and after a few years we had the opportunity to buy up the old paintworks. It had suffered a bit of bomb damage, and originally we only wanted it for storage, but we

66

noticed that the machinery was more or less intact, and there were a few chaps nearby who had worked there before the war, so we thought we'd have a bash at producing a bit of paint. There was a ready market at the time as the post-war building boom eventually got underway. We specialised in heavy-duty exterior paints, and they sold well, particularly among the trawler owners who were more concerned with their boats lasting well rather than looking pretty. Unfortunately, we allied ourselves too strongly to the trawlers, so when the fishing declined, so did our business. We tried to produce a range of interior domestic paints, but by then the big DIY chains were starting up and we couldn't compete. We lacked the money to give the firm the necessary refit, so the business slowly died."

There was a lengthy pause on the recording, obviously put in for effect, before the story continued.

"Anyone in the business with any sense at the time should have seen what was going on, but judging by the way certain departments were continuing to spend in the same old way, it is apparent that many of you didn't see the writing on the wall until the works closed. It had always been my intention to leave the business to family, some of whom, quite frankly, couldn't hope to hold down a real job elsewhere. I had a few small investments set aside for my retirement, and it was thanks to Clive that I chose to put some of this money into a little venture involving some computer internet group. I didn't understand a word of their jargon, but evidently they did quite well. Purely thanks to luck, I took my money out just before some sort of 'bubble' burst, leaving me with a few million."

Norman had known exactly how this would go down with the assembled vultures, and he left an even longer pause during which there were open shrieks of delight and evidence of mutual congratulations being exchanged.

Winstanley Pearson cleared his throat loudly and declared, "Ladies and gentlemen. Ladies and gentlemen. Please."

The smiling face on the screen appeared to look down on them, and then the performance continued.

"Obviously, I've spent some of this, but with other bits and pieces of investments, it still leaves a tidy sum. So what do I do with it? I'll start with my sister Marjorie and her family."

A small group of people at one end of the table almost leaned forward in unison to pay particular attention to their part of the payout. Clive recognised Marjorie, an elderly gentleman he took to be her husband and two former employees Clive knew to be Marjorie's children. Conscious of the fact that he would have the rapt attention of that section of his audience, Norman continued his performance.

"Well, Marjorie, you knew you were always my favourite big sister, and I could never hide my disappointment that you chose to marry Luke; the great useless lump turned idleness into an art form. The only thing he ever contributed to the marriage was the two children, assuming he managed that unaided! Turning to you, Carl, as the eldest, I had hoped you would have made a bigger contribution, but you obviously inherited your father's idleness, and the only labouring you have ever done was under the illusion that the world owes you a living. Your wheeling and dealing cost the firm tens of thousands with your ill-conceived initiatives, and I was so grateful when I was able to move you into personnel where you could do marginally less damage. Your brother Leonard was different. Hello, Leonard, you never tried your hand at the cut and thrust of business; you never tried your hand at anything really and were more than happy to drift along in the post I created for you as 'product development officer'. Drawing the salary you did for your minimal efforts bordered on illegal."

Marjorie and her children were visibly indignant at these comments but waited patiently to see what they were to receive. Norman now turned his attention to others.

"My younger brother Michael had the good sense to marry Lucy. Michael was never as lucky as me in business but certainly a lot luckier in love. Things would have been so different for me if my fiancée hadn't run off with that former Italian prisoner of war." Norman paused for a moment as if reminiscing about his earlier years before snapping back into his address.

"However, that's all water under some Venetian bridge now; perhaps it worked for the best as it gave me plenty of time to concentrate on my work to support the rest of you. Getting back to Michael and Lucy, sadly their contribution to the family firm in terms of manpower was little better than Marjorie's brood. Starting with Fiona, who I am sure will be here as she never misses a chance to dress up. Hello, Fiona. For years, you only turned up at work to flirt with the staff, and the fact that you didn't contribute more to the family workforce was a constant source of amazement to me. Still, you were undoubtedly the most popular member of the family on the shop floor, and in the store room, and the canteen, and, it is rumoured, at least once in the car park."

"That's a lie," protested a rather attractive, if somewhat gaudily dressed woman in her early forties, "I've never been so insulted in my life."

The solicitor strove to quieten her as, after a well-spaced pause, Norman continued his evaluation of those around the table.

"Michael's other children, the twins Estelle and Gordon. You might reasonably have expected that the law of averages would have dictated that one of them would have some inkling of what work was about, but no. Neither of them has done a full, let alone honest, day's work in their lives. Given the opportunity, they would let their famous 'business' breakfast run into their 'business' lunch, which would only conclude in time to go home."

There was general uproar in the room as the assorted family members made their objections as to the way they had been treated, and Winstanley Pearson was only able to regain control by having Miss Selhurst pause the recording and by informing the group that there were to be certain bequests that they ought to listen to. The veiled promise of having inherited something was enough to bring the meeting to order.

The recording was restarted, and Norman's show continued with an apology.

"I admit that I am responsible, in no small way, for how things have turned out for many of you. In my misguided effort to support you, I did too much, and you never had to stand on your own feet. I wanted to give you all the start I never had, but the way things have turned out, I must bear a lot of the blame for almost taking the family from rags to riches and back again in two generations. I have decided, perhaps too late, that I am not going to automatically pass on what money I've got to the family as certain of you no doubt expected."

There was a dramatic pause as the figure on the screen gave the impression of deliberating before announcing, "I've decided that those who asked less shall receive more."

The room fell silent as the assembled crowd tried to make sense of this last statement, but they didn't have to wait long before all would be explained.

CHAPTER NINE

All eyes were on the large screen as Norman went into the details of his last wishes.

"Despite the fact that I have been putting food into the mouths of many of my family over the years, I have been aware that I have been used, so I decided that I would keep my own tally to see if anyone actually valued me rather than my money. I hit upon a simple way to do it. In that time, anyone who contacted me for social reasons rather than for a desired financial benefit would score a point each time they did so. I decided to discount birthday and Christmas cards sent out of a sense of duty rather than as a sign of any real interest in the recipient. Naturally, begging letters or telephone calls trying to obtain money did not score. Likewise, any supposedly social letter that made veiled references to obtaining gifts or money did not count. For example, when Estelle informed me how sad it was that her little Tristram had hoped to go on the school skiing trip but was afraid he would let the family down as his skiing outfit was past its best! I would rather have had an open and honest request for money, although he still wouldn't have got it. After years of sending presents for birthdays and Christmases, I had, rather optimistically as it turns out, expected some thank you letters. I got the one: from Leonard's youngest thanking me for the football kit. Unfortunately, I had sent him a radio-controlled car that year."

There was a growing sense of unease in the family ranks as they started to appreciate that they might not get all they expected from Norman's estate. Their fears were realised when he went on to give details of the outcome of his self-devised popularity research.

"The plain truth is that none of the family scored at all."

There was uproar in the room as the family members made their protestations at being 'cheated' in this way, so once again the screening had to be interrupted, and the solicitor took some moments to calm the disgruntled crowd by making it clear that they would have to watch the rest of the recording to discover exactly what they were to inherit. It was only the suggestion of some reward that induced the group to calm down, and the screening was able to continue with Norman announcing, "You're probably wondering who did come out well on my little tally." There was rarely a question where the unspoken answer was more predictable.

"Maisie Clark, not only did you work well for the company for nearly 20 years, but you have written to me a couple of times since, just to let me know how some of the ex-workforce have been getting on. And in all the time I knew you, you never asked for a penny, and I thank you for your loyalty and friendship. But the outright winner of this contest? Clive!"

Clive was amazed to hear his name, and he stared at the grinning face on the screen in utter disbelief. The assorted family members around the table were similarly surprised, but as the fact sank in, they looked at Clive with ill-concealed loathing because this outsider had obviously won the main prize.

"I guess you're a bit surprised to hear your name given out, but you shouldn't be," explained Norman. "Every year, you send me an informative letter with your Christmas card, and you do the same with my birthday card. I've even had numerous postcards from you to let me know how you are getting on. In all these, you never once said anything that could be seen as a request for money or gifts. That shouldn't surprise me because there can be few people who value money as little as you do.

As an employee, you were extremely good at improving the firm's financial position, but your own finances seemed to matter little to you. In all my years at the paint plant, you are the only person I ever had to ask to take a pay rise, and then, at the top of the tree, you give it all up and take a massive pay cut to go and work helping others. I never understood why you did it, but in some daft way, I admired you for it."

There was a pause that seemed to last for ages before Norman concluded his announcement.

"The details of exactly who gets what will be announced by my solicitor. I must point out that it has cost me a lot in fees to ensure that this will cannot be successfully contested; it's watertight. Thanks for turning up; that's me finished, well and truly finished by the time you hear this."

The picture faded, and the strains of 'On Ilkla Moor Baht 'at' struck up from the brass band on the soundtrack. This was not enough to drown out the sound of the family members sharing their views on the proceedings so far.

It took Winstanley Pearson a while to establish silence for announcing the details of the will, which he did by way of giving a synopsis rather than reading it verbatim.

"Copies of this last will and testament are available for you to read at your leisure later, but in essence the document makes the following bequests. Michael and Marjorie and their respective spouses and children are to receive equal shares in the ownership of the former Hargreaves paintwork and the plot of land upon which it stands."

There was a muted air of satisfaction among the family until the solicitor added,

"The late Mr Hargreaves would point out that the plant, as you are no doubt aware, is non-operational. He would also point out that the site could become valuable real estate – just as soon as the land is decontaminated due to the presence of many poisons in the ground dating back to the times when heavy-duty industrial paints were produced there. Mr Hargreaves calculates that the project could become profitable eventually, but only if the family are prepared to work hard at it."

This was not what the family wanted to hear, and there were numerous vociferous objections, largely centred upon doubting the late Mr Hargreaves' sanity as well as his parentage. Eventually the solicitor restored order and went on to say, "And now we have the matter as to the disposition of the remaining part of the estate. As Mr Hargreaves outlined, the bulk of the money is to be divided between Mrs Maisie Constance Clark and Mr Clive Alexander Peter Sullivan in direct proportion to the positive communications they sent him. To explain the reasoning behind the amounts to be received by the said parties, I must quote directly from the will."

Mr Pearson carefully moved some sheets of paper on his desk, and then, with perfect solicitor's diction, he read, "To my former cleaner and good friend Maisie Constance Clark, I leave seven hundred and twenty-eight thousand pounds."

The family benches erupted with shock and indignation at this announcement, but with a magnificent display of projection, the solicitor continued to read the next part of the will.

"This sum represents half of her entitlement, the second part of which is to be given to her 12 calendar months after the first payment."

The family members were almost stunned into silence, and Winstanley Pearson took the opportunity to read from the next part of the document in front of him.

"I recognise that Maisie is a trusting soul, and I hope that by allocating her money in two halves like this she may be able to learn how to manage such a sum of money in the first year before the second amount becomes payable. It is the same logic that has persuaded me to leave two million pounds to my former colleague Mr Clive Alexander Peter Sullivan to be made available at once and the residue of his inheritance to become available to him after 12 calendar months and in that way, he cannot blow the whole lot in a single year."

There was a moment's relative calm before Michael Hargreaves got to his feet and shouted,

"I've had about as much as I can take of this lunacy, this travesty of natural justice. I can assure you, Mr Pearson, that I, that is the entire family, will be contesting this will so that we can get back what is rightfully ours from these, these snakes in the grass." His concluding remark was accompanied by a dramatic gesture in the direction of Maisie and Clive.

Mr Pearson looked Michael Hargreaves full in the eye before declaring, in his impeccable solicitor's voice, "You are, of course, at liberty to take that course of action if you so wish, but I would strongly counsel against it. Your late brother was insistent that this will should be watertight, and I can assure you that, to use the late Mr Hargreaves' own words, it is indeed 'as tight as a duck's arse'."

Quite at a loss as to exactly how to respond, Michael Hargreaves turned to the family members around the table and declared, "That's enough of this legal charade, I think we will be leaving." At this point, and with a dramatic flourish, he rose and made for the door before stopping, looking directly at Winstanley Pearson and announcing, "You will be hearing from my solicitor."

As the family members noisily exited from the room, they failed to hear as Winstanley turned to Miss Selhurst and quietly said, "That should be an interesting communication; currently I am his solicitor. I'm sure when he calms down, he will see sense, but he won't be happy."

Throughout the last part of the meeting and since the announcement of their inheritance, Maisie and Clive sat in a state of almost shared shock. Neither had said a word. Eventually, Maisie turned to the solicitor and, in a faltering voice, asked, "What did he want to do that for? Was he mad like they said? I mean, I hardly knew him."

"I feel Mr Norman Hargreaves may have been eccentric, but he was far from mad. During the drawing up of the will, I did try to persuade him to adopt a more conventional approach, but he wanted it his way. I did have a good deal of time to discuss his arrangements, and while I must adopt a position of neutrality as to the allocation of the estate, I must confess to agreeing wholeheartedly with the way he chose to allocate his money. It might be suggested that the Hargreaves clan have lived off Mr Norman for years, that they might be described as indolent parasites that between them have sucked just about every penny out of the business. It is not for me to comment on such accusations, but I must say that Mr Norman did see sense and realise that he was doing them a great disservice by giving them too much financial help over the years."

The solicitor then turned to his assistant and declared, "Miss Selhurst, I think these two could do with a stiff drink. Would you do the honours?"

Miss Selhurst duly went over to a large cabinet and returned with a small tray with three glasses and a decanter. Carefully, she poured a generous measure into each glass before handing one to each of the three people seated around the table. Clive took a generous mouthful and swallowed to discover it to be brandy rather than the sherry he had expected. Clive had heard that brandy should be administered for shock, and he certainly got a shock as the brandy burned down his throat. Maisie was experiencing no such problems, and having finished the first glass, she set about the second that Miss Selhurst offered. Clive put his glass, with its remaining contents, on the table so as not to tempt a refill.

"There are a couple of other items that Mr Hargreaves wished each of you to have," announced the solicitor. "They come as a sort of joke on his part."

This is what Clive had expected of the day, but he was more than prepared to be the butt of a little joke after the afternoon's revelations.

"You first, Mrs Clark," continued Winstanley, who appeared to be getting into the mood of the impending hilarity. "The late Mr Hargreaves was aware of the fact that, unlike his 'parasitic family members' – his words, but I share the sentiment – you were never a clock-watcher, so he has left you his office clock, which incidentally has been independently valued at well over eight thousand pounds."

"I love that clock, cleaned it religiously for years, but I just took it to be worthless."

"With a similar penchant for the ironic, the late Mr Norman, knowing how much you disliked driving, has left you his old car, Mr Sullivan."

The solicitor appeared to find these bequests mildly amusing, but Clive and Maisie only smiled weakly, both being completely overawed by the unfolding events.

"The clock can be delivered to your house whenever convenient, Mrs Clark, but Mr Hargreaves stipulated that you, Mr Sullivan, must drive the car away today or forfeit ownership of it. Should you wish to accept this particular example of Mr Hargreaves' generosity, then you can do so because the appropriate paperwork has been obtained, and the car is currently parked behind our premises as we speak. The office will be closing at six o'clock, by which time you will need to take up your option on it, or it will be put up for sale and the money shared between the Hargreaves family members."

Clive's first instinct had been to turn down the offer of an old car, but the thought of it being sold to put a few pounds into the Hargreaves' family coffers was not very attractive when he thought of the way they had behaved towards him and Maisie during the afternoon.

"OK. You're on!" declared Clive triumphantly.

"Bravo, sir," announced Winstanley with obvious delight. "Well, the sooner we get the details of the finances sorted out, the sooner you can remove the car from the premises and claim your dues."

The business for the day was soon concluded, and the solicitor explained to the still bemused beneficiaries that the first part of their money would be transferred to their personal bank accounts immediately, with the remainder being made available in exactly one year's time.

CHAPTER TEN

The solicitor was in the process of ushering Clive and Maisie out of the conference room as Sally and Conrad entered the reception area.

"Thank you so much, Mr Pearson," exclaimed Maisie, throwing her arms around him and then planting a very firm kiss on his lips before turning her attentions on Clive.

"Oh, Clive, what an afternoon."

As Clive tactfully extricated himself from Maisie's exuberant hug, he caught sight of Sally.

"My word, Clive, this Hull air certainly does bring out the animal in you," teased Sally. "Just what sort of a will reading was it?"

"It was not exactly what I was expecting," answered a still slightly bemused Clive. "Not at all what I was expecting, in fact."

The solicitor addressed the two beneficiaries, "Thank you for your attendance this afternoon. We shall be in contact in due course, but in the meantime, Mr Sullivan, don't forget the item behind the office." He then placed the manila folder on his secretary's desk and left the room.

"Behind the office?" remarked Sally. "Sounds intriguing. Anyway, hurry up, or we'll miss our train."

"That won't be necessary, the train, I mean."

"What do you mean?"

"Norman left me his car in his will." Clive knew this wouldn't necessarily clarify matters, so he quickly added, "I've got to take it today or forfeit it; it's parked round the back."

"You've got some weird ways of doing things in Hull. What's wrong with leaving someone a few pounds or something manageable like a wristwatch or a gold ring or a book token?"

"Well, he did leave me something else."

"Oh?"

"Yes. Two million pounds."

"Oh that's OK then; leave the car, and you can hire a helicopter to take us home," suggested Sally flippantly, but as she looked at Clive's face, she went on, "You're not joking, are you? You don't make jokes like that; he really left you two million pounds?"

"Well, not exactly."

"I knew it. You had me going for a while there."

"No, the two million is only the first instalment; I get the rest after a year."

Sally found herself standing open-mouthed at this last bombshell but was brought back to reality by Miss Selhurst stating, "Those are indeed the conditions of Mr Hargreaves' will, madam."

Clive suddenly had an alarming thought and asked the secretary, "The car isn't a two-seater, is it? I can't see Norman ever having a sports model, but it would be awkward with the three of us."

"Oh no, sir," she replied. "But why don't you come through and see for yourself? I'm sure there will be enough room."

Miss Selhurst took a bunch of keys out of her desk before escorting the three visitors through a store room at the back and into a small courtyard at the rear of the premises.

"There you are, sir, your new car."

Clive couldn't see anything for a large black vehicle immediately next to the rear door of the solicitor's office. In response to his obvious confusion, she tapped her hand on the side of the large black car that almost blocked their exit.

"This is it, sir, Mr Hargreaves' old car."

"I'd love a cup of tea," came the appreciative comment from Conrad.

Clive carefully squeezed past to get to the front of the car before exclaiming, "It's a Rolls Royce!"

"Yes," replied Miss Selhurst in a matter-of-fact way. "It's a bit old, but he looked after it. It should get you home all right. It's got a tank full of petrol anyway."

Clive took a close look at the size of the vehicle and the narrowness of the alleyway into which it had been squeezed. He gave a moment's thought to leaving it, but then, mindful that the Hargreaves family would thus have benefited financially, he decided he would have a go. With some difficulty, Conrad managed to get into the cavernous rear of the car, taking his seat like some wealthy Arab potentate while Sally sank into the luxurious leather of the front passenger seat. For a while, Clive stared at the array of dials and switches in front of him and played with them until he had a rough idea of how the essentials worked before eventually turning on the engine. It was already quite dark as a rather nervous Clive edged the car out of the twisting alleyway and onto the main road. He had intended to stop outside the front of the solicitors and check if there were any final details, but having got this monster moving, he just wanted to get out of the narrow streets of the old town and on his way home.

The car travelled at a very sedate pace. Conrad sat in the rear seat, obviously delighted with this new form of travel and looking completely at ease in such opulent surroundings. He briefly explored the drinks cabinet, then played with the window controls before settling back to simply enjoy the experience. Sally tried to engage Clive in conversation, but it quickly became evident that it took all his concentration to negotiate the streets of Hull in this monster of a car,

Things were going well for the first 20 minutes or so, but then, just as they were on a relatively clear stretch of road, a police car pulled alongside, and its blue lights started to flash. Clive quickly checked the speedo. He certainly wasn't exceeding the limit. On the contrary, it was obviously his very nervous driving at 22 miles an hour that had alerted the police officers to the possibility of something being worthy of further investigation.

Clive pulled over and lowered the driver's window as the officer approached.

"Good evening, sir," said the officer in the sort of voice that suggests servility rather than respect. "Would you mind giving me your name and address, sir?"

"Clive Sullivan," started Clive, but he was quickly interrupted by the officer.

"Don't tell me you're Clive Sullivan, the rugby player?"

Clive was amazed that anyone would have heard of his less than illustrious rugby career, but then it dawned on him that the policeman was obviously referring to the great former England captain of that name, who he remembered had played for both the Hull rugby league teams in an outstanding career.

"No, obviously I'm not that Clive Sullivan."

"I see. You are just another Clive Sullivan whom we happen to have pulled over as he is driving along Clive Sullivan Way, the very route that the people of Hull selected to honour an individual that many of us still hold in the highest esteem. It's almost as if it was the first name that came into your head. Do you happen to have any identification on you, sir, other than an old cigarette card that might feature Clive Sullivan on it? A driving license would suffice to stop my unreasonable scepticism."

As the luckless driver was checking his pockets in a fruitless search for identification, the police officer changed his tack.

He sniffed loudly before asking, "Been drinking, have we, sir?"

"No. Certainly not," replied Clive indignantly before remembering the small dash of brandy he had recklessly tried at the solicitors. "Well, yes, sort of, it was medicinal."

"I'm sure it was, sir, you'd be surprised how much medication some people take. Would you just step out of the car please, sir?"

Clive did as he was asked, and it was at this point that he saw the second police officer, who was sitting in the patrol car engaged in conversation on the radio.

"Would you blow into this please, sir? Please continue until I say stop." Clive blew into the breathalyser and then waited for the officer to check the readings.

"Well, it seems you've been lucky on this occasion. Is this your car, sir?"

"Yes, it certainly is. Why, is there a problem?"

At this point, the second police officer joined his colleague, and there was a hushed exchange of words before the first officer turned to Clive and asked, "Could I have a look at your insurance documents, sir?"

"Actually, no. I only got the car today, but the previous owner had it insured for all drivers."

"The previous owner! And can the previous owner confirm this?"

"No. He's dead."

"How very inconvenient, sir; you see, our records show this vehicle to be owned by a Mr Norman Hargreaves of Chisholm House in Hedon. Our switchboard staff don't seem to be able to get a response from him, but we could always send a patrol car round; I'm sure Mr Hargreaves could clear this up for us."

It was beginning to dawn on Clive that things weren't going too well.

The patrolman cast his professional eye over the vehicle and its occupants. He was intrigued by Conrad, who was obviously trying to shrink down out of sight. These innocent attempts to avoid the flashing blue lights were interpreted as the antics of someone with something to hide. The officer turned his attention to Sally.

"And could I have your name please, madam,"

"Sally Livingstone."

"And your address, Miss Livingstone?"

"It's Doctor."

"I see," said the police officer knowingly. "Doctor Livingstone, I presume you don't expect me to believe that."

Before Sally could respond, the policeman turned his attention to Conrad and gestured to him to lower the window.

Clive knew that things were not going to improve when the police officer bent down to the open window and started to say, "So far, we've got a former international rugby star and an intrepid explorer. What about you, sir?"

Clive winced as Conrad declared loudly, "I'd love a cup of tea."

The police officer strolled back to his colleague in the patrol car, leant over and said, "Better get back up; we've got some nut who claims to be a rugby star, another is supposedly Doctor Livingstone and some wise guy who thinks we are a travelling refreshments unit. They are all driving around in a car that appears to have been stolen, and the previous owner may have been killed in the process. We could be filling in paperwork for a week, but it might be seen as less than diligent if we just let them go."

Within minutes, another patrol car and a police bus had appeared out of what was becoming quite a good deal of mist, and the collected police officers gathered near the travelling trio.

"No point taking them back into Hull Central nick. We have had reports that it's packed in there as they're still processing the drug smugglers they picked up in this morning's raid on the ferry," suggested a police sergeant. "Best take them down to the local office to try and sort it out."

Ten minutes later, the complete entourage had arrived at a small local police office, and the sergeant set about trying to establish what exactly the group had been up to. Fortunately, he had assured himself very quickly that this was not part of some highly organised criminal gang, but the story still sounded a little far-fetched. To his credit, the officer soon realised that Conrad was somehow different, and having satisfied himself that he was not actually the victim of some bizarre kidnap plot, he switched his attention to Sally and Clive.

"So tell me, exactly what sort of a doctor are you?" he asked Sally.

"I hold a doctorate in counselling psychology, and no, I don't routinely carry my certification around with me, and it wouldn't be appropriate for me to take you on as a client to demonstrate my proficiency."

"I see," replied the police officer, somewhat at a loss as to what else to say. He turned to Clive in the hope that he at least might give less confusing answers.

"And you, sir, claim to be Clive Sullivan, I gather?"

"Largely because I am Clive Sullivan, not *the* Clive Sullivan, just a Clive Sullivan."

"And someone gave you a Rolls Royce motor?"

"Yes," replied Clive, who thought it best not to confuse matters by mentioning the millions he had inherited as well. "We were at Pearsons' solicitors this afternoon, and Mr Pearson explained that I had to take the car today."

"And which particular solicitor did you speak to?"

"Winstanley Pearson, ring him up and ask him yourself."

"And tell me, sir, where exactly was the solicitor's office?" asked the officer, who appeared to recognise the name and looked as though he might be starting to think that at least part of Clive's story was true.

"Near the Land of Green Ginger, it was Pearson, Pearson and Wentlock. I had their letter, but I must have left it in the office in the excitement."

"Much as I would love to spend the rest of the evening with you and your colleagues," intervened Sally, "I must concur with my colleague's suggestion that you might consider a quick telephone call to Mr Pearson's office to collaborate our version of events."

It only took the police a few minutes to get through to the solicitor's office, and Sally and Clive listened to snippets of the police officer's side of the conversation. The sergeant explained the nature of his enquiry and then was heard to say, "And can you describe the individuals concerned, miss?" There was a short pause before the officer repeated the message he was receiving. "Middle-aged, stocky build. Attractive young brunette, slim, smartly dressed, dapper gentleman with a penchant for tea. And you can confirm that they legally took delivery of one Rolls Royce motor car today?"

After the sergeant had listened for a few more moments, he apologised for bothering Miss Selhurst, put the phone down and looked up at Clive and Sally.

"Well, that seems to have cleared up our little misunderstanding. What can I say? You can understand our suspicions, can't you?"

"I concede that it might have seemed an unlikely story," admitted Clive.

"And it was the name, sir. Clive Sullivan is one of our local heroes. The officer thought you were taking the great man's name in vain."

"I'll remember that next time I come to Hull, I'll change my name."

The sarcasm was lost on the officer, who shuffled some papers together on his desk and then said, "I'm glad we were able to sort it, sir, and now I'd better get back on the mean streets of Hull and catch some real villains."

"Yes, you never know," interjected Sally, "there might be a crime spree going on with dozens of people impersonating sporting legends; sometimes it's hard to sleep soundly in one's bed."

The sergeant smiled politely and made to get up, but as he did so, Sally put her hand gently on his arm and said, in a quiet, reassuring way, "You are a naturally suspicious man, Sergeant, which is an admirable quality in someone in your profession but don't let it carry over into your personal life. You are more sensitive than you let on and have considerable unused capacity that you have, as yet, not turned to your advantage."

"Thank you, Doctor, thank you," replied the police officer before clearing his throat brusquely and heading out into the night, leaving the three travellers and two of the other police officers who were taking the chance to grab a quick cup of coffee.

"He's a softy really," commented one of the policemen, looking in the direction the sergeant had left." I'm Jack Creamer, and this is Paul Downer, by the way, aka Cream Cake and Doughnut. We know your names."

"Cream Cake and Doughnut," said Sally. "The very mention of them makes me remember how hungry I am."

"Steady on, madam," said Jack playfully. "You can't have both of us."

"I wouldn't dream of it," rejoined Sally. "I know my limitations and stick with middle-aged, stockily built men." The way she cheekily looked at Clive, and the reference to Mr Pearson's description of him over the phone only served to embarrass him as she knew it would.

"We haven't eaten since our midday snack; look, Conrad has even eaten the sandwiches that Minnie made him. Poor lamb must have been really hungry."

"So what are your plans now?" asked Paul.

"We'll get in the old banger and head off home to the delights of Leicestershire," replied Clive at the sudden memory of the Rolls Royce standing outside.

"I wouldn't even dream of it in this weather, mate."

"What weather? It's a bit misty, but that will clear once we get away from the river."

Paul took a sharp intake of breath like a plumber about to break some very bad news to a customer. "It's got a lot worse since we picked you up; it's the worst fog we've had in years, can't see your hand in front of your face, and the reports from the Met boys say it stretches nearly all the way to Birmingham. The motorways will be lethal for those daft enough to risk them. Do yourself a favour and stay over till the morning. I'm a specialist driver, and there's no way I'd willingly head off for Leicester tonight."

"We'll just have to sleep in the car until it clears then," declared Clive, in a rare moment of decisiveness.

"I wouldn't do that if I were you," commented Jack. "For a kick-off, you can't just park up and spend the night just anywhere, and secondly, it gets bloody cold in a car overnight; take it from someone that knows."

"So what exactly do you suggest we do?"

"If I were you, I'd book into a hotel for the night."

"Any ideas as to where? It could take us hours to find a hotel," asked Clive, conscious of the fact that he found driving the Rolls difficult enough in fine weather.

"There's Big Ethel's place. That's less than half a mile away."

"Big Ethel?"

"Yes. Big Ethel's a retired copper who took over a small hotel earlier in the year. It's been undergoing a refurbishment, but I'm sure they would be keen to put you up if they've got any space."

"Tell me, Jack," asked Sally. "Do you detain a lot of hapless travellers just to drum up trade for former colleagues?"

"It's a good idea, but we don't even get commission on bookings. Big Ethel might just make us a bacon sandwich if we take you along, though. If you follow us, we'll escort you to his place if you want."

"Jack, if you can take us where we can get a warm room and a decent meal, I will personally own up to every unsolved crime in Hull over the past 20 years," said Sally, offering her wrists to take the handcuffs.

"And I was her accomplice," added Clive, copying the gesture.

Keen to join in, Conrad proffered his hands and declared, "I'd love a cup of tea."

CHAPTER ELEVEN

The Lanscombe Park Hotel turned out to be one of those small hotels that had started its life as the home of some wealthy Victorian industrialist, and it had been extended over the years in a reasonably tasteful way, but it was evident that more work was needed to restore it to anywhere near its former glory. The police car, closely followed by the Rolls Royce, passed through the gateway and parked in front of the hotel. Clive was concerned to see that the small car parking area was relatively full. He was worried that there might not be any rooms still available, but more immediately, his concerns were about how he would park such a large vehicle in such a confined space. He needn't have worried as the two police escorts were almost fighting each other for the chance to park up the luxury vehicle. Jack managed to grab the car keys, leaving Paul to escort the weary travellers into the small vestibule.

"Good evening, Paul, great to see you," enthused a smartly dressed man behind the reception desk. "Brought us some more victims of the fog?"

"Hello, Big Ethel, yes, and I hope you've got somewhere for them tonight."

The proprietor was not exactly how Sally had envisaged Big Ethel would look, and it prompted her to enquire, "Why Big Ethel?"

"Well, I am over six foot six."

"Granted, that bit makes sense, but the name Ethel wouldn't seem to be an obvious choice, not even here in Hull."

The proprietor saw that he would have to clear the issue up, so he explained, "It goes back to when I was a new copper on the beat. I was under the wing of a seasoned old copper on one of my first night shifts in the docks area, and we met a woman who explained that she did work for sailors. In my innocence, I assumed she worked for the seamen's mission in the area, and I congratulated her on the fine work she was doing. She seemed genuinely surprised when I expressed my admiration for the selfless way that she and her colleagues were prepared to offer a hot meal and a warm bed to any matelot unfortunate enough to find himself in a strange port. It turns out that the services she was offering were of a more personal nature. My partner that day didn't bother to explain the nature of her employment until after we had left her, but he couldn't wait to let the guys at the nick know. It turns out that the seamen's friend was a well-known trader by the name of Ethel, so I became Big Ethel. I tried to lose the name, but my 'friends' wouldn't let me."

"Evening, Big Ethel," chirped Jack as he arrived, having parked the car expertly. The hotel owner looked at Sally and shrugged.

"I'm afraid I've only got two rooms left," announced the owner, keen to change the subject. "It's a twin and a double with a shared bathroom, but I'm afraid it's in part of the hotel that's still being done up, and the central heating is not all it needs to be at times. It should be comfortable, though, if you can manage in two rooms?"

Clive turned to Sally and said, "I can share the twin with Conrad, and you can have the double. I don't think we'll find anywhere else now."

"Fine by me," she said. "And can we get something to eat, please? I'm starving."

"I'm sorry," said the proprietor, "the chef had to cry off this evening because of the fog, but we could probably manage a sandwich."

"That's typical of my luck, stranded with my own little millionaire, prepared for an expensive meal at some secluded hideaway in Withernsea, and what do I get? A sandwich somewhere in Hull."

"You're a long way from Withernsea, madam," interjected the owner who had overheard the remark.

"Aren't I just! Never mind, we would love a sandwich, a stack of sandwiches, any bread, any filling, as long as it's food. Please. In the meantime, I'd love the opportunity to have a wash before 'dinner'."

"Certainly, madam. Let me show you to your rooms. Ah! I see you don't have a lot of luggage. Perhaps you would like to avail yourself of one of our Lanscombe Park Emergency Traveller's packs? It's an idea we got from our travels abroad when the airlines lost our luggage and provided us with the bare essentials for an overnight stay. We've put together this little pack, including a toothbrush, shaving equipment and a unisex nightshirt. We had planned to put it all into a smart little bag with our logo, but it's still being discussed with the printers."

"We'll take three of your finest," responded Clive. "And then could you show us to our rooms?"

The hotel owner leant down and produced three cellophane bags containing assorted coloured articles, and he placed them on the reception desk. Each of the group took an emergency pack and followed their host up the stairs. They stopped in a corridor, and Big Ethel led them into a comfortable room, although the décor was a little dated, and he explained the arrangements.

"This is the twin room. As you see, it's not been revamped yet. And this door leads to the communal bathroom with rather a nice shower rather than a bath as such. Now if we go through the other door here, you find we are in the double bedroom. Oh, you will notice that we are still on proper keys in this wing rather than the swipe card system, so please be careful with them as we don't want to have to replace them. Now, I'll go and get those sandwiches ordered. Perhaps you'd like to have them in the residents' bar? I'll see you down there in a few minutes."

Having done his formal introduction and without bothering to wait for an answer, the proprietor turned and went about his business.

While Sally prepared to have a wash, Clive led Conrad into the twin room. "Which bed would you like then? They appear to be equally soft."

Conrad walked over and sat on the nearest, and his "I'd love a cup of tea" assured Clive that the decision had been made, so he wandered over to the wardrobe, took out one of the assorted coat hangers and hung up his jacket before collapsing on the bed. He looked over at Conrad, who was busying himself looking through some of the assorted brochures that had been left in the room to advertise the delights of Hull.

"I know it's not your usual bed, old boy, but it's only for one night. By the time you've had your sandwiches and a couple of pints, you'll sleep like a log."

The mention of pints galvanised Conrad into action, and he started to get up.

"Not just yet, Conrad, Sally's getting ready, and we have to wait for her."

Conrad turned his attention to his emergency bag, which he carefully opened, spreading the contents on the bed. He was particularly taken by the large T-shirt on the front of which was a colourful advert for a brewing company. It was obvious that the 'nightshirt' had been acquired as a result of some brewery's promotional scheme. Conrad held it up to himself and smiled at Clive, who couldn't help but be struck by the incongruity of his usually conservatively dressed friend with a large orange shirt emblazoned with the strapline *Bull's Bitter – get some down yer neck*. Clive picked up his pack to see just what delights he had to look forward to when he heard a knock on the door to the bathroom. Having been used to spending hours waiting for Maureen to 'freshen up', he was surprised that Sally had finished so quickly, and he called her in.

"You look," he paused, "different, er nice, fresher."

Sally was struck by his inability to compliment her, and for once she resisted the temptation to tease him.

"Thanks. A quick wash, a comb through the hair, and the application of some make-up, and the job's done. Now, if only I could get some food inside me, I'd feel half-human."

Clive put the emergency pack he was holding on the side of the sink, and they went down for supper.

The small bar was already quite full, but Clive found a vacant table, and his friends encamped around it while he obtained two pints of bitter and a glass of white wine. After a rather large gulp of beer, Clive felt himself starting to relax a little after what had, by any standards, been an eventful day. Big Ethel duly arrived with a large plate of sandwiches, which he placed before them, saying, "There you are. One plate of assorted sandwiches. I made them myself. They're a bit uneven, but we only had unsliced bread left, and I'm not good with that bread knife."

The plate of assorted bread shapes looked rustic rather than gentile, but none of the group cared.

"I think I ought to warn you," said Sally earnestly, "I think one of your Michelin stars might be in jeopardy, Big Ethel. But they look fantastic to me."

The plate of sandwiches was soon finished off along with the round of drinks, and Sally rose to her feet and looked at Clive. "Care for another? Conrad will want to get his quota."

"No, let me," protested Clive.

"I daren't do that. You may be a millionaire, but I'll be no kept woman," she said in a deliberately melodramatic way. "Here I am, a simple country girl, and you here on your old stomping grounds, breathing the Hull air and at risk of turning into an animal at any moment. I just daren't risk it."

"Please yourself, you daft ha'peth. Mine's a pint then."

As Sally went off to get some drinks, Clive took the opportunity to look at the fellow guests. The room had taken on almost a party atmosphere, and Clive guessed that most of the people there were fellow travellers escaping the fog. The famous British reserve had been broken by experiencing shared adversity. The group on the next table seemed determined to have a good time, and their frequent bouts of good-humoured laughter were interspersed with the flash of a camera. The nearest member of the group leant over and shook hands as he announced, "I'm Reg. I see you were escorted in by the police. I was one of their guests today." Aware that he may have given the wrong impression, he went on, "Not as a prisoner, you understand. I was reporting on the big drugs bust. There was a press conference, and this is as far as I got on my way back to Manchester. Bloody fog! Still, it's a good opportunity to run up some legitimate out-of-town expenses." With this, Reg turned back to his increasingly merry group.

Sally arrived back with the drinks and said, "We'll have to let people know what's going on. Len and Minnie are more than capable of looking after themselves, but Mousey June will want to be informed. I won't be missed, but you'll need to let the family know."

"They're so used to me getting back late that they probably wouldn't notice, but you're right. I'd better do it now. Would you look after my drink?"

Clive had hoped that Nicky would have answered the phone, but it was Maureen's voice that he heard, and so the conversation was not as pleasant as he had hoped it would be.

"Hello, darling. I just wanted to let you know that we are stuck in Hull with the fog, and it doesn't look like we will be able to travel until tomorrow."

"The fog? Why should that stop the trains? Where exactly are you?"

"It's complicated. Norman left me a car, and the police stopped us, and it was foggy so they brought us here to a small hotel. It's very comfortable, and Sally is helping look after Conrad."

"Sally?"

"Sally, you remember Sally from the barbecue? She's helping me look after Conrad."

"Oh yes, the one with the drunken husband! So when will you be back? What about the dog? Josslyn is picking me up early for the convention. This is all very inconvenient."

"I thought that was last weekend."

"No, that was Accrington; this is Brussels. I told you all about it, but you obviously weren't paying attention, as usual. I suppose I'll just have to ask Mother to help out again. I'd better contact her right away before it gets even later."

With that, the conversation ended abruptly, and Clive found himself holding the receiver and listening to the dialling tone so he knew Maureen wouldn't hear him when he added, "And by the way, I've come in to a couple of million pounds." He replaced the receiver and rejoined Sally.

He returned to his seat to find Sally laughing at what had obviously been an amusing anecdote from Reg on the adjoining table. Even Conrad was looking appropriately jovial, and for a while Clive felt to be actually enjoying this enforced stayover. He thought about the way Maureen had responded on the phone, but he was more surprised at his own attitude; he really didn't feel all that upset that he had been unable to share his good news with his wife. His self-analysis was soon forgotten as the group of fellow stranded travellers set about enjoying the evening.

Conrad was obviously having a good time as his second drink lasted appreciably longer than usual, but eventually he began to look slightly unsettled as he felt the need to retire.

"Shall I show you to your room now, Conrad?" asked Clive, only to receive the customary reply, which this time made it clear that Conrad was ready for bed.

"If I get Conrad settled, we can have another drink before going up ourselves," suggested Clive.

"Fine. I'd better give Mousey June a call and let her know what is going on. Goodnight, Conrad. See you in the morning. We'll have another trip in the Rolls Royce."

It was a very happy, if tired, Conrad who was escorted to his room. Clive gave him a few moments in the bathroom to prepare for bed while he lay on his own bed. After a few minutes, Conrad emerged in his new night attire, and Clive couldn't help but think that though the T-shirt was not in a style one would normally associate with Conrad, he still seemed to wear it with some style and it was with a degree of sincerity that he announced, "Very smart. I'm just going to have a chat with Sally; we'll see you in the morning."

It was at this point that Clive realised that there was only one key for the room, and being reluctant to lock Conrad in, he decided to leave the door unlocked. He was about to slip the key into his pocket when he remembered Big Ethel's remark about not losing it, so he slipped it into the lock on the inside. They clearly had nothing by way of possessions, and Conrad was not a wanderer. Indeed, he would soon be settled in his own style of deep sleep from which virtually nothing could arouse him until he decided to get up in the morning. Clive left Conrad in front of the wardrobe mirror doing his last-minute check of his new shirt and, having waited in the corridor for a couple of minutes until Conrad's room fell silent, he made his way back to the bar.

"All settled?" asked Sally.

"Nothing will rouse him until he decides to wake, probably about half past seven. Did you get through to June?"

"Yes. She only flapped a little bit, but I assured her that we could just about manage Conrad between us. Obviously, I didn't tell her about your inheritance. I didn't want to steal your thunder."

"Eh? What thunder?"

"When you go in to announce your resignation, to tell her that you wouldn't work for their crumby organisation even if she performed her full act there and then on her desk top, Burmese python and all."

"I hadn't thought of that."

"What, demanding the full tawdry show as an inducement to stay?"

"No, resigning. It never occurred to me. I really love my job. I work with friends. I think I'd rather just give the money away. I bet the old bugger knew that; Norman, I mean."

"They do say that a fool and his money are soon parted, but a kind man and his money are in danger of parting company even quicker. We need to toughen you up, my boy."

"So I can become a Counselling Psychopath like you?" he laughed. "You certainly had that police sergeant going there; he really believed you are a doctor."

"I really do hold a doctorate in counselling psychology. I really am Doctor Sally Livingstone."

"Of course you are, and I've got a doctorate in arse-elbow differentiation from the University of Hard Knocks."

"Hard Knocks will accept anyone these days, but a doctorate is a doctorate. You're not having me on are you, Doctor?"

"No. It took me two weeks of hard work, but I did it. Trust me, I'm a doctor."

They both laughed at this reference to what had almost become Sally's catchphrase. There was a moment's silence, during which they each took a sip of their drinks before Sally announced, "Sorry, but I wasn't lying to the police sergeant. I really, really am a doctor."

Clive had almost convinced himself that he knew when Sally was winding him up, but he was still unsure, and he asked, "So what was all that you said to the sergeant about being suspicious and he shouldn't be afraid of his sensitive side; was that psychological counselling?"

"No. That was good old-fashioned fortune cracker philosophy, stating something obvious that could apply to most of the adult population. They're also called Barnum statements," revealed Sally. "They give the impression that the speaker has some mystical insight into the kind of person they are addressing. For example, I could look at you and say that at times you have serious doubts about whether you have made the correct decision or done the right thing. Am I right?"

"Absolutely!" replied Clive before thinking for a minute and adding, "But you could say that about just about anybody."

"You're learning."

"Clever. I thought people called you 'Doc' because of the Livingstone name, like a bit of a joke."

"Most people assume that, and I'm really not bothered about being called by my title, except when dealing with petty officialdom. It was useful when Steve and I had the counselling business, but it doesn't help much in our line."

"You're not trying to tell me you moved from running your own business to working for 'a bowl of rice a day', are you? What kind of idiot would do that?"

"Sure, the money was nice, but it can get pretty heavy with the emotional involvement. I know you're not supposed to do it, but both Steve and I would bring our work home, so I opted to do something different."

"So you really are a doctor?"

"Trust me."

The rest of the evening passed in a most enjoyable fashion, with the assorted travellers being entertained by Reg's anecdotes about the minor celebrities he had interviewed for his paper over the years. Clive was impressed that Reg did occasional articles in the very paper that Maureen had delivered to their house every morning, although he couldn't bring to mind any of the numerous special pieces that Reg listed as having been his particular contributions over the years. One by one, the occupants of the bar made their way to their rooms until it was only Reg's table and Sally and Clive who remained, so they rearranged the chairs to make one larger group. Before the evening was out, Clive, who by now was feeling particularly sociable, had treated the group to an account of their somewhat unusual day by which they were suitably impressed. Reg offered to buy a celebratory drink, which Sally and Clive politely refused, but they did agree to a celebratory photograph being taken just to remember their big day by. Clive scribbled his name and address on a beer mat so that the photographs could be sent on before Sally announced, "Come on, Clive, we'd better be getting off to bed. I suspect we may have another interesting day ahead of us tomorrow."

The couple bid the small group goodnight and set off for their rooms. On the way upstairs, Clive offered to let Sally use the bathroom first and asked her to tap on the bathroom door when she had finished so he could prepare for bed. The plans changed a little as soon as they got to their corridor, and Clive tried the door to his room and found it was locked.

Conrad must have routinely locked it just as he locked the door to his room in Kitchener House every night.

"Never mind," said Sally. "You can get in through my room and the bathroom."

"Thanks. Sorry about this. I suppose it was just habit to make sure he was secure."

"No problem, but please don't let anyone see you sneaking into my room," she added in a playfully furtive voice.

Sally stood back to let Clive into her room.

"I can honestly say I've never had such an eventful day. It has been great fun. We didn't get to Withernsea, but thanks anyway." She kissed him on the cheek before adding, "Goodnight, I'll knock on your door when I've finished in the bathroom."

"Goodnight. I'll let you know when we are awake in the morning," replied Clive before turning to go to his room. It was at this point that the day decided it had one more little trick to play on them as Clive found the connecting door to his and Conrad's room was also locked. His attempts to tap on the door to awake his roommate met with no response from within, but it did attract Sally's attention.

"What's the matter?" she asked.

"Conrad's only gone and locked the door from his side, and he's not responding."

"By the time you make enough noise to wake him, you'll have half the street awake. You know what he's like!"

"So now what?"

"You'll have to share my room."

"I can't do that," replied Clive, with a slight suggestion of panic in his voice, "I'll sleep in the car."

"It will be freezing out there, and with your luck, you'd probably get accused of trying to steal it again."

"But I can't stay in your room."

"I'm not suggesting a night of unbridled passion, but staying in with me is the obvious solution. We'll just put the spare pillows down the centre of the bed as your first line of defence in case I lunge at you during the night."

Clive was decidedly uneasy about the proposition but realised it was the obvious solution. There was no convenient sofa or even a chair he could curl up in, and even the bathroom didn't have a bath in it. He briefly considered the prospect of curling up in the shower cubicle, but the room was already starting to cool down as the central heating had long since shut down for the night. Sally's room seemed the logical, if daunting, answer.

"OK. I guess you're right. I'll just get my emergency bag, and you can use the bathroom." Clive opened his bag to put his toothbrush and toiletries on the side of the sink, glancing briefly at his large pink nightshirt before turning to her and asking, "Would you do me a favour and swap shirts?"

"I invite you into my room, and straight away you want to share your fetish for cross-dressing. This Hull air really does something for you!"

"No. It's just that I'm not sure about this shirt."

"Because it's pink?"

"No. It's just that I don't like a shirt that announces that I'm *Bull's Brewery's babe of the month*, it doesn't seem right."

"Fair enough; I wasn't exactly impressed by the prospect of wearing my purple number announcing that I might need some depilatory work because *Bull's Burton Best puts hairs on yer chest*. So it's a deal."

Preparing for bed was a succession of embarrassments for Clive as he and Sally made their separate ways to and from the bathroom and then ultimately to the bed. The manoeuvres did not phase Sally at all, so it was no surprise that she made her way into bed first while Clive stood, trying to look respectable in his T-shirt, while trying to think up any plan that would avoid him having to get in beside her.

"For goodness sake, Clive, you'll freeze to death. Get into bed," she badgered him, "I won't bite."

Clive dutifully climbed into the bed, which suddenly seemed very small.

CHAPTER TWELVE

Clive had hoped that he would be able to fall asleep quickly, get up in the morning and return to some kind of normality, but Sally was still mentally turning over the events of a somewhat unusual day.

"So what now, then?" she asked.

The question unsettled Clive even more, and he was quick to respond, "Sleep."

"No, I didn't mean immediately." She giggled. "I meant about your money and everything; it's bound to make a difference. How did the family react?"

"It was Maureen on the phone. I didn't tell her."

"Didn't tell her!" she said, sitting up in bed. "You inherit a few million pounds, and you don't tell your wife?"

"I didn't have time. She was busy implying that I was being a nuisance, and she rang off to go and arrange cover for her early start in the morning."

Clive recognised that this would seem a pretty lame excuse, but it was the truth, or at least it was the part of the truth he could make any sense of. Beneath the obvious truth was a vague feeling that it just did not seem important to tell her or it was too important because the money would assume a disproportionate importance for her. Either way, he was glad that Sally didn't press the subject.

"Will you keep working? It's a lot of money; you don't need to do another day's work if you don't want to."

"I know, but I'd miss Conrad and Minnie and Yorkshire Len."

"And me? "

"Yes, particularly you," he answered, almost shocked at his own openness. "Better get to sleep now, or we'll be good for nothing in the morning. Goodnight."

Sally slipped back down into bed and, turning her head towards him, said, "Goodnight, and thank you."

If it wasn't for the obvious difficulty that Clive had in waking up the next morning, he would have sworn that he hadn't slept at all. In his semi-conscious state, he tried to focus on what had been going on in his life over the last 24 hours. The reality of his inheritance and the fact that he had shared a bed with Sally began to sink in. He turned to see if Sally was still there and was relieved to find she was not. He sat up and tried to figure out just how he was going to organise the complex procedure of everyone getting up and washed. He needn't have bothered because Sally came out of the bathroom to announce, "Morning. Conrad and I are ready. You can use the bathroom, and we'll see you at breakfast." She gave him a warm smile before gently laying her hand on his arm and saying. "There you are, I told you I wouldn't bite."

The fact that Clive had uncharacteristically hung some of his clothes up meant that he didn't quite look like he had dressed himself in a pile of assorted dishcloths, and he was almost presentable by the time he got down to breakfast. He joined Conrad and Sally and, thanks to the fact that the chef had been able to get in, they enjoyed a rather hearty cooked breakfast.

"I could take to this lifestyle. I am thoroughly enjoying this meal," exclaimed Clive.

"That's more than can be said for Reg's party," said Sally, nodding in the direction of a table full of individuals who were considerably quieter than they had been the previous evening. Reg raised a glass of orange juice in a weak toast directed at Sally, who smiled back.

"They certainly know how to party, those journalist people," commented Clive. "But I'm glad I wasn't trying to keep up with them, I can't stand hangovers."

The last time he had suffered such a fate was after the notorious barbecue, and Clive felt it unwise to remind Sally of that. Instead, he added. "I bet he doesn't remember to send those photographs on. In a couple of week's time, he'll probably find that beer mat with my name on it and wonder what the hell it is. Still. It was a fun evening."

"It certainly was, I haven't laughed so much in years, and I certainly needed it. Thanks again."

"For what?"

"For just letting me share your bizarre day. Come on, we'd better settle the bill and be on our way."

The three happy travellers picked up their luggage, which still consisted solely of their emergency packs and headed to the reception area. Big Ethel, looking very smart, not to say pleased at the way the fog had contrived to bring him so much out-of-season trade, totted up the bill, and it was only when he announced the very reasonable total that a thought struck Clive. He only had about 50 pounds in cash, and his credit cards were still in his old wallet in his work clothes at home. Maureen had always impressed upon him that his bulky wallet spoiled the lines of his smarter suits, and he had only transferred cash to his slimline, fancy Italian wallet that he carried in his suit. Sally noticed Clive fumbling with the notes in his wallet and saved the day by announcing, "Let's put it on my card, and I'll see if Mousey June will stump up some of it."

Clive could have kissed her. But simply thanked her and headed out to the car. He was pleased to see that most of their fellow escapees from the fog had left, as had the fog. He opened the huge boot, and they each ceremoniously put in their 'luggage' before getting into the car in their usual places.

As the car pulled out of the gates, Sally turned to Clive and said, "It could only happen to me. I spend the night in a hotel with a millionaire, and I end up picking up the tab. It had better not be like this when we go to Withernsea. If I am to be whisked away for a romantic sojourn at the coast, I don't expect to have to pay for it."

After a few moments, she began to giggle. He had grown to love that giggle and was almost reluctant to stop her. Eventually his curiosity got the better of him, and he had to ask, "So what's so funny now?"

"It's just that, well, as I paid for our wild night in Hull, does that make you a gigolo?"

"A gigolo? Don't worry, I can't afford to develop a reputation like that. I'll settle up later."

"Shame. I was enjoying having a gigolo and one that doubles as a chauffeur as well."

The morning continued without incident, and all three occupants of the car were almost in holiday mood as they enjoyed the stately journey home. It was decided that they would leave Sally's car parked at her friend's house for a few more hours while they delivered Conrad home.

The Rolls looked decidedly out of place outside Kitchener House and caused more than the odd raised eyebrow and twitching curtain in the houses facing onto Verona Road. Minnie was delighted to see her Conrad back and to see him arriving in such style. "Eeh, I thought it was the queen popping in, but better still, it's our Conrad. Come in, and I'll put the kettle on for us all."

Conrad walked into the house, but not before brushing the bonnet gently with his hand and saying, "I'd love a cup of tea," in such a way that he appeared to be thanking the car for the ride.

"Best make it a quick coffee then, Minnie," suggested Clive. "I've got to get back home and see how Arkwright is."

"I'd better give June a call to let her know we are all back," suggested Sally. "And to see if we can get a bit of extra staff cover for this afternoon. After all, we did technically do an overnight duty last night."

"You've got more chance of hell freezing over; good luck though," said Clive while secretly thinking that, despite the moments of acute embarrassment that had been caused, he would gladly have spent more time on similar overnight duties.

Clive resigned himself to enduring another of Minnie's coffees while she gave a full account of all that had happened since the previous day. This amounted to very little, but she was pleased to give Clive and Conrad a full update. Clive was pleased that things had been as uneventful as he had expected, and Conrad was content to just listen to Minnie's account as he sipped his coffee and enjoyed a biscuit.

It was a while before Sally returned, and she was not in the best of moods.

"That bloody woman is the most penny-pinching, small-minded, anally-retentive jobsworth that was ever put on this earth to annoy the rest of us."

"We don't get any time off in lieu this afternoon then?"

"Not only that, she didn't feel she could authorise a claim for our overnight accommodation expenses without putting it to the full steering committee at the next meeting, and she made it clear that they would probably be disinclined to support our claim, which was in fact a mini break for us. She was almost putting the case for us to take the time out of our holiday entitlement. I nearly told the over-officious, self-opinionated piece of swamp life what she could do with her job. In the end, I told her we had had one hell of a riotous night in Hull and would have to have an early finish today before I told her that I hope her python eats her."

"Nice try; you didn't really say that about her python, though, did you?"

"Nothing ever really gets at you, does it, Clive? You just blithely stroll along life's highway thinking the best of people despite the fact that they always let you down."

"Not always. You haven't."

"I told June I'd cover until this evening, and then I'd have to get home," said Sally, adeptly changing the direction of the conversation.

"I'd better get home and sort Arkwright out, and then I will be back about dinner time to make sure Conrad has settled well after his recent adventures. I can take you to pick up Steve's car then if you like."

"Thanks, but it will be fine where it is for a couple of days. I'll walk home later, that'll give me time to unwind, and then I should get a good night's sleep, an undisturbed night's sleep," she added pointedly. "Last night was just too much excitement for me. All that Hull air."

By the time he arrived home, Clive was beginning to feel he was getting the knack of driving his new motor, and he managed to park it in his drive with relative ease. He looked up and down the road to see if it had caused the sort of nosey interest that he had noted before and wasn't too disappointed when he realised that his arrival had gone unnoticed. Arkwright was pleased to see him and bounded around the kitchen until he could be placated with a biscuit. The commotion brought Pru through into the kitchen from the front room.

"Hello, darling, who brought you home?" she said, gesturing in the general direction of the drive. "I looked out the front to see that majestic motor, so Maureen was right; you have been on a little holiday."

"Hello, Pru. It's a very long story, and it wasn't a holiday; it was work," replied Clive, conscious of the fact that he sounded rather like his wife.

"Then I'll put the kettle on, and you can tell me all about it, particularly about the lovely car."

Clive told Pru all about his day, or rather he told her about most of it. He chose not to mention his previous night's sleeping arrangements, partly because he found the prospect of telling her very embarrassing. He didn't doubt that she would believe what had happened or not happened, but he knew she would tease him about it. That part of the saga was glossed over.

He concluded his story by explaining why he had phoned home the previous night and how he had not had time to let Maureen know about the little matter of the money or the car.

"So she doesn't know?" asked Pru, trying to look casual as she poured a cup of tea for him.

"No one knows except you and Sally."

"When are you going to share your little surprise with her and the rest of the family?"

"It's not as easy as that, Pru. I had some half-baked idea about gathering them all together and gently breaking it to them, but we never seem to be together. Much of our routine communication is through notes, and it didn't seem appropriate to leave a recorded telephone message or a post-it note on the fridge door just saying *Dad's inherited a few million pounds*. Apart from anything else, I suspect that people might not entirely have believed it."

"I suppose it isn't the sort of situation you find yourself in every day, but you've got to tell Maureen somehow before she picks it up from someone else."

"I know, but she's on one of her trade missions to Paris or somewhere, and she never leaves a contact address."

"Brussels, she's in Brussels," Pru corrected him. "She rang about an hour ago to say they are staying over to Sunday now. You could use the dial-back feature to get her number."

Clive was less than enthusiastic about the idea of having to disturb his wife on one of her business trips, even with what was really very good news, but he dialled the appropriate number and listened carefully with a pen poised to catch the latest caller.

"It's no good, Pru," he said as he put the receiver down. "The last number recorded was a local one, I've written it on the pad, but I don't recognise it. Probably one of those telesales companies trying to sell me a new conservatory. They must have rung since Maureen did, so now we can't get her number."

"That's strange. I didn't hear the phone ring; it must have been while I had the vac on. Never mind, unless she rings back, she will get some rather nice news when she gets back from Brussels."

For the rest of the afternoon, Pru pumped him for more information, and gradually he filled out the details for her while being very careful to avoid the sleeping arrangements.

"How do you intend to broach the subject with Nicky and Sebastian? They are likely to be home soon, I was expecting Nicky by now, and Sebastian sometimes gets home early on Friday so he can prepare for his weekly night out with his friends."

"This is just getting silly, Pru. Maureen will want to know first, but I can't be expected to keep it a secret until Sunday, can I?"

"I'm sure she'll understand, darling," said Pru, with no real conviction in her voice. "After all, you did try and tell her."

The decision as to how and when to tell the children was largely taken out of his hands when Sebastian and Nicky arrived home together shortly afterwards.

"Whose is the motor on the front?" asked Sebastian eagerly the moment he came through the door.

"You're not going to tell us that your old boss actually left you something valuable?" asked Nicky intuitively.

The topic had been opened, so Clive felt compelled to bite the bullet and let the children know at least the outline of what had happened.

"To bring you up to date on the soap opera that has become my life, it broadly goes like this," started Clive. "We went to the reading in Hull. Well, it wasn't so much a reading as a film show, and it appears that Norman left the factory to his family, and the rest went to Maisie, a former cleaner and me."

"And you got the motor, Dad? Fantastic!" enthused Sebastian.

"Yes, I did, but I also got an amount of money," continued Clive, trying to break the news as gently as he could.

"How much?" asked Sebastian with his usual lack of subtlety. "You'll need a packet to run that beauty outside, or you'll have to sell it."

"I wasn't planning on keeping it anyway. In answer to your question, Maisie got a lump sum, which was half of her inheritance, and she gets the other half in a year's time. And in answer to what will no doubt be your next question, she got just under three-quarters of a million pounds."

Clive was aware that despite his best intentions, the tension was building, so he went straight on.

"It would appear that Norman felt he couldn't trust me with my full amount in one lump sum because I'd fritter it away in a few weeks, so he left me two million now with the other half in a year's time."

There was silence for a moment, and then Sebastian threw his fist in the air, shouting, "Yes!"

Nicky was less dramatic and walked over to Clive, kissed him on the cheek gently and said, "Well done, Dad." She paused for a moment and then asked, "Did you and Sally have a nice time in Hull?"

"Yes. It was eventful with the fog and everything, but it didn't turn out too badly."

"And what was Mum's reaction?" asked Nicky. As ever, she seemed to be more concerned with people than money.

"She doesn't know anything about it – the money, I mean," he added unnecessarily.

It had been a perfectly innocent evening with a colleague. True, they had shared a room, they had shared a bed, but nothing had happened, and yet he still found the memory embarrassing with a touch of guilt thrown in as well.

"We don't have a contact number for her in Brussels," added Pru. "And she won't be back until Sunday night."

Having established the size of his father's inheritance, Sebastian was not interested in the minor details, so he borrowed the keys to the Rolls Royce and went to investigate it. In the meantime, Nicky wanted to know all about her dad's trip to Hull, so he spent a good part of the afternoon giving her all the details; well, not quite all the details. By the time Clive had to set out for his evening session at work, Pru and Nicky were making plans for him to celebrate his good fortune, and Sebastian had mentally planned out how to 'invest' a good part of his dad's new-found wealth. As Clive was leaving, Sebastian casually asked him if he was planning to drive to work, and he got the expected answer, "It's easier on my bike than bothering to get that thing out."

Sebastian was quick to take his opportunity and asked, "Any chance of me borrowing the car tonight then, Dad?"

"No, I don't think so," replied his father, "I am reliably assured that that particular model can go at a comfortable 110 plus miles per hour, and I don't want you to prove it."

"I wouldn't be drinking."

"If you bent that car, you wouldn't even be breathing. Leave it where it is."

CHAPTER THIRTEEN

It was a chilly evening, but Clive thoroughly enjoyed the short bike ride to Kitchener House; it seemed that he had got a bit of normality back into his life. When he arrived, he caught the smell of something Minnie was cooking for dinner and noticed the table set out for three. Minnie was stirring something in a pan while encouraging her two boys to take their seats at the table.

"Come on, our Conrad, it's your favourite; beef casserole, lots of vitamin B to build up your bones." She briefly acknowledged Clive before going on to say, "Get yourself on that chair, Len, or you'll be getting no pudding later."

"All reet, lass, stop tha mitherin'. Anyone 'ud think tha were me mother. Evenin', mester Clive, Minnie tells me th'as done all reet for thisen wi' a new motor. Ah shall hev to touch thee for a couple o' bob for a pint or two if tha's so flush."

Clive reflected on how fast the news was spreading, and still Maureen didn't know. He didn't have long to ponder the matter as Sally came down from checking that things were ready for the bed time routines.

"Hi Clive, come into any more money today? More importantly, how did the family respond to yesterday's windfall?"

"Mixed. Nicky and my mother-in-law were very happy, Sebastian has spent most of it in his mind's eye, but Maureen still doesn't know a thing."

"Oh dear, that doesn't sound at all good. Never mind, I'm sure she'll be all over you like a rash when you tell her the good news."

"I'm sure it will work out OK. But she does like to know what's going on, bit of a control freak is my wife."

"You're so easy-going that you give anyone the chance to control you."

"Fortune cracker philosophy?"

"Sorry, occupational habit, must remember to stop giving unwanted advice."

"No problem, Doc. The advice is no doubt the very best, but we don't always find it easy to take advice, however good and however well-intentioned."

Clive managed to persuade Sally to leave on time because she had obviously had a rather demanding couple of days, and she did not protest as he insisted that she should get off home. Clive covertly supervised the group for the rest of the evening, but the general contagious air of excitement meant that they were late getting to bed, so it was well past two o'clock before he finished the last of the paperwork. He went through the motions of filling out his timesheet, including the enforced night away, although he knew he had no chance of being remunerated. With his recent good fortune, he couldn't pretend to be too bothered, but he felt his claim might support Sally's request for extra money. Having finished his administrative duties, he listened at the bottom of the stairs to confirm that his charges had settled before he quietly slipped out of the door to cycle home. He loved cycling home in the early hours after work; he had the roads to himself and that satisfying feeling of having done a good shift. This evening was particularly enjoyable. The weather had turned even colder under a cloudless sky, and as he meandered along, he entertained himself by watching the moisture in his breath turn in to steam-like clouds. What did he need of money and big cars? He liked being Caring Bill, he liked his friends in his job and above all, he liked it when things were simple. Perhaps if he gave it all away? But then what would Maureen say?

Maureen: even when she knew nothing about his inheritance, she still seemed to be complicating his life. "Are you a man or a mouse, Clive Sullivan?" he muttered to himself. He knew the answer, and anyone listening that night would have been unsure if it was Clive or his bike that was squeaking.

Clive was a little later getting up the next morning, by which time Sebastian had gone off to work. Saturdays were often the best time for business, and the would-be wonder salesman tried to get in early. Nicky was planning to go and watch her boyfriend playing rugby in the afternoon and was meeting friends in town for a bit of shopping first. Clive was sad that Nicky wasn't there for a chat over what was often a leisurely breakfast on such a Saturday when he wasn't working the early shift, but he was determined to make the most of his day. A bacon sandwich, a jug of coffee and a book of poetry. It sounded good to Clive.

His blissful morning was interrupted by Arkwright's manic barking alerting him to the fact that the phone was ringing. Clive put down his bacon sandwich and picked up the receiver.

"Hello, Clive here."

"What the bloody hell have you been up to?" screeched a very irate voice, "I leave you for a couple of days and this!" The vocabulary was unusual, but the voice was unmistakably Maureen, and she hadn't finished.

"How could you? And to find out in my own paper. I'll be the laughing stock of the ladies golf club. And you didn't think to tell me. I should have known. How could you? After all I've gone through for you."

Maureen was quite capable of getting somewhat heated in her exchanges with Clive, but this time she was going for meltdown. Clive tried hard to get a word in but effectively had to wait until she had run out of 'how could yous' before he was able to proffer. "What are you talking about, darling?"

"Don't you darling me you, you rat. You know full well what I'm talking about. And after all I've put myself through for you, working my fingers to the bone to bring up your children. And you do this. I just don't know how you dare."

Clive briefly considered the prospect that she may have gone mad or partaken of some strange Belgian spirits for breakfast but then guessed that it must be the inheritance. Somehow she had got the news. He was expecting her to be put out because she wasn't the first to be informed, but not to this extent. He had never been any good at understanding women, but this episode was proving to be impossible.

"I did try get in touch to let you know, but we didn't have a contact number and—" Clive didn't have time to continue as Maureen, having got her second breath, was up and running again.

"Thank you. Thank you very much," she said with undisguised sarcasm. "You were going to phone and tell me. That was so kind of you."

"I didn't want to tell Pru and the children first, but it just sort of happened that way. They were all very pleased, though."

"You told them? You told them about it. They were pleased? But I have to learn about it in my morning paper. How insensitive, how heartless, I'm coming home early. This is going to get sorted. If she thinks she's going to steal the main prize after all I've put up with, she's got another think coming."

The line went dead, leaving Clive to try and make sense of the call and to plan what he could do to patch things up. He tried to remember just what she had said, but it was a blur. What was she going on about a paper for? It struck him that Norman's executors had probably been obliged to put some announcement in the paper about the estate. That must be it, but what did she mean about someone stealing a prize? She was probably just upset.

Clive's musings were disturbed by the phone ringing again. Perhaps this was Maureen. Perhaps she was going to apologise for her outburst. Stranger things had happened, albeit not that often.

"Hello, darling," he ventured tentatively.

"Clive? It's me, Sally."

"Thank goodness, I could do with a friendly voice; Maureen has just been on the phone, ranting about not being told."

"Have you seen your paper this morning?"

"No, if Maureen's not here, Sebastian takes it in to work. I can't cope with all the sensationalist trash that they put in. Why?"

"I think I know how Maureen found out."

"Don't tell me. The paper printed details about the will in the legal notices section?"

"Not exactly, but it does go into some detail about the inheritance. I think you had better get round here to Kitchener rather quickly; the water's getting decidedly murky."

"Murky! What do you mean, murky?"

"They have got hold of the story, and I can see why Maureen wasn't too pleased. I think it best if I don't try and explain on the phone. See you soon."

If Clive had ever had even a passing understanding of the plot, he had lost it now. Two phone calls, one that made hardly any sense and another that only seemed to make it more complicated.

"What's going on, lad?" he asked Arkwright, who was keeping a careful eye on the barely touched bacon sandwich. "Women! I wish I had even a faint idea of what drives them. Anyway, Arkwright, it's an ill wind that gets the dog an extra breakfast." With this, he carefully took the bacon from his sandwich and put it in the dog's dish. "I'll be back soon, lad;

don't pine too much," he added needlessly as the dog was engrossed in his bacon.

It seemed that Sally had been keen to see him quickly, so he took the car. Within a few minutes, he was drawing up outside Kitchener House, and Sally was soon outside to meet him.

"Have you still not seen the paper?" she asked.

"No, I got round as quick as I could, as it seemed urgent. What exactly has the paper got to say about Norman?"

"It's not so much what they say about Norman; come inside and I'll show you."

Clive was still baffled by what was going on, so he followed Sally into the house.

"I suppose you ought to read it yourself, page four, you can't miss it."

Clive had expected to have to search through endless small boxes of tiny print but his mouth dropped as soon as he found the page. There at the top of the page was a picture of two people obviously enjoying a shared joke and looking to be having a very good time. It was Clive and Sally, and a closer inspection showed them to be sitting at a table he recognised as being in the bar of the Lanscombe Park Hotel. He looked up at Sally, half expecting some witty little comment, but she just looked at him. Clive began to read out aloud.

"*Social worker celebrates his millions.*"

Clive looked up, "I'm not a social worker. Can't they get their facts right?"

"That's not all they got wrong," added Sally.

Clive read on.

"*Clive Sullivan, fifty-two-year-old father of two, caught celebrating his recent multi-million-pound inheritance with his attractive young girlfriend, thirty-year-old Sally Livingstone, during a secret stay at a discreet hotel near Hull last week. Sullivan had just heard that he had inherited twenty million pounds in the will of his former employer, the industrialist Norman Hargreaves, who made his fortune in the paint industry. Mr Sullivan was also left the late industrialist's luxury Rolls Royce car, but he needed a police escort as he drove it to his hotel hideaway to escape the attentions of the late Mr Hargreaves' family. A spokesman for the family, Mr Michael Hargreaves, the dead man's brother, said that the family felt cheated by the terms of the will, but their solicitor felt it was not worth contesting it. Meanwhile, Mr Sullivan is seen living it up with his young girlfriend in their hotel love nest."*

Clive lowered the paper and looked at Sally. He was almost speechless, but he managed to say, "Twenty million? Police escort to hotel hideaway love nest?"

"Attractive young thirty-year-old! I like that," added Sally, trying to lighten the tone a bit before adding, "You can see why Maureen was a little upset."

Clive slumped into a chair, groaning, "Maureen, of course, I'd forgotten that for a while."

"I suppose that the idea of her working hard while you inherit a fortune and we're at it like rabbits could just niggle her a bit. Don't worry about it; she'll see the funny side in the end. How on earth could she believe all that? About us and everything?"

"I just remembered that I told her that I'd told Pru and the children about this. She probably thinks I've been parading my mistress in front of the family before telling her!" Clive picked up the paper again and looked at the page more carefully.

"Ah ha!" he declared. "That explains it; the article's by Reg Royston. No wonder he was keen to try and get us to have an extra drink or two. I suppose it was easy to get a bit of background on Norman and put a few things together to make a story, but why did he have to put that in about us being associated romantically with each other?"

"Sex sells papers."

"But there wasn't, isn't any sex, is there?"

"It's a bit late to ask me now; you had your chance in our love nest but blew it."

Clive was in his own personal turmoil and in no mood to be teased. He looked at the paper again and spotted something that made the situation even more worrying. He pointed to the photograph and said, "Look, look where my hand is."

"Where?"

"It looks like I'm lunging at your chest. Maureen will kill me."

"Don't be daft. It's a perfectly respectable photograph, and nothing untoward was going on. Believe me, I'd have noticed."

"I know that, but what will Maureen think?"

"Clive, they must have taken dozens of photographs that night; they were sure to find one that showed us in a somewhat frivolous state. Don't worry about it."

Their conversation was curtailed by the arrival of Minnie with two cups of coffee on a tray. As she moved the paper to clear a space on the table for the tray, she saw the photograph and commented. "What a nice photograph, I always knew you two would make a lovely couple. I'll just put these down here and then leave you to your courting."

"Thanks, Minnie," responded Clive, knowing it was pointless trying to convince her that she had misunderstood the situation. She had come up with the most obvious interpretation of what the picture showed, and it was not difficult to understand why many people would come to a similar conclusion. This realisation did nothing to reduce Clive's feeling of dread at the prospect of having to face up to his wife on her return from Brussels.

CHAPTER FOURTEEN

As he drove home, Clive tried to develop a plan of action for facing Maureen. It wasn't enough to know that he had done nothing wrong because he knew the blame would undoubtedly, if unjustly, be heading his way. He tried to rehearse his response; it had never helped in any previous encounter with Maureen, but he clung to this forlorn hope. He went through the imagined conversation in his mind. He would have to get in quickly to pre-empt her accusations. Perhaps, "I'm not surprised you are upset, darling. It must have been a shock to see those ridiculous stories in the paper. I appreciate it looks like we are having a party in the picture, but it's probably one of those touched-up photographs, you know what papers are like, all sex, drugs and rock and roll." His gambit needed some work, but it was a start.

No sooner had Clive climbed from the car than Pru came out to visit him.

"Darling, I just had to rush round, I tried to phone, but you were obviously out. Have you seen this morning's paper?"

Clive wondered to himself if there was anyone who hadn't seen the article with its incriminating picture but limited his answer to, "Morning, Pru. Yes. It's all a pack of lies, and that ridiculous touched-up photo!"

"It's a good job Maureen's in Brussels; it wouldn't do to have her finding out this way." Pru looked at him before adding, "You poor darling, she has found out, hasn't she. But how?"

"With my luck, the paper probably sent a copy by personal courier to her hotel."

"A lot of foreign hotels get proper papers routinely delivered from England. Just your luck."

His mother-in-law's concern about how her daughter would react did nothing to comfort Clive, and he felt that the gloom was deepening as he followed Pru into the kitchen.

"Coffee, Pru?"

"I think I'd rather have something a bit stronger. Got any of that nice white wine?"

Clive collected a bottle of Pru's favourite and opened it. "To hell with it, I think I'll join you," he said, taking two glasses from the cupboard, "I need something to steady my nerves."

At Pru's suggestion, they studied the newspaper article. Clive was less than keen but knew his defence depended on him anticipating what Maureen was going to say.

"It says you got 20 million here," Pru pointed out.

"Pure fantasy, a nice round figure. They probably did a bit of background reading on the paint business, assumed it was still a profitable concern, got a figure and doubled it. I tell you, I got two million and, like Maisie, I get my other half in 12 months' time."

"It's a pity they mentioned your love nest."

"There was no love nest. We were caught in one of the worst fogs in years, and the police didn't escort us to the hotel. Well they did, but not to protect us from Norman's family. They actually warned us not to consider driving back in the fog. It was all so innocent."

"That's a shame. You deserve a bit of fun."

Pru's comment was something of a surprise as well as being less than helpful to Clive in his private state of panic. They sipped their wine and tried to prepare for the arrival of Maureen, but Clive was aware that the more he disclosed, the less credible it seemed.

They hadn't been planning for long when Nicky arrived, brandishing a copy of the paper that contained the evidence for the prosecution, but before she could ask, Pru said, "Yes, we have seen it. Quite a story!"

Nicky was her usual smiling self, and she went over to her dad, kissed him on the cheek and declared, "I was having lunch before going to the match when Stan saw the article and pointed it out to me. I tried ringing home, but you were obviously out or busy. I must say, Dad, you're a dark horse. Who'd have thought it? You and Sally in a love nest in Hull. The romantic spirit still burns bright, eh? I know I said I liked her, and she was the older sister that I would always have liked, but I'm not sure if this is the best way to get her into the family."

"I don't think your dad is in the mood for jokes, Nicky."

"Sorry, Dad, but who in their right mind is going to take that load of horse feathers as the truth?"

"Your mother," answered Clive.

"I see your point, but surely even she will see that it is pure journalese. We have people at the university studying journalism; they could make extracts from the Highway Code sound salacious."

"And your mother would believe it. Don't forget that she reads that particular sort of tripe in that paper every day."

"But you can see it's rubbish. They've given you a few extra years while shaving a little off Sally's age. It gives more scope for the dirty older man and young bimbo scenario. If they don't have all the facts, they fall back on the tried and tested clichés. Sex sells papers."

"That's what Sally said but there wasn't any sex."

"Hard luck, darling," added Pru in a less than helpful way.

"Mum may be a bit shocked to find out this way, but she'll get over it. In a while, we'll all be looking back at this and laughing. I think I'll join you in a glass of wine if I may."

For a while, the two women tried to help Clive get a better perspective on his situation, but even after two glasses of wine, he felt only slightly less uneasy about facing up to Maureen.

The peace was broken by Sebastian's arrival with yet another copy of the paper.

"Yes, we've all seen it," said Pru before Sebastian could utter a word.

"Great news, isn't it," blurted out Sebastian, "I read it at work. I tried getting hold of you on the phone but no reply. Anyway, I thought, who needs to stay on in the saleroom for the afternoon now that we're millionaires?"

"We? We're millionaires?"

"Twenty million! Even better than I thought."

"The 20 million is a lie. The paper made it up, you idiot," pointed out Nicky. "Surely you don't believe everything you read in the papers; you put those second-hand car ads in all the time, and you know they're works of fiction."

"A lie?" asked Sebastian, who was obviously very disappointed.

"I'm afraid so," said Clive. "But I'm more worried about what your mum's going to think about it."

"I know it's a bit of a disappointment for her, Dad, but you've still done pretty well out of it."

"It's not just the money; what's she going to say about Sally?" asked Nicky, with obvious disapproval of her brother's insensitivity.

"Sally who?"

"The one in the picture. There with Dad."

"Oh her, she looks nice, although I'd put her at slightly older than 30. Friend of yours, Dad?"

It was quite obvious that Sebastian could not see beyond the money, and the implied infidelity had not been seen as a matter of any importance.

"When did Mum say she would be back?" asked Nicky.

"She didn't exactly, but she seemed keen to get back very quickly to sort things out. How long does it take to get from Brussels?" The ensuing conversation showed how little any of them knew of Maureen's travelling routines. It was assumed that she would have gone via the tunnel on Eurostar, but none of the group knew how that linked in with the rest of the travel arrangements. No one was actually sure if she hadn't flown to wherever. All they did know was that she had taken her car, but was that now parked up at some airport or at the railway station? It transpired that the car was at neither venue as it was, at that moment, pulling on to the drive.

The family were so engrossed in their conversation that they failed to notice Maureen until she walked into the kitchen clutching her own copy of the damning paper.

"Hello, darling," said Clive, trying to seem casual. "How was Brussels?"

"Belgian," came the curt reply before she declared, "And now, if I might interrupt the party, I think we have things to discuss, Clive."

This was not the furious, semi-hysterical woman who had spoken to him earlier on the phone. This was far worse; this was Maureen in her cold calculating mode. When she was like this, she reminded him of Margaret Thatcher but without the caring, compassionate side. He followed her through into the front room, and the rest of the family knew that they weren't expected to follow, and they were glad of it.

"I see it's true," she declared, looking out at the Rolls standing on the drive.

"Oh yes, that's true, but not the rest. You know what rubbish these papers put out for the gullible masses." Clive realised that he was starting to gabble a bit and that Maureen was, in fact, part of the gullible masses who regularly read that particular paper, so he belatedly added, "Not that all the readers are like that, believing all that rubbish; I mean." His bleating tailed off, and he walked in what he intended to be a casual way over to his usual chair and sat down. He tried to regain his sense of calm. He wasn't going to just take it all. He'd done absolutely nothing wrong. He knew he had to be firm, but at that moment he felt about as firm as a soup sandwich. It was time to put his rehearsed speech into action.

"I had hoped to tell you about it all in person, but then I had to explain things to Pru about the delay and things, so I ended up telling the children as well. But only the money and the car, not about staying with Sally, not that there was anything to explain until the newspaper article mentioned her." Clive knew from Maureen's stony silence that he hadn't got off to a good start, and although he was now in a hole of his own making, he continued to dig.

"It all started with Norman leaving me the car, which he said I had to take away there and then or forfeit it. Well, I thought you might like it, but there was a mix-up with the insurance, and the police took us to the station to sort it out, which they did, but it was foggy by then, and they said we ought to stay at Big Ethel's until it cleared."

"Police? Big Ethel?"

"That's not his real name, of course. Ethel was a lady of the street that he once knew. He only had the two rooms left, but I said I didn't mind sharing. We had supper in the bar afterwards, and we were chatting with the guy on the next table, and somebody took that photo. It turns out that Reg does articles for the paper, and he must have misread the situation with Sally and me and our relationship. Not that we have a relationship as such, except we're friends, as you know. And the photo, it's probably been touched up."

"I can see something is being touched up," commented Maureen icily.

"No. No, that's the camera angle. I wasn't, I wouldn't, and Sally said she would certainly have known if I had."

"Perceptive young woman," observed Maureen sarcastically.

Once again Clive's old plan of rehearsing his argument had failed miserably, so it only remained for him to add, "They didn't even get the money right. I only got four million, not twenty."

"The money isn't important," she said calmly. "It's the deceit. Twenty-five years blissfully married and then this." She pointed at the paper. Clive was more than a little surprised at this comment. Since when had money been unimportant to her, and since when did 'blissfully happy' describe their marriage? Peaceful co-existence perhaps, but hardly blissful.

"I need time to get used to this new situation. It's been a shock, as you can imagine. I feel so let down," she continued, with an air of hurt innocence. "And to hear about it in such a way. It was all too much!"

"It's only a silly report in a paper."

"A paper that many of my friends happen to read. What are they all going to think? My husband fondling a young woman at some wild party. How will it affect the business?"

"The business can take it, and we've got the extra money now."

"The money means nothing to me. It's our marriage."

Clive was amazed at what he was hearing. Money had been what had driven Maureen all her life. She had carefully selected Clive when he was a young man with what appeared to be a very lucrative career in front of him and would probably have been quite content to be supported by him for the rest of her life. That had all changed when he altered his career path after his 'breakdown'. Clive assumed that this was just another of a long line of incidents in his life where he had been completely unable to fathom out what women were all about.

"I need time to think, to reconsider my position," she continued. "My bags are still packed in the car. I'm going to stay with a friend for a few days. Oh, and if you do want to let me know anything, please don't announce it in the paper. You can contact me at this number." She scribbled a telephone number on the back of one of her business cards and gave it to him, saying, "I'll need a while, and then I will get in touch to let you know where we go from here."

Clive slipped her business card next to the telephone on his way through to the kitchen where she was announcing, "Your father and I need time to sort things out. I'm staying with a friend for a few days. Don't worry, we still love you. I'll be back in a day or so to collect some fresh clothes."

Maureen kissed each of the children in turn and then turned to her mother. "I'm so sorry things had to turn out like this, Mum. I'll be in touch" She walked out, leaving a rather bemused group.

"She's not happy," suggested Sebastian. "You'd think she'd be over the moon with the news."

"Shut up, Sebastian," chorused Nicky and Pru.

The children wandered off to their rooms, leaving Pru and Clive in an awkward silence for a while, which was eventually broken by Clive.

"Well. It looks like we're having a trial separation."

"How will you know when it starts?"

"Pardon?"

"It's just that you've been effectively separated for years; you've just happened to share the same house."

"It's not been as bad as that," answered Clive, but with no real show of conviction. He thought back to the early days when they had shared things; their ambitions, social lives, bank accounts and a bedroom. It had all gradually changed until his change of career had highlighted their differences.

Even so, he liked being married. He liked the predictability, the comfort and the family home, and he didn't like the current feeling of uncertainty.

"I know she's my daughter, Clive, but she's never been what you would call a loving or devoted wife or mother. She has always manoeuvred to get her own way, and for years she was happy to live the life of the young executive's wife, but she's never been one for sharing; it had to be her way."

"She just needed to feel comfortable, and she wanted the best for the children."

"Maureen has never wanted the best for anyone other than herself; even in nursery school, the teachers reported that she would monopolise the play equipment, and in primary school, they wouldn't let her be milk monitor because she would only give out milk to those she wanted to ingratiate herself with. She once told her career officer that it was her intention to marry a millionaire."

"Children are like that; egocentric, but they grow out of it."

"I wish Maureen would. I know that her dad and I have to take a lot of the blame; we indulged her, even competing for her attention when the marriage wasn't going too well, and we created a spoiled product."

"Don't beat yourself up over it, Pru. I know she's a little self-centred, and I know that I probably didn't help. I just loved providing for her; the little presents, the surprise treats, that's what I worked for. She was very disillusioned when I quit the paint works."

"Yes, she did have a pretty good life in Hull; she was such a lady of leisure that she eventually got bored. Remember how she set up that little business venture for a bit of pin money? Not that the money was important at that stage."

"It soon took off. The house was full of cardboard boxes full of little bottles and labels. Like a modern-day seller of snake oil, except it was largely cod liver oil that she was buying in bulk at the fish docks and selling on in an expanding range of wonder treatments," added Clive.

Clive remembered how the initial foray into the health foods business had diversified to the point where it was now a small concern importing cheap cosmetics and selling them on to the public as 'natural' products. At the same time, the business premises had developed from a small room in the house to the garage, a small unit on an industrial estate and now a much larger and smarter unit that employed a small group of packers and the lovely Josslyn. Clive was never entirely sure if Maureen saw Josslyn as an employee or a fashion accessory, but her frequent references to him made it clear that she valued whatever it was that he did. The business had done well, and by the time Clive had changed careers his financial input was hardly critical.

CHAPTER FIFTEEN

Clive and Pru's reminiscences were disturbed by the sound of the phone. Clive had begun to dread answering it as he currently only seemed to receive bad news, so he was pleased to hear Sally's voice on the other end.

"Hi Clive."

"Sally. I can't tell you how nice it feels to hear a friendly voice. Are you OK?"

"I'm fine, thanks, but I can't say the same for June."

"Why, what's happened?"

"She's a bit upset about the Hull trip; well, not so much upset as put out."

"The Hull trip?"

"Yes. It seems she wants to see us about it. She suggests at the end of your shift tomorrow, about five. I can come in early."

"On a Sunday! Mousey June? She rarely leaves her office, and she never works on Sundays. It must be important to her; the last time she ever turned out at a weekend was when they temporarily lost old Jacob from Trafalgar House, and we haven't lost anybody."

"True," agreed Sally. "But the Trafalgar House staff weren't photographed in their love nest and had it emblazoned across the pages of a national paper."

"What absolute rubbish. What the hell has it got to do with June what we get up to, even when we don't get up to it? See you tomorrow then."

He put the receiver down and realised he had been short with Sally, and it certainly wasn't her fault. As he stood there by the phone, trying to calm down a little, he happened to notice the number he had scribbled on the pad when he had traced the last caller on the day Maureen had rung from Brussels. It was the same as the contact number she had given of the friend she was currently staying with and which she had written on her business card. Initially, it struck him as strange, but then realised that this must have been the friend whose call had cancelled out the record of the Brussels call – someone else who seemed to be in this conspiracy to mess up his life.

The normally easy-going Clive was less than happy as he worked through his shift the following day. Sundays were usually an enjoyable time at Kitchener House as he supervised the preparation of lunch before he would take one or more of his friends out for a walk, sometimes to the Prince William, but today he just wanted to make sure that everything was in order; he was determined that he wasn't going to give June anything else to complain about. By the time Sally arrived, the house was pristine, thanks almost solely to Clive's efforts. He knew that his role was supposed to be one of supervising and encouraging the residents to do as much as they could for themselves, but today he wanted to make sure there was nothing out of place. It also meant that he could vent some of his anger on the cleaning.

"Hi Sally, I'm sorry if I was abrupt with you yesterday; I know it's not your fault. I just feel that I'm a character in some arcade game, and everyone is trying to shoot me down."

"That's OK," she said with a smile. "And, anyway, I do deserve to take some of the blame."

"You? It's not your fault. You're just an innocent bystander, collateral damage," protested Clive.

"Thanks, but I could have kicked myself when I thought back to that evening at the hotel. I should have known that

Reg would use that story. And to think we posed for all those photos. I should have seen through it, but I didn't. We were being stitched up, and I didn't spot it."

"Hang on a minute; don't forget that I was taken in as well."

She smiled and then, trying not to sound too patronising, said, "I know, love, but you have a bit of a track record for being taken in; I should have known better."

Clive would have liked to have protested, but he knew she was telling the truth and after a few moments simply added, "Perhaps. But it's still not your fault."

All this only served to fire up Clive ready for their appointment with June. He was more than ready to tell her exactly what to do with her python.

Right on time June arrived, and Minnie showed her into the kitchen where the whole family, including Sally and Clive, were waiting. Clive was amazed when June announced,

"I do love coming out here to Kitchener. It's such a friendly place, and you always keep it so clean and tidy."

Minnie was delighted at this acknowledgement of 'her' efforts, and she offered June a cup of coffee. June had visited enough residential settings to know that it was best to decline, and instead she spent a further 10 minutes chatting, largely with the residents and glancing at the house diary. She was absolutely charming, and Clive felt as if he'd been caught flat-footed, having psyched himself up for a showdown. After a while, she announced, "It's been lovely meeting up like this, but if you'd excuse me, I'd like to have a word with Sally and Clive, perhaps in the front room?"

As they followed June through, Clive felt himself preparing for what must surely be the big scene he had been anticipating all day. The staff group made themselves as comfortable as the situation permitted, and then June pulled a sheet of paper from a file and slid it onto the coffee table in front of Sally and

Clive. They recognised it immediately as a photocopy of the article that had caused so much trouble.

"I received this as a fax yesterday," started June. "It was sent by the chairman of the steering committee after he saw it in his paper, and he is less than happy about it. I don't read the paper myself; I find it often gives gutter journalism a bad name. I assume you have read it?"

"It's absolute rubbish," protested Clive, somewhat more vehemently than he had intended. "It was just an innocent enforced stayover. Sally and I have absolutely nothing to hide."

"I am absolutely certain of that, Clive," added June swiftly. "And even if it was your own little 'love nest', it is none of my business. I know you well enough to know that if you were planning such a romantic rendezvous, you wouldn't have taken Conrad with you anyway."

"Thanks for the vote of confidence, June," said Sally. "So, if you know we weren't involved in some steamy orgy in Hull, what's the problem?"

"What I think isn't important, it's what the steering committee thinks," added June defensively.

"In what way?" asked Sally bluntly, as she sensed uneasiness on June's part.

"The steering committee seem to be of the view that if you two were…"

"Going at it hammer and tong?" suggested Sally, much to Clive's embarrassment.

"I was going to say 'romantically involved', then you might not be as diligent as the steering committee might wish, given that you are working in a residential setting."

"I understand," said Sally. "But don't the steering committee realise that we could probably take the odd break from our sexual gymnastics, at least long enough to check the residents were still alive?"

"If the steering committee is so concerned about moral rectitude," interrupted Clive, "then why don't they seem concerned about Liz and Alan at Trafalgar House? Their relationship has been an open secret for years."

June looked uncomfortable for a few moments, and then she pulled herself to the front of her chair. "You must promise not to tell a soul that I told you this," she said in a conspiratorial way, "but I keep picking up messages on the office grapevine to suggest that the steering committee would love an excuse to get rid of you."

"So all this time I've been feeling paranoid, and now I find that people really are out to get me," added Clive.

"Oh, it's both of you they would like to lose."

"So what have we done to deserve that? Surely the committee aren't getting uptight about us exposing Conrad to the sleazy side of our relationship in Hull?" asked Sally.

"I wouldn't mention Conrad being there," said June, raising a finger to her mouth. "You see, they don't know anything about that; he wasn't mentioned in the article. If the steering committee knew he was there, they would have felt they had good grounds to ask the full committee of the housing association to dismiss you summarily."

"But it's in all the paperwork we submitted before the trip; they're bound to find out," said Sally.

June tried hard to suppress a smile and went on, "The paperwork at my end has somehow got lost. The outing couldn't have happened without official clearance from me, so Conrad was here all the time. After all, they can interrogate him as much as they like, not that they are likely to, and they won't get anything from him except his love of cups of tea."

"Ah, but the house records are all perfectly up to date, and we can't lose those," said Sally. June smiled broadly before delivering her answer,

"I guess that if an unscrupulous couple were to take the last week's records from out of the file and replace them with a less comprehensive account, then have it signed off as usual by their line manager, then no one would be any the wiser, and I could pop round tomorrow to sign any such paperwork in my capacity as your supervisor."

Clive and Sally were dumbfounded, and it was some moments before Sally had a sudden thought and asked June, "So why do the committee want us out? We're efficient, too efficient with our paperwork, it would appear."

"You are both obviously intelligent people; you know the company are always going on about not making the profits they would like and…" She paused for a second before continuing. "They are keeping their cards very close to their chests, but I guess they are currently formulating plans to close one of the residential units and reallocate the residents. You know that Kitchener is currently underused, given the staff we need to put in, and it seemed that one solution was to move the residents to use the capacity we have elsewhere."

"You can't split up Kitchener; they've been together for years. They're a family. They just gel together so well. You can't do it," declared Clive.

"Believe me, I don't want to split up the family any more than you do, and I don't want to lose what are undoubtedly my best staff, but the chairman has his mind set on 'rationalising', not that he ever had a lot of mind to set."

"So who is the chairman of the steering committee at the moment?" queried Clive.

"Councillor Hodge is taking his turn. Not the most gifted member of the group, but he's been around so long that they thought they'd better let him have a turn," explained June.

"Councillor 'King of Smut' Hodge," exclaimed Sally. "He's got such a reputation in the council chamber that women won't share a committee room with him unless they outnumber him four to one. He's a time-served ball of slime who could find sexual innuendo in a prayer book. He sees himself as irresistible to all women when the truth is that his halitosis is his most attractive feature. As Minnie would say, 'he puts the vitamin C in creepy,' and she'd be right."

"You have obviously met him. How unfortunate for you," commiserated June. "So you know that you can't appeal to his better nature; he hasn't got one. He will get his way and close somewhere, so be very careful. All he wants is a case to present to the full housing association committee. For the moment, I will tell Hodge that I carried out an unannounced inspection today and found everything in perfect order and that I have questioned you about the newspaper article, which you have assured me is a gross misrepresentation of the truth. It would help if you could persuade the paper to print a retraction, but I wouldn't hold out much hope. On a completely different subject, I think I will come over tomorrow to inspect and sign the diary, perhaps about 11. It's such a pity that you haven't been able to take any of the group out recently." June gave them both a knowing smile before preparing to leave.

"Thanks for doing all this, June," said Clive before impetuously kissing her on the cheek.

She was a little surprised by this unexpected show of affection but turned to Sally and said, "I don't know what you've been doing to him, but keep up the good work."

"I think it was the Hull air, June. It brings out the animal in him."

"I must take my Gavin to Hull," commented June.

As they were showing June out through the kitchen, they found the 'family' sitting around the table enjoying one of their regular chats where Len and Minnie were exchanging their usual banter while Conrad beamed contentedly and added his occasional comment about a cup of tea. The staff stopped for a moment so June could say goodbye, and Minnie took the opportunity to say, "It's been lovely to see you again; it's nice to have friends round for a chat."

"Tha's reet there, woman, 'avin friends round of a Sunday meks it sort of 'omely. Tha can work thisen in t'ground all week, but on Sunday tha can get thi feet up an' just enjoy t' luxury of bein' at 'ome. Grand!"

"I'd love a cup of tea," added Conrad to show his agreement with the sentiment.

June smiled at the trio and then at the staff before declaring, "This is a lovely home."

After their supervisor had left, Clive and Sally took the house diary and removed the incriminating record, which Clive carefully put in his pocket, and Sally declared her intention to write an alternative version after Clive had gone home. In the meantime, they sat down to try and make sense of all that June had indiscreetly disclosed.

"Who would have thought that Mousey would turn out to be one of the good guys?" asked Sally.

"Typical!" commented Clive. "Just when I expect a woman to react in a particular way, she ups and behaves completely differently. You're right, though; I had got completely the wrong idea about her. Still, they do say you can't judge a book by the cover."

"Clive. You can't even judge a cover by the cover," she teased him. "That's what I love about you."

Clive smiled. Sally understood him but still liked him; that was something important to hold on to in what were very difficult times for him. How could such an inheritance cause him so many problems so quickly? Many people would not understand his dilemma; many would dream of inheriting so much money and have elaborate plans as to what they would do with it, but for Clive it was just an unfortunate complication in his life.

"By the way, did you manage to explain it all to Maureen? Is she back yet?"

"Yes, I did explain it, but I don't think I managed to get the message across too clearly."

"Oh dear, Clive, was she mad?"

"Not in a wild sort of throwing things around sort of way."

"That's good."

"No it isn't. You can dodge thrown objects, and I have certainly got used to coping with verbal attacks, but this was like trying to reason with a block of frozen steel: if steel does freeze."

"She'll calm down, or warm up, soften up or whatever. She'll see the funny side, and things will be back to normal. Once you've had a chance to chat it through."

Clive wondered why everyone seemed convinced that this situation was one that he would look back on as having been hilarious, and it certainly didn't seem remotely amusing at the moment, so all he could think to say to Sally was, "That could be difficult. She's moved out while she decides on what to do next, but currently we appear to be experiencing what celebrities refer to as a 'trial separation' effective as of yesterday."

"Oh, Clive, I'm so sorry."

"It's not your fault. I'm fed up telling everybody it was innocent. One lousy photograph and a piece of pure fiction and my wife walks out. And she says she couldn't care less about the money. I think that shocked me almost as much as her decision to have a bit of time on her own to think things through. For years, she has got at me for not having a lot of money, and now I have a lot of money she doesn't want it, or me!"

"Would it help if I explained the love nest fiasco? I do have a bit of experience at that sort of thing."

"Experience of love nests?"

"Experience of counselling people!"

"It's a kind thought, but at the moment I think it best to leave it as it is. If she just sits down and thinks about it, she will see that I am hardly likely to have got attached to a woman like you. I mean an 'attractive young thirty-year-old'. I'd be out of my league." Clive realised he had almost paid Sally a compliment again, so he quickly added, "You're a doctor. You know how dangerous such excitement could be for a man of my advanced years."

CHAPTER SIXTEEN

One benefit of working irregular shifts is the general absence of that Monday morning feeling, as Monday is as likely to be the last as the first day of a shift, or it could even be a day off. This did not prevent Clive from feeling rather low that morning. His wife had walked out, and he now realised his job was in jeopardy, and all the time he felt annoyed because he didn't feel he had done anything to deserve it. He went through his usual routine, setting out the materials for breakfast for the children and himself before giving Arkwright the first of his breakfasts. Sebastian came down first, and over his cup of coffee he casually discussed the somewhat dilapidated condition of his car before going on to declare that Clive was absolutely right about his son's habit of driving too fast. Clive would be the first to acknowledge that he was easily taken in, but even he was aware that he was being softened up for some sales pitch. Clive expected some request for money for a new luxury car of some sort, probably a Mercedes convertible, so he was pleasantly surprised when Sebastian announced, "I can't go on driving fast cars, I need something more reliable, dare I say it? More conservative." Clive's mind raced to imagine just what his son was pitching for now. He had more or less convinced himself that his son was after the Rolls Royce when Sebastian continued.

"A second-hand Volvo estate, that's what I need. Good for my image, bit of prestige, but nothing too fast." Clive was amazed but less than surprised when Sebastian announced, "We do happen to have a suitable model coming on to the forecourt soon, and I'm sure I could get a very good price on it for you."

"For me?"

"Well, no, for me really, but now that Mum's taken her car, if my old heap breaks down you wouldn't want me to borrow the Roller, would you?"

"You're right on the last point."

"And you know how Mum worries about the way I drive my sporty little number. Volvos, on the other hand, sound, safe and sedate. I can't go on being a boy racer all my life, can I?"

Clive suspected he was being a fool to himself but felt obliged to say, "We'll see. Things are a bit complicated at the moment. I'm not even sure if the inheritance money has made it to my account yet."

"Thanks, Dad. I'll look into it further in case you decide to go ahead with it."

Having achieved as much as he could in this ongoing round of negotiations, Sebastian finished his coffee, and after his usual preening session in the hall he set off for work.

Clive settled to his toast as Nicky came down.

"Morning, darling, the kettle's boiled. Did you want anything special today?"

"Morning, Dad. Nothing special. Perhaps you could get on to Fortnum and Mason's and ask them to deliver some caviar and fresh figs?"

"Very funny, but I'm not sure they could deliver before you set off for university."

"I'll just have some toast then, thanks."

After a few moments, Nicky looked up and asked, "I didn't really want the figs and caviar, but you have to accept that your financial status has changed more than a little, so what are you going to do with your money?"

"Your brother seems set on helping me spend a lot of it."

"Surprise, surprise!"

"The truth is that I have no idea. I was confused by the whole thing from the start, but now with your mum disappearing for a few days and complications at work."

"You mean Sally?" asked Nicky, almost sounding optimistic.

"No, not that sort of complication; the future of Kitchener and its occupants looks unsure."

"Poor old dad. Mum will be back soon. She won't be able to resist the lure of the money."

"Sally! That's unkind; your mum told me that she's not interested in the money."

"Yes? And I hear the pope's not a Catholic. Face up to it, Dad. Mum loves money and what it can buy; it doesn't mean that she's a bad person, but she's never been one to go out of her way to do things for others. And you're so soft she'll get the lot."

Clive was about to remonstrate more forcibly when he noticed that Nicky was on the point of tears, so he said, "Nicky love. Your mum and I have been together a long time. Our marriage isn't the classic one. I know it's not all happy families and conventional, but we have a relationship of give and take."

"So when is she going to stop doing all the taking?"

Clive decided that the conversation was going nowhere. He knew that after numerous such chats he couldn't convince Nicky, and he was getting to the point in life when he was finding it increasingly difficult to convince himself. Perhaps he was just too stubborn to accept that, despite his Herculean and often single-handed efforts, the marriage was not a strong one.

They sat in silence that was broken by the sound of the letterbox and mail falling onto the hall mat, and then more mail, and then more. The two looked at each other before Clive ventured, "Lot of mail. Is it someone's birthday?"

Nicky went out to the hall and, after a few minutes, arrived with an enormous pile of letters, which she tried to place on the table. The stack spilled over onto the floor, prompting Clive to add unnecessarily, "Lot of mail today."

"There's more on the hall mat."

Clive wandered through to the hall and returned with another collection of assorted envelopes. In the absence of any space on the table, he dumped them on the work surface before picking up a small handful, which he sorted through, systematically reading the names of the addressee, "Mr C. Sullivan, Mr C. Sullivan, C. Sullivan, Clive Sullivan, Mr C. Sullivan, C. Sullivan. It must be my birthday!"

"This lots all for you as well, Dad, and these," added Nicky. "We'd better sort them out. Give me a hand to clear a place on the table."

After a few minutes, there were two sets of mail. One set containing 10 envelopes was addressed to Maureen Sullivan, while the other mountain was for Clive.

"Someone's having a laugh," suggested Clive as he opened the first letter and scanned it. "This one is suggesting I might want to consider taking out extensive home insurance, so it's for the bin."

"This one looks more official, Dad," declared Nicky, passing him an impressive-looking envelope in better quality paper and with a small crest on the back. "It may be important."

Clive opened the letter and unfolded the communication inside. He read in silence for a few moments before announcing," It's from some firm of solicitors offering to act on my behalf to collect some other money that I am entitled to. That's just what I need! Someone else to dump money on me."

Nicky took the letter from his hand and read it more carefully before saying, "I shouldn't worry about them burdening you with more money. If you check out the second paragraph, they point out that you have to agree to retain them to act on your behalf in claiming the money which 'may' be due to you.

In other words, you pay out their initial fee of £785, and they will claim money on your behalf if it turns out that you have any due. Later, no doubt, there would be a further request for fees to cover some other aspect of their work and so on. Don't hold your breath waiting for that investment to pay out."

"But it's from solicitors. It says they can sort it all out."

"It's a scam, Dad. Anyone with a passing knowledge of even the most basic desktop publishing packet could run one of those off on the computer. A few pence for good quality paper and envelope and it looks convincing enough. These parasites send out letters to a few hundred people, and even if only a small percentage gets back to them, they are in the money. By the look of your mail you've got onto what is called a suckers list."

"Suckers list! I'm not a sucker."

"Dad, I love you, but you're King Sucker of Suckerland. You are a con man's dream; you are so nice that you see the best in everybody."

Clive recognised himself quite clearly in what Nicky was saying, and all he could think to say was, "So I'm possibly being targeted?"

"By the look of your mail, I would suggest that it's a nailed-on certainty, and I would venture to suggest that all this is not unrelated to your appearance in the paper. Twenty million is a big prize."

"But it wasn't 20 million."

"The truth is immaterial; the paper says you got 20 million, so that's what the reading public believe, and that's what all the con men want a cut of."

"I don't need all this hassle at the moment. Let's just bin this lot and forget it."

"You can't do that without at least opening those that don't look like circulars. You're bound to get some legitimate mail;

what happens when the Hull lawyers want to get in touch with you, for example? You can't afford to miss their letters."

"Oh Nicky, it just gets more and more complicated. It's going to take me ages to check this correspondence out, and I'm at work soon."

"I've got an hour before I need to go in. Would you like me to at least sort out those that are obviously circulars? I can leave the others unopened for you to check out when you get home. After all, there may be something personal from your girlfriend."

Clive gave a weak smile and said, "That's nice of you, but if you do see anything from your big sister, feel free to open it. I assure you we have nothing to hide."

Clive was relieved to close the door on this latest upset in his life and to cycle off to work.

At Kitchener House, Minnie was busily helping Conrad with his domestic chores, which meant that she demonstrated how the job should be done until she had completed the task single-handedly while Conrad watched. His usual impeccable clothing was suitably protected by an equally smart apron, which was completely unnecessary, but he was content to bask in all the attention she was giving him. Clive checked out the recent bogus entry in the diary file and smiled to himself: no mention of Conrad's presence in Hull.

Just before 10 o'clock, Clive was surprised to see Sally turn up, and having politely turned down Minnie's offer of coffee, they sat at the kitchen table for an impromptu staff meeting.

"I wasn't expecting you this morning, Sally. Can't you keep away from the place?"

"I just felt I had to come round and get my claws into the man I have stolen from his wife," she said.

"Eh?"

"I am reliably informed, in some remarkably colourful language, that I am personally responsible for snatching you away from your wife and dragging you off to Hull to indulge in some rather base activities. Those weren't the actual words used, but you get the drift."

Clive was obviously even more confused than ever and for a moment seemed unable to decide how he ought to respond, so he merely repeated, "Eh?"

"I had some rather unusual mail today, Clive, among which was a rather poorly written letter expressing disgust at my part in the orgy on Humberside. Some nutter obviously read the article and decided that as part of their personal moral crusade they should point out that I was a Jezebel who would 'rot in Hull'. I think that's to be my fate, but the spelling is a bit suspect, and they should have used a sharper crayon."

"I'm so sorry, Sally. How could anyone think that of you?"

"Don't worry about it. I found it rather amusing, although I was a bit worried about the curse of having to rot in Hull. I had a couple of other letters offering me moral guidance. It's interesting that some of them seem to have great difficulty putting into words what we were allegedly up to. I haven't heard the term 'rumpy pumpy' in years, and the writer seemed unclear as to whether we were having rumpy pumpy or doing rumpy pumpy."

"I have no idea, but in our case it was neither," said Clive who felt a lot easier over the offensive letters now that he saw Sally's obvious lack of concern.

"I had two letters from people I haven't heard from in years and haven't missed during that time, who suddenly want to get in touch. I don't know whether it's because I have a rich boyfriend or because they find my notoriety interesting."

"I'm sorry," repeated Clive. "I've had a bit of mail myself this morning. I left Nicky sorting it into obvious junk and probable junk, but there must be over a hundred letters."

"And I thought I had problems."

"We opened one or two, and most seem to be just offering me services; double-glazing, insurance, financial advice, etcetera, but one was an obvious scam trying to get money from me."

"You can expect a lot more of those. I'm afraid it's open season on Clive and his 20 million."

"Nicky said as much this morning before I left. She seems to think I may be a bit vulnerable, and I know she's right."

"At the moment, Clive, you are a lamb among the circling wolves of the financial underworld. I realise that we are told that the wolf will dwell with the lamb, but rest assured, the lamb has a short tenancy in that particular dwelling. If we don't instil a bit of good old-fashioned cynicism into you, I calculate you won't have any money left by Christmas."

Their conversation was curtailed by the early arrival of June, who flopped down onto a chair.

"I'm sorry I'm early, but I just had to get out of the office this morning," she explained. "I've had Councillor Hodge and the treasurer for a breakfast meeting."

"Yech!" exclaimed Sally. "The very thought of facing up to that sleaze ball at breakfast time, no woman should be expected to cope with that."

"I had no choice. I find it more than a little distasteful to put up with the smut fest, but it is worse when I have to fight like hell to stop them ruining everything the organisation is supposed to stand for. I try to explain that we are a non-profit making group to provide reasonable homes for our clients, but they want to show an appreciable profit. If they had their way, we'd close down most of the houses and have the residents three to a room in the remaining few. It just seems hopeless at times. It's so nice to come down here and spend time with you all. I spent 10 very happy years working in just such a house before I was persuaded to go for promotion. I should never have done it; for a few pounds a week extra, I gave up the very aspects of the work that I enjoy. And I know that it's no secret that I'm no good at doing the timesheets and staff rotas. I once managed to arrange for one member of staff to do three shifts at the same time in different houses! It looked fine on my planner with all the little coloured pins, but it was never going to work."

"Just take it easy for a while and I'll get us a coffee," said Clive before turning to Minnie, who was busily preparing lunch and saying, "My turn to make the coffee, I think."

"While you're here, you'll want to see the house diary, won't you?" asked Sally knowingly.

June took the file, and after only a cursory glance, she signed the appropriate section and handed it back. Minnie and Conrad joined them, and they all sat around the table and enjoyed a decent cup of coffee. As they were clearing away, June asked, "I don't want you to feel that I'm getting under your feet, but would you mind if I stayed on for a while to help out?"

"Not at all," answered Sally, a bit at a loss as to exactly what they would do with such a preponderance of staff but not wanting to disappoint June.

"That would be lovely," added Minnie. "We can get our Conrad doing a bit of cleaning and leave the love birds to their Humpty Dumpty."

June looked understandably confused, while Sally made a mental note to be more careful what she said in front of Minne in future.

"I'm sure that Minnie and Conrad can look after me for an hour," said June. "So why don't the pair of you take the time to have a 'staff meeting'. With all that's been going on, you need some time to catch your breath and you, Clive, need to sort out just what you intend to do now that you have got all that money."

Clive was glad of the opportunity to talk things over with Sally. He knew he was not an unintelligent man, but he was an innocent in what was proving to be a very dangerous world, and he knew that he had to learn very quickly or the wolves would have him.

CHAPTER SEVENTEEN

"You mustn't assume that every request for help or cash is genuine," said Sally, "In fact, it may be wise to assume that everyone who gets in touch, particularly after your recently reported good fortune, is trying to part you from your money. There are lots of genuine needy causes, but you can't solve all the problems in the world, even with all your new-found riches."

"I know," he answered, "Norman was right; I am hopeless at looking after my own money. I wish it could all go away."

"It soon will if you're not careful. You've got the money; you have a responsibility to make the best use of it. If it's not too wild a suggestion, why don't you buy something you want?"

"What would I want? I've got everything I need."

"There must be something; you still keep turning up to work on that squeaky old bike, for example."

"I've got some oil in the garage somewhere."

"Do something wild and frivolous; buy a new can of oil. Better still, get yourself a game plan for what you want out of life and sort out your money accordingly."

"I guess a lot depends on when Maureen comes back. She was always good at looking after the money, but now she says she's not interested in the money at all."

Sally spent time outlining some of the basic scams that can be used for separating a mug from their money, and with the majority of the ploys, it was obvious that without some support of an adviser, Clive would have been fooled into giving money away. Sally outlined a typical ploy for Clive.

"You might receive a letter or even an initial telephone call that informs you that you've won hundreds of thousands of pounds in the national lottery of some foreign country."

"I hope not!" commented Clive.

"Don't worry it's never that simple. The letter then points out that there are specific problems about releasing the money to you; there are legal costs, local revenue laws, or international money exchange complications. It doesn't matter what the reason is, they are all equally bogus. They ask you to forward some money so they can sort the matter out for you. They don't ask a lot compared to what you are told you will gain from the arrangements, but after a while there is another letter to say that you need to pay a little more. This can go on for months until you realise that you're being taken for a ride or your money runs out. They prey on your greed initially, and then when you are 'hooked', you don't want to risk stopping as you've already 'invested' a lot of money. There are similar scams related to a holiday that you have won in a raffle you don't remember entering. These plans have some kind of bait, but they all ask you to pay to get it."

"I've heard of those schemes, but I wouldn't be tempted to send money," said Clive. "And, anyway, I wouldn't particularly want to get any more money."

"I agree that you're less likely to fall for a scheme that plays on your greed, but I've only outlined a very simple one; the people that run these things are very clever; as soon as the public becomes wise to one, they try something else. There is another type of approach that was tailor-made to relieve you of your money. It's the straightforward begging letter, not that they are straightforward. These can take an infinite number of forms. There is a simple letter that relays a 'sob story'. These are designed to tug at the heartstrings and, once again, they will probably start by requesting a relatively small amount of money. The stories may contain horrific details of suffering, and they will often express confidence that a fine man such as you, no doubt influenced by God, will send a few pounds. In return, they will put you on their suckers list, and they or like-minded groups will inundate you with further requests."

"Nicky mentioned that I'm a bit of a sucker myself."

"No?" replied Sally with feigned disbelief. "Smart girl, your Nicky! You are just too trusting, Clive. When you get a letter from someone who purports to be sitting in an African hovel with a blind child and a husband who has AIDS in a country ravaged by war and famine, remember that it may have been written by some reprobate sitting in a smart office in London who has hundreds of identical letters ready to send out."

"But there is a lot of suffering in the world. How do I know that letter isn't genuine?"

"You're right. It may be impossible to tell if a story is a fabrication, but there may be a clue; if the article appeared in the paper on Saturday, it is hardly likely that someone in an isolated part of the world will have picked up on it and have a letter on your mat by Monday morning."

"So what do I do?"

"I'm sorry, but you just have to assume that every communication you get is from a rogue who wants your money. If you want to give money, then do what I do; allocate what you want to give and select decent charities to do what they can with your money."

"So it's fine if it's a charity?"

"Would that life were so simple, my innocent little friend! There are charities and there are charities and there are groups that pretend to be charities."

"Pretend?" asked Clive despairingly.

"Let's say I want to declare that I'm a charity. I could get myself an emotive title, *The Livingstone Trust for Poorly Kiddies and Sick Puppies.* I then collect lots of money; I'll put you down for ten thousand."

"Fine by me."

"I then use a small percentage of the money doing some pretty ineffectual work with puppies and children, having previously deducted running costs and my not inconsiderable wages. When you give money to genuine charities they have their legitimate expenses, but the good organisations ensure that the vast majority of any money collected goes to the target group who need the help."

Clive felt that what little control he had over what was going on in his life was swiftly slipping away.

Having finished working with Conrad and Minnie, June came in to say goodbye before returning to her office. She seemed distinctly perky as she announced, "I really enjoyed that. Minnie is a marvel, but Conrad isn't in any danger of breaking into a sweat when he's working, is he?"

"Conrad sees himself as decorative rather than functional," said Sally.

"I must get back to the office. I'll log this session down as an unannounced inspection and support it with a healthy report on what you are doing. I think we need to be as positive as we can, given the current financial climate and what we discussed previously," she said pointedly.

"Still no new developments then?" asked Sally.

"No. But Sleaze Ball Hodge is pressing hard to get his way."

Shortly after June had left, Sally announced, "Well, I'd better be on my way. I'm going over to pick up Steve's car, I'll see you tomorrow afternoon, and we can continue our lessons on advanced cynicism then."

"I'd forgotten about the car. Things just seem to have been so hectic over the last couple of days."

"Yes. I've got a lift over there later. It will be good to get it back in the garage."

Suddenly Clive was hit by one of his rare moments of inspiration and blurted out, "Why don't we go out to the pub for a meal tomorrow?" Sally was slightly taken aback by this apparently impetuous move, which was so unlike him, but before she could respond, he added, "I mean all of us, Minnie, Len, Conrad and yourself, my treat. It will mean that Minnie doesn't have to cook," he added by way of explanation, "And as you will be on duty anyway you can do part of your shift in the pub!"

"Sounds good to me, Minnie rarely gets out. Are you sure you can afford it?" she teased him.

"I think so. You said I ought to spend money on things I want to spend it on. We can pop round to the Prince William, they are used to our gang going in there, and Bill does a reasonable, if limited, selection of bar meals."

"I'll look forward to it," said Sally.

Clive could hardly conceal his delight at the response; at last he had something to look forward to in his life.

When Clive arrived home, he saw Pru's car on the drive and, on entering the kitchen, he found her looking at the results of Nicky's mail-sorting session.

"Hi Clive, I see you're quite the popular boy, aren't you?"

"It's a nightmare, Pru. I'll have to sit and sort all that lot out later in case there is anything important among the garbage."

"Yes, Nicky explained when she rang me this morning. I hope you don't mind, but I've offered to have Arkwright over at my house for a while until you get things sorted out here."

"Thanks, Pru, you're a darling. I just don't seem to be able to get any sort of order into my life at the moment; just when I think I'm nearly in control, something else crops up. Knowing that the dog is catered for will take a load off my mind. Where is the little fella, by the way?"

"That's the strange thing. I couldn't find him when I arrived, so I assumed you might have come home and picked him up and taken him back to work with you, but then I found him."

Pru motioned for him to be quiet and led him upstairs. Creeping along the landing, she pointed into Maureen's room. Clive peered into his wife's room, and there was Arkwright, in the middle of Maureen's bed with his feet in the air, snoring contentedly.

"Cheeky little monkey," started Clive, but then his amusement faded, and he turned to Pru and declared, "You know what this means, Pru? She's not coming back."

Clive knew that Arkwright had never entered Maureen's room in all the time he had been living with them. The little dog obviously felt that it was now safe to go in.

Pru sensed Clive's disappointment and by way of consolation, said, "It might not be that bad, Clive." Then her attitude changed abruptly, and she declared, "What am I saying? You're better off without her, darling. It grieves me to say it about my own daughter, but she's hardly been the perfect wife all these years. It was all right at the beginning, she was delighted to have married a solicitor's son when she could play the little wife, impressing her friends with the home you were working to provide for her, then there were the babies she could dress up and brag about, but in the meantime you were becoming less and less central to the plot. It was bad enough when you didn't show any interest in following your father into the family business, but she never forgave you for leaving the paint plant."

Clive listened without attempting to interrupt her. He was mindful that his own daughter had expressed similar sentiments that very morning and numerous times in the past.

"Oh Pru!" he exclaimed when she had finished. "I know it wasn't perfect, but she gave a bit of shape to my life; it was all so normal. Granted, it was hardly exciting, but it suited me in a way; she was my personal organiser, and we did get on most of the time."

"Clive darling. Neighbours, friends at the pub, colleagues at work and even commuters you meet regularly on the bus, those are the people you might reasonably hope to get on with, but in a marriage there should be more."

Clive felt completely beaten down, not least because he couldn't think of any counter-argument at that moment. Maureen's own mother and daughter were accusing her of being a bad wife, and as her husband he seemed unable to come up with any reasonable response.

"She's not left you completely, Clive; she'll want her part of the money."

"Now you're wrong there, Pru. She was quite adamant that she wasn't interested in the money when she last spoke to me. Why should she bother? She's got plenty of money coming in from her business," said Clive with some feeling of satisfaction that he could say something in his wife's defence."

"We'll see," commented Pru, not wishing to continue the discussion. "I see Nicky has made a good start on the junk mail. Why don't we have a cup of coffee and check some of them out?"

Leaving Arkwright to his slumbers, the pair descended to the kitchen and Clive put the kettle on.

Before they could start to read any of the letters, the doorbell rang. Clive went through and opened the front door to a smartly dressed man in his thirties who smiled broadly at Clive and, waving his arm in the general direction of the house, announced, "God has brought great riches into your life. Riches that he shares with you that you might share with others. Amen."

Clive thought this was a particularly short prayer, and he appreciated the brevity, but before he could respond, the young man continued.

"Better is a little with righteousness than great income with injustice, Proverbs chapter sixteen verse eight. We in the Church of the Repentant Miser understand that we all grow by giving to others, for we know from Luke six, verse thirty that we must 'Give to everyone who asks of you, and whoever takes away what is yours, do not demand it back', and we know it to be true."

"The Repentant Miser, is that a local church?" asked Clive, not so much out of any interest but to stop the preacher before he quoted the entire bible.

"We are wherever we are needed, and the world has much suffering, so we are needed everywhere. We are thus your local church."

"Strange," commented Clive, "Holy Bill is the vicar round here, and last time I saw him at the pub, he was still under the impression that he worked at Saint Benedict's."

"We obviously don't interfere with the work of other churches; we are specialists in promoting inner contentment among those who are burdened with commercial problems. We help promote global justice by relocating wealth to where it is most needed. You, of all people, will appreciate the wisdom we receive from Ecclesiastes chapter five verse ten, 'Whoever loves money never has money enough; whoever loves wealth is never satisfied with his income'."

"Oh, that explains it," said Clive. "You obviously need to speak to my wife, and she's not in. Good afternoon." With this, Clive closed the door and returned to his junk mail.

"Who was that?" asked Pru, without looking up from a letter she was perusing.

"Oh, just some church guy offering to make me feel better by taking some of my money away, the religious equivalent of blood-letting. Anything interesting in the mail?"

"That pile is complete rubbish offering a range of services you don't want. That pile comprises a whole batch of raffle tickets that you obviously never asked for but which you might want to sell to your friends on behalf of a whole host of different charitable organisations."

"If I lived to be a hundred, I'd never acquire enough friends to sell on that lot," said Clive.

"This lot here are largely begging letters. I've read one or two, and they range from being harrowing to being laughably naïve. So what do you intend to do with them?"

Clive was momentarily despondent but then started to formulate a general plan which he tentatively outlined to his mother-in-law.

"Pru darling," he started, in a matter-of-fact sort of way. "You are obviously better at sorting out the genuine from the deceitful mail; would you consider taking on the job of dealing with this lot? I'll pay you for it, of course."

"It's a deal. I get two bottles of wine per hour, none of your cheap rubbish either," she replied.

Clive was delighted, not least because he felt that, at last, he was starting to take control of his life a bit.

"Darling, you are worth far more. Do you want to take this lot to your place or sort it here?"

"Seems silly to cart it over to my place. I'll nip over tomorrow for a couple of hours if that's OK, and bring Arkwright back so he doesn't forget where he lives. I somehow doubt that this is the last of your unsolicited mail, but we'll get it sorted. Oh, by the way, if I find anything that is obviously personal, I'll put it to one side for you."

"Like love letters from my attractive thirty-year-old girlfriend?" quipped Clive before Pru had a chance to bring the matter up.

"You could do a lot worse than her; Nicky says she is lovely."

"I'm pleased that you both appear to be in favour of the relationship, but I'm not sure what Sally's husband would make of the idea."

"Shame," said Pru.

CHAPTER EIGHTEEN

The following morning, Clive didn't bother opening any of his mail. If anything, he had received more than the previous day, but mail-checking duties had been delegated to Pru, and he felt good to have made an executive decision. Pleased with the feeling that he had started to turn his life around a little bit, he had decided over breakfast that on his way to work, he would drop in at the garage where Sebastian worked to look at the Volvo estate. A quick phone call had enabled him to arrange this with his son, and it was only later that he realised that Sebastian's place was quite some distance out of his way, so at the last minute he realised he would have to take the Rolls.

Clive's subsequent arrival at the showrooms meant that the young salesmen were falling over themselves to serve him. As luck would have it, Sebastian was out on a test drive with a prospective customer, so it was a young Sebastian clone that eagerly showed Clive the car he had expressed interest in. When Sebastian arrived back, he was quick to join his father by the side of the estate car he had singled out.

"Lovely, isn't she, Dad? Magnificent bodywork, relatively low mileage, typical Volvo, solid reliability. A bit conservative for some young people I suppose, but then I've got to grow up some time."

Clive let the sales patter go on for a while as his son listed the virtues of this particular model that was obviously better suited to a middle-aged couple for nipping to the supermarket once a week. After a while, Clive said, "Very impressive, Sebastian. Reliable and solid, certainly not built like a sports car.

However, your colleague, who kindly gave me his sales pitch, did point out other qualities, among which was the fact, and I quote him directly, that this model 'goes like shit off a shovel'. A 'wolf in sheep's clothing' was another phrase he was keen on. 'Understated power', 'gut-wrenching acceleration for such a big car.' Need I go on?"

Sebastian was deflated and simply added, "Perhaps I'll keep looking."

"Good idea, son," said Clive, who was inwardly jubilant that for once, albeit because of the fortuitous intervention of Sebastian's colleague, he had seen through an attempt to fool him.

With his new-found confidence, Clive purposefully strode over and got in his car and for once he seemed to suit it.

Conrad was delighted to see the car arrive at Kitchener House, and he was obviously keen to get in and take up his place in the back.

"Make yourself at home," suggested Clive, "but I'm afraid I won't be going anywhere in it."

Conrad appeared content to just sit in the car and enjoy the luxury. Clive mused that all Rolls Royce models should offer a Conrad as an optional extra as he seemed to have been made for the car.

Minnie was preparing vegetables for lunch; she liked to get them done quite early so they had plenty of time to boil. "Morning," she said and then, by way of explanation, she pointed to the pan and added, "Greens. You need plenty of vitamin G at this time of year."

Clive spent the remainder of the morning working with Minnie in the forlorn hope that he would be able to help her create something a little more appetising than her usual bland offerings. After lunch, Minnie washed up and did most of the drying while Conrad picked up the odd plate and dabbed it with a tea cloth, for which Minnie heaped praise upon him.

As they sat with their coffee after lunch, Clive worked with Minnie to decide what they needed when next they went to the shops, while Conrad retired to his seat in the car. Minnie was quite capable of shopping on her own, though she did have difficulty with the money and had no sense of the appropriate cost of items. Her main problem was that she tended to shop for the same items every time. Left to her own devices, she would have a house full of milk, eggs, butter and one or two other staples. The intricacies of home management were too much for her. She wouldn't have attracted a second glance in a supermarket as she filled her basket, but she just didn't know what to put in it. A lifetime of people doing all that for her meant that she still needed a fair degree of support.

The pair had just assembled a reasonable shopping list when they were disturbed by the sudden arrival of two men in dark suits who strode into the kitchen.

"I'm Councillor Hodge, chairman of the steering committee, and this is our treasurer, Mr Tennett."

The officious introduction and the rude entry into what was effectively someone else's home annoyed Clive, and it took a degree of self-control not to reprimand the councillor for his display of bad manners. All he did say was, "Good afternoon, I'm Clive, and this is Minnie. This is her home." He added the last part with particular emphasis to try and remind the councillor, but it was a wasted gesture.

"Yes, I know who you are; you were in that blasted article. I see it's all true about the car and everything; by the way, you do realise that one of the patients is messing about with your car. Damn great thing! I could hardly get my car on the drive."

Clive was losing what little patience he had left, but he tried to remain calm.

"That is Conrad, who I invited to sit in my car for a while, and I would point out that he lives here too, and he is not a patient. As for the article, I'm sure that no one in their right mind would believe all the salacious rubbish that is regularly churned out by that particular muck-raking rag."

The last comment was made in the full knowledge that the councillor was a regular reader, but by this point Clive was starting to get fired up, as was Hodge, who responded by saying, "It may not be one of those wishy-washy liberal broadsheets so favoured by social worker types, but it exposes corruption when it finds it. Enough of that, down to the purpose of this visit. The committee have become very concerned about the damage to the organisation caused by bad press, so the treasurer and I have been sent to carry out a proper inspection."

"June did an unannounced inspection yesterday, and although she was too professional to disclose the details, she did appear completely satisfied with what is going on here."

"June isn't accustomed to doing such inspections as thoroughly as we might wish."

"Naturally after a working lifetime in these sorts of settings, she is hardly likely to be as competent as someone who runs the family hardware business."

Clive realised that this last remark about Hodge's family business interests was not likely to pour any oil on what were fast becoming troubled waters, but he was past caring.

The councillor and his silent partner spent some considerable time scrutinising the staff diary file, which was in perfect order, and spoke to Minnie before walking about the house to carry out their inspection. They were less than happy when Clive refused them access to the bedrooms, explaining that the residents must have their privacy respected. This led to what is euphemistically referred to as a full and frank exchange of views. Clive was so furious that he found he had finished an entire cup of Minnie's coffee before he realised what he had done.

By the time Len arrived home, the two committee members had thankfully left. He had arrived back early and had been badgered into going up and getting a 'proper' wash by Minnie, so by the time Sally arrived, Clive and his friends were all sitting ready for the planned trip out to the pub for dinner.

"Don't bother taking your coat off, Sally. I suddenly feel the need for a pint to calm me down."

"Why? More junk mail?" she asked.

"That's the least of today's events, but I'll tell you about it over a pint. I assume you'll be on your usual orange juice as you're on duty, so you might as well drive if you don't mind. It's turning rather chilly for Minnie."

Sally was impressed by this decisiveness on his part. She took the keys from him and said,

"The Rolls? Are you sure you trust me to drive it?"

"Sally, it's only a car. In the hotel in Hull, I trusted you with my body; the car's nothing like as important."

Sally smiled but couldn't come up with one of her usual witty responses. She couldn't help but feel that there was something strange about Clive today; he seemed somewhat intense. "Right, everybody!" she announced. "Your transport awaits."

The short trip to the pub was a particularly jovial affair with almost a party atmosphere developing in the car. As they arrived at the pub and tumbled from the car, one might have been excused for thinking they had already enjoyed a few drinks. The party entered the bar to be met by the landlord, who greeted Clive with, "Well, if it isn't Rich Bill with his usual party and his lovely girlfriend."

A number of Bills at the bar raised their glasses in the group's direction, accompanied by comments expressing their pleasure at seeing them and gestures towards the small notice board. Looking at the board, Clive could clearly identify an enlarged photocopy of the notorious newspaper article.

"You don't want to believe all you read in that rag," Clive advised the landlord. "And just to make it clear, Sally is not my girlfriend."

The landlord appeared genuinely surprised at this last piece of information from Clive and by way of apology, said, "Oh, I just thought, having seen you in here before, and you just seemed like a natural couple."

Sally smiled before adding, "Thank you. It seems that we have managed to give a lot of people the wrong idea but believe me, we didn't spend the night in our little Hull love nest."

"Hard luck, Bill," said the landlord to Clive.

Clive ordered drinks for his group before offering to buy drinks for his regular friends in the bar and warning them that he wasn't going to make a habit of it because he had not actually inherited 20 million.

The party from Kitchener House soon settled in well. Len joined some of his friends at the bar and treated them to his various Yorkshire dialects, Conrad sat in his usual seat sipping his beer, and Minnie sat beside him.

"So you've had a rough day?" asked Sally.

"You could say that," replied Clive. "Not unrelated to the fact that Councillor Hodge and one of his cronies came along to give us a special inspection."

"Sleazeball!" commented Sally.

"Yes. It got off to a bad start when he burst in without showing the common decency of knocking. It went downhill from there. He couldn't see why I wouldn't just let him wander into any of the bedrooms without permission of the owners; he insisted upon calling the family 'patients' and was a little put out when I called his regular daily paper a muck-raking rag."

"I can see he wouldn't be too pleased about that, but it could have been worse."

"It was. He made some comment about the article and suggested that he could understand my wanting to show you a good time in Hull. He said that he would have been tempted to do the same."

"He should be so lucky!" declared Sally.

"That's what I said, more or less. What I did infer was that he would only stand a chance if you were in a coma, and he didn't have a face that looked marginally less attractive than a bulldog's bum."

"The Diplomatic Corps are crying out for people like you, Clive, but thanks for the support."

"The general good-natured banter we were enjoying was augmented by Minnie's well-intentioned insistence upon calling him Councillor Sleaze Ball at every sentence end."

"Oh dear! I wonder where she picked that up from," said Sally, glancing towards Minnie, who broke from her conversation with Conrad long enough to give her an enigmatic smile.

"It would appear," concluded Sally, "that what happened today has shot down any chance of Councillor Sleaze Ball supporting any attempt to keep Kitchener House open."

"I rather think Conrad put the issue beyond any doubt."

"Conrad?"

"Yes, I had insisted that Hodge couldn't just go where he liked, but he's not strong on listening. He managed to get up to Conrad's door while I was otherwise engaged. Conrad had managed to get up to his room to seek sanctuary from all the commotion, and when he heard someone trying the handle, he came to see who it was. Hodge, with his usual lack of tact, muttered something offensive about Conrad and tried to push his way past. Poor old Conrad didn't like being manhandled in such a rough way, so he punched Hodge. It was beautiful.

One minute the sleazy councillor is trying to force his way into the room then, smack, and the offending intruder is toppling back into my arms while Conrad calmly closed his door on the scene. It was a treat to watch. Hodge was all for calling the police, but as I pointed out, and as was witnessed by the treasurer of the steering committee, it was Hodge who instigated the violence. The strange thing is, I could have sworn I saw the treasurer smile as he recalled the incident. They left shortly after that, and Hodge made it quite clear that we had not heard the last of the matter, but by that time he had reverted to his comments about our activities in Hull and the disrepute into which we had brought the organisation."

For a while, Sally sat in what appeared to be a stunned silence before she smiled and said, "Sleaze Ball." She giggled. "Bulldog's bum!" She giggled again and then added, "And Conrad hit him?"

Conrad looked up from his pint and, as if in acknowledgement, raised his fist slightly and said in a sheepish voice, "I'd love a cup of tea."

Things had not gone as well as they might for the Kitchener crew that afternoon, but you wouldn't have guessed it from the party atmosphere in the Prince William that evening. They all enjoyed a very passable meal and a few drinks. Clive, in particular, enjoyed the opportunity to unwind, and one or two drinks offered by the assorted Bills meant that he was very pleasantly relaxed by the time Sally announced that his carriage was waiting.

"If it's OK by you, I could run you home and then take the crew back to Kitchener," suggested Sally.

"Thanks. Sounds like a good idea; I somehow don't feel it would be a good idea for me to drive now. I'll pick the car up some other time," he added casually.

As they drove to Clive's house, he found himself wishing it was a longer journey. The car's heaters soon created a cosy atmosphere enhanced by the mellowing effect of a few pints of bitter. All this, and a good friend to act as driver. Clive was happy. All too soon they arrived at his house and parked on the road outside. Clive was reluctant to end such an evening and would have liked to have asked his friends in for a coffee, but he knew Conrad would need to get home to bed. Clive got out and walked round to the driver's side as the driver's window slid down silently. "Thanks for a lovely meal," said Sally and the same message came in various ways from those in the back.

"My pleasure, we must do it again very soon," suggested Clive. "Goodnight." He decided it was not a good idea to kiss Sally goodnight in case she thought he was only acting under the influence of the beer, but he needn't have bothered because as he leaned forward to wish goodnight to those in the back of the car, Sally kissed him gently on the cheek.

"Thanks again," she said. "Now hurry inside in case you're seen here with your Jezebel."

CHAPTER NINETEEN

Clive was pleased to see that Nicky was home when he got in. "Hi Dad, who was that who dropped you off?"

"It was Sally and the gang from Kitchener. We've been out for a meal at the Prince," he replied.

"You should have invited them in for a while, now that Mum's not here to object."

"I would have, but you know what Conrad is like. I didn't want him falling asleep here; we'd never have wakened him."

"Of course, but it would have been nice to see Sally again. Have you had a good day?"

This apparently innocuous question prompted Clive to give a full breakdown of the day's events, from the victory of seeing through Sebastian's Volvo ploy to the pugilism following the Hodge inspection. It had, by any standards, been a full day, but Clive's days were becoming increasingly eventful.

"Poor old Dad, life's really got it in for you at the moment," commented Sally before giving a little laugh and adding incredulously, "Conrad, the sweetie, smacked him?"

Clive knew that such behaviour was not to be condoned, but he couldn't help chuckling himself as he explained, "Yes. One punch from Conrad and I had my arms full of Councillor Hodge. But you have to remember that Conrad was an aggressive piece of work before his accident, and I suppose it was just some deep-seated instinctive response. Very effective too!"

"Gran told me that you have asked her to look into the mail thing for her," said Sally, changing the subject. "She seems really pleased to have the responsibility."

"Good. I just haven't got the time to sort out all that, what with your mother going walk-about and now the future of Kitchener looking so bleak."

"It's a complete pig's bottom of a setup, Dad, and now I think I'm going to complicate things a bit more."

"I'm sure anything you say can't make things any worse, so what is it?" asked Clive, while praying that she wasn't going to ask how he felt about becoming a grandfather.

"It's Stan," started Nicky.

"Good chap that Stan," exclaimed Clive, just to make it easier for Nicky in case his fears were to be realised.

"Well, he's asked me to marry him, Dad."

Clive tried to conceal his sense of relief and restricted his comment to, "And how do you feel about that?" His immediate response had been to hug her and say how pleased he was, but he sensed a problem.

"I don't know. I get on really well with him, and I'm very happy at the thought of being with him. I love him, and I'm pretty sure he thinks the same way about me."

"I sense there's a 'but' coming."

"Not really, it's just that I haven't seen many examples that would recommend marriage to me as a lifestyle. Gran didn't cope for long, and you and Mum have gone for quantity rather than any credible quality of marriage. It's just not very inspiring, and Stan and I are very happy the way we are."

"So why consider it if things are fine the way they are?"

"Stan is really keen, he's sort of old-fashioned and just wants to settle down properly. He's asked me a few times over the last few months, but I keep putting it off."

"So it's not just a recent thing?"

"No, he asked me the first time when we were on holiday in July."

"That's good news in itself."

"What do you mean?" she asked. "What difference does it make?"

"Well, last July you weren't the daughter of a millionaire."

"How could you suspect Stan of being such a gold digger? I thought you liked him," said Nicky, sounding a little hurt.

"I think he's a great guy, head and shoulders, quite literally, above the other assorted misfits and general lower life forms that you've ever brought home. I liked him from the start, but first of all, it's not me he wants to marry, and secondly everyone has been telling me not to take anyone at face value. I'm just pleased that he made it clear that he loved you before you became an heiress."

"You really have changed, haven't you, Dad?" asked Sally without any trace of criticism in her voice.

"Everyone has been telling me I'm too trusting, and I see that you've just got to be a little wary at times. As for Stan, I'm pleased that he makes you happy, and I like him whether you marry him or not. Have you mentioned the proposal to your mum?"

"No, I haven't seen her to speak to for a while and, anyway, I don't think she's the ideal person to seek out for advice on marriage. I suspect she would be pretty pleased about it, though, because Stan's parents are both doctors!"

"Yes, that would do nicely for her. I haven't heard from her myself for a while. I did expect her to be round, if only to pick up some clothes."

"She'll be in touch soon enough. You're worth a great deal to her. She has a few million reasons not just to walk out of your life."

"It's a terrible thing to say, Nicky, but I'm afraid you're probably right."

"Never mind, Dad. Pru and I will stick by you. After all, you did say I was an heiress."

The couple spent a while discussing some of the general letters that had arrived, and they were both astounded by the audacity of some of them. In many cases, the appeal was made bluntly but in others all sorts of ploys were used to attract the attention of the reader before slipping in the request for money. Clive felt he was at last starting to gain some insight into the murky world of the confidence trickster, and his air of total naivety was slowly dissipating. When Nicky finally decided to go off to bed, she kissed her dad on the cheek and said, "Thanks for the advice about Stan."

"What advice? I didn't give you any."

"I know, but I felt I got good advice, and that's all that matters."

Shortly after Nicky had gone up to bed, Sebastian arrived home. He got himself a bottle of his special Mexican beer from the fridge, opened it and sat down at the table with his father.

"You were right about the Volvo, Dad," he said, sipping a mouthful of the designer brew from the bottle neck. "It turns out that it was not entirely suitable, a bit on the fast side, as you suggested."

"Like excrement flying off a garden implement?"

"Sort of." Sebastian looked at Clive and smiled before continuing, "You've changed a bit, haven't you, Dad?"

"I am reliably informed that I had to, or I would have been penniless by Christmas. I've been learning some hard lessons, but I'm getting there. Speaking of Christmas. I appreciate your present car is a complete pile of junk that kicks out noise and fumes that do more environmental damage than a Lancaster bomber, so I thought that, for the sake of the neighbourhood, I might consider buying you a better motor for Christmas. Something a little more refined, perhaps. Check out the market and come back to me with a few ideas. Let's say with a ceiling of ten thousand pounds. I would stress that this is not to be seen as setting a precedent for all future Christmases, but just a way of letting you share in Norman's legacy. I had planned to do the same for Nicky, your mum and Pru, but I suspect your mum might have her own ideas."

"Thanks, Dad, I'll get right on it tomorrow. With that sort of money, I should be able to get something pretty tasty through the trade and nothing too racy, honest."

"We'll see about that," observed Clive, displaying some of his new quality of cynicism, "I don't suggest that you drive around in a fossil of a car, but don't expect me to be too keen to buy a model that could become your coffin."

"Fair enough, and thanks again, Dad, you're a star."

As he sat on his own in the kitchen later, Clive reflected on the fact that even after showing some of his new-found cynicism to his children, they had both gone to bed happy with what he had done. It was a strange new Clive who sat there contemplating what the next few days might bring. Surely life had to calm down soon.

The following two days were blissfully uneventful, but the day after that was somewhat different. Clive had used the lull in the drama that had become his life to get to grips with the junk mail a bit. Pru had been marvellous, doing all the initial sorting and presenting Clive with the few letters that he might be interested in, and with uncharacteristic ruthlessness, he had discarded most of them. Among those he had been forced to acknowledge as being of some particular interest was one inviting him to an extraordinary general meeting of the steering committee called by Councillor Hodge for the following Friday evening. The letter was worded in Hodge's usual rude way so that it was not so much an invitation as an order to attend. While Clive's initial response was the temptation to tell the sleazy councillor what he could do with his committee, he decided that he ought to attend to stand up for the residents of Kitchener House.

The impending meeting did not stop Clive from enjoying the intervening days, during which he took the opportunity to inform Pru and Nicky of his wish to give them a special Christmas gift as he had promised to do with Sebastian. Both Nicky and Pru had initially objected to the idea, but Clive convinced them, so Nicky reluctantly decided to accept, saying that she would use the money towards setting herself up in a flat with Stan, and Pru was persuaded to have some work done on her garden in the spring to make it a little easier to manage.

Clive had still heard nothing from Maureen, and he was a little surprised to find that he didn't miss her much. It wasn't unusual for her to be away for days at various conventions, fairs and sales promotion events, and with his shifts it meant that they might barely meet in the house. They hardly ever went out socially as she didn't like the pub, and he didn't like the affected social soirées that Maureen often claimed she had to attend.

Clive and Sally met a couple of times to try and devise a strategy for the Friday meeting in an attempt to defend their jobs, but more importantly to protect the residents of Kitchener and to prevent them from being split up. Even after extensive collaboration, neither Clive nor Sally felt optimistic that Friday evening as they waited in the room above the local Co-op that was the regular venue for the steering committee. Most of the members were already assembled, and Clive noted that he had met many of them before. Sally and Clive exchanged pleasantries with June, who acted as secretary to the committee, but deliberately chose not to sit with her in case this might alert Hodge to the fact that they were allies. The rest of the group, apart from a sprinkling of staff members, were a mixture of local councillors and general members of what Clive referred to as the big hat brigade, largely well-meaning people who regularly gave up their time to support the sheltered housing group.

The main business and day-to-day running was carried out by the chairman and a few paid officers, and the full committee was largely a rubber-stamping group to endorse what had previously been decided. The general murmur of conversation in the room was shattered by the entrance of Councillor Hodge and Mr Tennett.

"Good evening, ladies and gentlemen," started the chairman, "I must apologise for having to call this extraordinary general meeting. I am aware we are all very busy people, but there are certain issues related to the organisation that, I regret, we must deal with without delay. You will no doubt have seen the article in the national press that reported on the activities of two of our employees and their recent assignation in Hull. While this matter caused a certain degree of unwelcome gossip about certain of our staff members, I must assure the committee that the incident has no bearing upon the subject of this meeting."

"So why bother mentioning it?" said Clive in an aside to Sally that could be heard by the entire meeting.

Hodge ignored the comment and, clearing his throat, he continued, "Our treasurer, Mr Tennett, and myself have had reason to examine the accounts of the society, and we have cause to express some concern as to the parlous state of those said accounts. It is apparent that, if we maintain our present spending levels, the group will be in a position of being unable to invest in further expansion. Over the years, the group has failed to make sufficient profit to set aside funds for the said expansion, and our projections prove that the organisation will be running at a small loss in 10 years' time. I call upon Mr Tennett to explain the figures in greater detail."

The treasurer rose to his feet and asked for a number of prepared documents to be passed around. There was a rustle of papers and the hum of conversations around the table. Hodge called for order in an overly officious way and asked

Mr Tennett to continue. There followed a fountain of accountancy jargon, during which attention was drawn to various paragraphs and graphs in the document, which had been efficiently photocopied in full colour and presented in cellophane-fronted document folders. Tennett droned on about the figures as only an accountant could and concluded by saying, "So it is clear that we have a limited range of options open to us and, I regret to say that we have to propose that Kitchener House should be sold off and the resulting cash used to prepare a 'war chest' to enable us to face up to the future expenditure shortfalls that we have brought to your attention."

"Thank you for that concise but illuminating report, Mr Treasurer," said the chairman with unseemly haste. "And now it only remains to ask the committee to adopt this document. Proposed by Mr Tennett, seconded by myself. All those in favour."

Before he could say another word, Sally rose to her feet and announced, "Mr Chairman, I am sure that I am not alone in thinking that the committee would wish to discuss this matter. After all, it seems nonsensical to gather such an eminent group of local citizens and then to pass up the opportunity of obtaining their views on such an important issue that does have major implications, not least for the people who have called Kitchener House their home for a combined total of over 35 years."

There was a murmur of approval among the great and the good, but Hodge was not impressed and tried to get rid of this irritation. "Mrs Livingstone," he began, "as a member of staff, you are here with the permission of the committee and as such you are not allowed to take part in the meeting."

"That's Doctor Livingstone," Sally corrected him before pointing out, "The constitution of the committee clearly states that any member of staff invited to meetings is to be regarded as a co-opted member of the committee and is be able to address the committee and have full voting rights on any issue or issues that are deemed to relate to the particular establishment within which they work."

Hodge had considerable difficulty hiding his fury, but speaking slowly he said, "Very well, Doctor Livingstone. Perhaps you would permit us to move on to the vote?"

"We cannot do that," interrupted Clive. "We haven't had an official motion or the option to propose any amendment to the said non-proposal. I am sure the committee would wish to have a chance to discuss this proposal in full after digesting the contents of Mr Tennett's comprehensive and highly illuminating document."

Hodge was starting to turn a rather florid colour and fought to try and regain his calm before stating, "I am sure we don't all wish to be here until midnight discussing the document."

"Of course we don't, I'm sure that all our respected members have lots to do in their busy lives, but I do have a proposal," added Sally with a sweet smile.

"I trust it's a sensible one," prompted the harassed chairman,

"I propose that each committee member be permitted to take away a copy of the report so that they can subject it to the scrutiny that it undoubtedly deserves, and I further propose that the said report should then be discussed in full at a meeting of the same members here present at a date and time to be decided by the chairman but not before two weeks has elapsed," said a rather jubilant doctor.

"I second that motion," added Clive quickly.

Another murmur of clear approval went around the room, and Hodge resigned himself to having to put the motion to the group. Only two of the officials voted against it. Shortly thereafter the meeting closed, and Clive and Sally watched the chairman sweep out of the door with Mr Tennett in tow and then listened to the bad-tempered stomping as they made their way down the stairs.

"I bet you're not on Hodge's Christmas list now," said Clive, "I didn't know anything about the constitution of the steering committee."

"Fortunately, neither did Hodge, serves him right."

"So you just made it up?"

"Would a doctor do a thing like that? I thought you were pretty quick with the motions and amendments jargon as well. We make quite a team. Did you notice June? She was finding it hard not to show her delight at the way Hodge was squirming. The trouble is that Hodge may just be bright enough to check the constitution, but at least we've got a copy of the document to see what they are trying to do, and we've bought ourselves a minimum of two weeks. I don't suppose we can put it off indefinitely, but we can make life pretty difficult for Sleaze Ball. By the way, did you see that faint bruising on his lip? If I didn't know better, I'd think someone had punched him."

CHAPTER TWENTY

Clive and Sally were eager to arrange an early date to discuss the report that pressed for the closure of Kitchener House, and they were pleased to be able to arrange a meeting when they were both free on the following Sunday evening. The Prince William seemed a suitable venue and so it was that they turned up there with their copies of the report. They got themselves a drink before finding a table away from the bar where they could discuss issues in relative privacy.

"So, Clive, you're the figures man. What did you make of it?" asked Sally as they settled to business.

"I found it all rather complicated."

"You mean you couldn't understand it either?"

"Oh no, I could understand it, I just found it complicated, too complicated," said Clive, but aware that he wasn't making himself clear, he went on to explain, "Any audit that is carried out should be as simple as possible. All businesses have assets and they have liabilities. The audit should set out, first and foremost, to establish what the company is worth before looking at what it has paid out and what it can reasonably expect to have to pay out in the near future."

"So they have to see what money they have got and what they need to spend?"

"Exactly. But in this report, they seem to have consistently undervalued the assets while assuming the worst in forecasting future spending. For example, the figures allow for an annual increase in staff wages of 12 percent for each of the next five years, but we know that we would be lucky to get three at the moment. The other figures also paint the blackest possible picture, but even with those forecasts the organisation has sufficient investments to just about cover any future shortfall."

"I must admit that when I read it, I felt the numbers almost balanced."

"And if the worst came to the worst, the association would make nearly two hundred thousand pounds selling off the plot at the bottom of the garden behind Kitchener House. But according to their figures, Kitchener House and the entire grounds aren't worth that much. Now the habit of undervaluing property is a legitimate accountancy procedure, but when you want to translate those liabilities into assets, that is by selling the property, you have to be realistic about what you could expect to make."

"That was part of the confusing bit in the report; they talk about 'residential units A to E' at one point, and you have to cross-reference that with a chart on the back page to see which is which, and elsewhere they are 'domiciliary units', and there are entire pages that seem to say nothing but which are sprinkled by phrases such as 'on costs,' 'commercial viability', front-end-funding' and countless other incomprehensible terms."

"That's what I meant about being too complicated. They give you lots of information you don't really need and hide what they don't want you to see behind a verbal smoke screen," explained Clive.

"I must admit that I couldn't understand some of the appendixes or even why they were in there. Why bother putting in a detailed summary of staff wages for the last five years and a full breakdown of total heating costs? To try and put the whole lot in the proverbial nutshell, they recommend selling off Kitchener House because it's the most expensive or least efficient in terms of running costs?" asked Sally as though she had grasped the message.

"Well that's what they infer, but if you compare it to Trafalgar House, you see that the annual running costs are more than Kitchener, and it is well known that Trafalgar is going to need extensive refurbishment soon."

"So selling off Kitchener is unnecessary? And if they have to sell off somewhere, it shouldn't be Kitchener anyway?"

"That's about it." concluded Clive.

"Clive Sullivan, you are magnificent. You have completely changed my views on accountants. I now realise that you are not all boring, unimaginative, superannuated train spotters with unimaginably low excitement thresholds."

"Steady on there, Doc. I was never actually an accountant as such as I lacked the necessary devil-may-care qualities, and I failed the medical."

"Well, you'll always be an accountant to me. But tell me this, my ledger-loving superhero; if selling off Kitchener makes so little sense, then why is Hodge so hell-bent on pushing for it?"

"That's a very good question, but I think we will have to do a bit more digging if we hope to get to the bottom of it. But we can't do anything about it at the moment, so why don't we join Beer Bill at the bar and have another drink?"

Clive bought himself another pint and another orange juice for Sally.

"Cheers," declared Clive. "Let's not let Councillor Hodge ruin our entire evening."

"Dirty Harry?" interrupted the landlord, "I thought I heard you mention his name earlier. He's barred from this place."

"Barred? I wouldn't have thought he'd have spent much time in here," commented Sally.

"Oh, he's never actually set foot in the place, but he's barred anyway; I've heard a lot about him from Council Bill. Isn't that right, Bill?" he asked as he drew another of the customers into the conversation.

"This is Council Bill; he'll tell you all about Councillor Hodge."

"Dirty Harry?" said the new member of the group. "He's got his face in so many troughs at the council offices, but he still comes up smelling of roses. He seems to know everything that's going on in every department, and if there's a few bob to be made along the way, he manages to do it. If he can't get his own way by stealth, then he is not averse to bullying people. He sails pretty close to the wind but nobody can pin anything on him. He's not the most popular member of the council. There have been a couple of informal enquiries into dealings, but he always walks away without formal charges being made. He's had numerous accusations of sexual harassment from the female staff, but no one seems prepared to take the charges forward."

"That sounds very believable," said Clive. "I've only met him a few times and he makes my flesh creep. He's now threatening to throw us out of a job and close down the house where our friends live."

"Conrad's family?" queried Council Bill. "The group you were in with the other night? Still, I wouldn't put it past old Dirty Harry; he'd throw his own grandmother out into the snow on Christmas Eve. His heart is as cold as a penguin's bum."

"He's got it in for us," explained Sally. "There's no reason to close any of our organisation's homes and certainly not Kitchener House."

Council Bill thought for a moment before suggesting, "If Dirty Harry is doing anything, there has to be something in it for him. Give me a couple of days and I'll make some discreet enquiries in the council offices."

Clive and Sally gave Council Bill details of the location of Kitchener House, and then the group settled down to their conversation, much of which revolved around the previous exploits of the obnoxious Hodge. Despite the shadow of Hodge falling over their chat, they enjoyed a pleasant evening, and Clive was sad when Sally announced, "Come on then, Clive, we need our beauty sleep if we are going to challenge the Ogre Hodge."

"Our separate beauty sleeps," clarified Clive to the rest of the group.

"Shame," said Sally. "I can still give you a lift home, unless you want to wander the freezing streets on your own."

Clive was pleased to take up Sally's offer of a lift; it wasn't a long walk, but it had turned very cold and there was even the odd pathetic flake of snow falling. Above all, he was just pleased to have a few more moments with Sally, though this time it was in her old car, and the heater had barely warmed up by the time they arrived outside Clive's house.

"Thanks Sally," he said, and then almost as an afterthought, he added, "Would you like to come in for a coffee?"

"It's late. I'd better not. Oh what the hell! I'd love to."

The kitchen was warm and welcoming as Clive ushered Sally in. He put the kettle on and set about putting fresh coffee into the cafetiere.

"It's strange that this is only the second time I've been in here," observed Sally.

"Yes. It's relatively close to work, and over the years you might have thought you'd have been round. Come to think of it, though, I don't even know exactly where you live. I come out of Kitchener and turn right along Verona Road and you turn left. As we said before, you work closely with someone, and yet you may know nothing of their lives in the real world."

Their conversation was interrupted by the noisy arrival of Pru and Nicky.

"Hi Sally," said Nicky enthusiastically. "Hi Dad. Sally, I don't think you've met my gran."

"The name's Pru," she said with a warm smile. "It's so lovely to meet you at last. It's about time I met my son-in-law's attractive young girlfriend."

"Pru, you are a very naughty woman. You'll embarrass Sally," protested Clive.

"After all we've been through together, I think I will cope," joked Sally.

"All what?" asked Nicky very quickly.

"I must spare your father's blushes, but you'll gather that Hull is quite a hotbed of passion. It must be true because I read it in the paper."

"Coffee anyone?" asked Clive in a vain attempt to steer the conversation onto a topic he would feel more comfortable with.

"Thanks," said Nicky. "Gran and I have been doing a bit of Christmas shopping, and then we went round to her place for a bit of something to eat. The shops were quite full, but then it's just over two weeks to Christmas. I don't suppose you've been out shopping yet, Dad?"

"Life has been a bit full recently, and any way I've sorted you two out."

"Yes, and thanks again, darling," said Pru. "I decided what I needed to do to get my garden in order; I intend to hire a couple of beefy off-duty firemen to sort a few things out for me."

"And what about the garden?" asked Nicky. "And will two firemen be enough for you, Gran?"

"As long as they're fit, darling."

"You must excuse my gran, Sally. We've tried to get her a more sedate hobby, but she's hardly ready for crochet circles and whist drives just yet," explained Nicky.

"And have you any idea what you'd like from me for Christmas for your proposed flat, Nicky?" asked Clive, still trying to get the conversation into potentially less embarrassing areas.

"I don't know, Dad. Stan is still keen on marriage, and if we do go with that plan, we might decide to save a bit more for the deposit on a house. I still can't make my mind up if I want to marry him or not."

"So you might be getting married?" prompted Sally. "But you're unsure if it's what you really want. Quite a dilemma!"

"It's silly, I love him, and I'd like to be with him, but, as I pointed out to Dad, our family has such a lousy track record as regards marriage," she explained before turning to Pru and adding, "No offence, Gran."

"None taken, darling," said Pru with a smile. "I make no bones about the fact that I was just unsuited to marriage; perhaps I'm too fickle, too lazy, too selfish or too easily bored. How about you, Sally?"

"Quite the opposite really. Marrying Steve was the best thing I ever did, and I never had a single regret. It could be a personality thing or just being extremely lucky to find the right man. But if I had my time over, I'd do the same thing again."

"I'm so pleased for you, Sally. You make marriage sound ideal," commented Nicky.

"Oh, it was never a permanent bed of roses, but I know it was worth the effort."

Clive marvelled at the way the three favourite women in his life got on so well and the fact that even so early in their relationship, they seemed to have no difficulty discussing personal things with each other. Men would need to know each other for years before discussing anything more private than the identity of the football teams they supported. He had never discussed his marriage with anyone at the pub, even to get a bit of sympathy. He listened as the women chatted on about a whole range of topics. On more than one occasion they discussed him, but he had given up any hope of turning the conversation in any direction. The three of them were quite comfortable discussing the recent events in his life and the less than stable nature of his marriage. Both Pru and Nicky were quite open about their feelings about the way Maureen had treated Clive, and he had long passed the point when he felt able to defend her so he just sat and drank his coffee.

Despite the women's tendency to occasionally discuss items that still made Clive feel a little uncomfortable, he enjoyed their late evening chat. Eventually, Pru declared that she must be on her way home and Clive walked her to her car.

"Nicky was right about her; she's lovely, and she obviously cares a lot about you; pity that she appears so genuinely happy about her marriage to Steve. Still. There's plenty more fish in the sea, and for a man in your position, as they say, the world's your lobster."

Clive didn't even bother to point out that he was still married to Maureen. The separation had somehow made it clear to him that they had never been really close, and it was equally obvious that Pru and Nicky had no objection to the relationship slowly sinking below the surface of the sea of matrimony. As Pru's car pulled away from the house, he was suddenly aware that Sally's announcement about how much she enjoyed married life had made him happy for her, but he was also aware of a vague feeling of envy for Steve. He was so deep in thought that he almost missed Pru's parting comments about inviting Sally to her party on Sunday.

Back in the kitchen, Nicky and Sally were clearing away the coffee mugs and generally tidying the kitchen.

"Sally's been telling me about the obnoxious Hodge; he's just the kind of pervert you wouldn't want to get stuck in a lift with."

"That's a pretty fair appraisal of him," agreed Clive. "But he's the type of malevolent little lizard that can make our lives very uncomfortable, and the only way we can have a hope of thwarting him is to find out exactly what he's after."

"Let's hope Council Bill can find something," suggested Sally., "But Hodge's reputation would suggest that he is very good at covering his slimy tracks."

"His attempt at bulldozing his way through the last meeting wasn't too subtle, but he probably wasn't expecting a lot of opposition. Now that he's been alerted to us, he may box a bit more cleverly," warned Clive.

"We'll see," said Sally., "But for now, I must bid you both goodnight. I'm supposed to be at work for 10 in the morning if Mousey June's roster is to be believed."

Clive walked Sally out to her car. It was bitterly cold, and Sally was glad to get into the car. She started the engine before winding the window down and saying, "That was fun. You should be grateful for having two such lovely women in your life. Best get a move on; I might see you tomorrow at handover."

"I may well drop in for coffee, as long as Minnie isn't making it, and we could draw up our battle plans."

"I'll look forward to it. Good night," she called as she pulled away up the drive.

Clive stood for a moment as she drove off. Sally was wrong. He didn't have two lovely women in his life; he had three. It was far too cold to stand there counting his blessings, so he hurriedly made his way back into the house.

"Sally seems very pro-marriage," observed Nicky when she saw her dad. "It's nice to see someone for whom marriage obviously works so well. I might have to rethink Stan's proposal. It's a pity for you though, Dad."

"What do you mean?"

"Well, as Sally is so obviously taken, we'll have to find someone else for you. Shame, I like her, and it is obvious that she likes you a lot."

"Sometimes I despair of you, Nicky. Sally is just a very good friend."

"Dad! How can you be so insensitive? It's obvious that she's keen on you, and it's probably only the fact that you're both married that stops her from telling you. Surely you can see how she feels about you?" asked Nicky, becoming increasingly exasperated.

"You've been reading too much romantic poetry. Sally and I get on well, but you mustn't read any more than that into it."

"What exactly would a woman have to do to get through to you that she fancies you? If a beautiful woman ran in here now, threw off most of her clothes and threw herself into your arms, what would you say?"

"I'd say she'd got the wrong house," answered Clive. "Now will you please stop trying to find me a partner?"

"Well, someone has to give you a shove now and again, Dad. How on earth did you ever manage to pick up Mum on your own?"

"I was young, debonair and fancy-free. I met her at a dance in the Conservative club, and our romance just sort of blossomed. We were married within six months," recalled Clive.

"How romantic, Dad."

The truth of Clive's early romance was fundamentally the same, but the version he recounted was one that Maureen had helped him to perfect over the years. It was true that they had met at the Conservative club, but Maureen was not attending a dance, she had an evening job working behind the bar that she had agreed to do just so that she could meet a 'better class' of prospective husband. It was true that he had been overwhelmed by her striking good looks, but it was also true that she had selected Clive because of his white-collar job and the fact that he was a solicitor's son. He was a far better catch than any of the men who worked alongside her in the biscuit factory during the day. Having secured her man, she was keen to get him down the aisle as quickly as possible, hence the whirlwind romance. With twenty-twenty hindsight, it was easy to see what had happened, but at the time it was all a happy blur and, for a while at least, the dream had worked for both of them.

"Stan's coming over tomorrow if that's OK, Dad? University is largely closed for Christmas, but he still has an assignment to hand in by Wednesday, so we thought he would be able to work better here."

"That's fine by me; I've arranged to drop in at Kitchener during the day to see Sally, so I will leave the pair of you to your business."

"Very tactful, Dad, but he really does have to get this assignment done."

"You must try and keep your hands off him then," quipped Clive, pleased to make a dig about her love life for once.

CHAPTER TWENTY-ONE

There was a faint dusting of snow on the roads the following day as Clive cycled to Kitchener House, and just a few flakes in the air as he pushed his bike up the side of the house before going into the warm kitchen. Minnie, with minimal assistance from Conrad, was doing some polishing in the hallway, but she quickly came through to greet Clive.

"The doctor's on the phone at the moment," she announced. "We were just going to have a coffee. Do you want one?"

"That's very kind of you, Minnie, but as you're obviously busy, let me make it," replied Clive, pleased that he had thus avoided another of Minnie's coffees.

After making up four cups of coffee, Clive informed the others that it was ready. Minnie came through, laden with a wooden box filled with assorted polishes and cloths which she carefully put away in a cupboard. Conrad came in wearing his apron, which as ever was as pristine as the rest of his clothes, and he sat down to his less than hard-earned drink. It was a while before the vague sound of Sally's conversation on the phone finished and she came in to the kitchen.

"I'm sorry, but do you think Clive and I might take our coffees in the front room as we've got a bit of business to get through?" Sally asked. Minnie and Conrad were pleased to get on with their break, so Sally led Clive through to the front, where she immediately explained the situation.

"I didn't want to discuss it in front of the others, but that was June on the phone. She wanted to warn us that Hodge has taken his concern over the newspaper article to the full committee of the association. Hodge, as chairman of the said steering committee, can recommend disciplinary action be taken, but such action has to be taken by the full committee."

"So Hodge wants the backing of the parent group to slap our wrists?" asked Clive.

"It seems so," agreed Sally. "But the full committee aren't due to meet until the 27th, so in the meantime Hodge wanted us to be suspended on full pay until we have a chance to defend ourselves at the meeting. June wanted to warn us that Hodge had initially wanted her to write and notify us formally."

"But that would mean that we would be suspended on the day of the meeting about the proposed closure," added Clive.

"I suspect that's exactly what Hodge was manoeuvring for. However, June has pointed out to the association's president, Sir Jack Stamp, that if we can be persuaded to take two week's leave, and we tack that on to the Christmas break, we would be due to return on the 27th, the very day of the full committee meeting. So we would be 'out of the way' and there is no extra cost to the association. We would have to use up two weeks of our holiday allocation, but we would not technically be suspended."

"If they'll buy that, it's fine by me. I have trouble using up my holiday allocation anyway," said Clive.

"It seems that Sir Jack is all in favour of the plan as it doesn't cost them any extra in staff wages. It is also a well-known fact that Sir Jack hates Hodge and wouldn't put himself out to do anything to please the sleaze ball – something to do with a failed planning application in the past. He is obviously less than enthusiastic about being used to carry out Hodge's dirty work over what he apparently sees as a relatively trivial incident. June suggests that we might like to make this gesture 'in the financial interests of the association' and commence our holiday tomorrow. What do you think?"

"I feel the need for a holiday all of a sudden."

"Good, I thought you would. June volunteered to draw up a provisional cover plan for staffing Kitchener in our absence. She said it should be OK if Sue comes back from Nightingale and June does some of the shifts herself. With that, Larry, and the other part-time workers, it should be fine."

"Let's do it then. I'll ring up June now and tell her to go ahead. I'll miss the family though."

"We can always drop in and visit. It's their home and, despite Hodge's scheming, we are not forbidden from entering the house," pointed out Sally before adding, "We could set off for a wild and bracing time in Withernsea."

"Withernsea is certainly bracing, but few brass monkeys choose to holiday there at this time of year."

Clive went off to phone June to ask her to put her plan into operation and to thank her for her help in thwarting Hodge's scheming. He then sat down with Sally and the others to inform them of the impromptu holiday plans.

"Are you and the doctor going somewhere nice for your holiday?" asked Minnie innocently.

"We don't know what our plans are exactly," answered Sally. "We've got some matters to deal with, but we'll no doubt try and get a break as well."

"And will we still be having our Christmas outing this year?" asked Minnie hopefully.

"Of course, Minnie," responded Clive. "And this year we can go wherever you like. Have a word with Len and Conrad and decide what you want to do."

The response was exactly as Clive had expected. Minnie made it clear that the Prince William was the ideal venue, and Conrad concurred with a definite, "I'd love a cup of tea."

Clive had tried in previous years to suggest alternative venues, but the family always settled on the pub. To them it was a familiar and friendly place where they were sure of being accepted, and Clive was pleased with their suggestion because he knew that Beer Bill would be disappointed if he couldn't put on a bit of an event for his special customers. The landlord didn't routinely put on Christmas dinners, but for the last few years it had been part of his own Christmas tradition to have the Kitchener family in for a meal shortly before Christmas. His food was nothing exceptional, but he and his wife always provided crackers and seasonal decorations on the table. The other regular Bills enjoyed the evening as well. There was always some taped Christmas music which was followed by a few carols, and the evening always ended with the drawing of the pub's Christmas raffle. It was a further tradition that there were three extra prizes that just happened to be 'won' by the Kitchener House family. Clive knew that the pub's Christmas raffle was to be drawn on the 22nd, and it had already been entered in the diary file.

"Well, I suppose the enforced holiday will give us a bit of time to work on a strategy to tackle Hodge's plans," said Sally as she sat with Clive in the front room later.

"And to see just what Maureen's intentions are. I somehow doubt she'll be rushing home for Christmas, but I haven't heard a word from her," added Clive.

"Oh, you poor dear," said Sally with a genuine show of concern. "I'd forgotten all about your problems, what with Hodge and everything. Do you think you ought to contact her? Try and get something sorted out? You can't just go on living in limbo."

"I had provisionally planned that if she hasn't been in touch by Friday, then I would have to ring her, but I'm not looking forward to it. It's not a good time of year with the usual family Christmas routines. Speaking of which, Pru is holding her Christmas cocktail party on Sunday afternoon, and she asked me to invite you. Sorry, I forgot last night. You were a big hit with her, and Nicky wants you as an older sister."

"I enjoyed the evening, and yes I'd love to come."

"Oh, and Steve as well, of course. It's open house at Pru's, and it would be good to meet up with him again."

For a moment, Sally was silent but then quietly said, "I thought you knew."

"Knew what?" asked Clive, with a sense of foreboding.

"Steve died."

Clive was literally shocked into a state of being totally speechless, and it was a moment or two before he could proffer, "I'm so sorry. What happened?"

"It's nearly four years ago now; ironically, he was visiting his sick father in Canada. It appears that Steve had some undetected heart problem and he just died."

Clive was once again at a loss as to what to say. He just felt it was impossible to believe, but he knew that unfortunately this was not one of Sally's attempts to fool him. After a while, Sally broke the silence.

"I thought you knew. I was off work for a week to go over and attend the funeral. We felt he would have wanted to be buried in his home town. I got some lovely flowers from work, and I'm sure you signed the card."

Clive was unable to make any sense of the situation; Steve, who was as strong as an ox, had suddenly died? It slowly started to filter back into his memory that there had been an announcement at work about someone who had died, and no doubt a collection would have been made and a card signed, but it couldn't have been Steve. Steve from the barbecue, Steve whose car they had borrowed, Steve who was so happily married to Sally.

"There was a member of staff who died, but that was a Doctor Luger or Lika or something. I just assumed it was someone who worked on the association's management committee."

"That was Doctor Lukar. That was Steve. When we married, we were both Dr Lukar, but I stuck to my maiden name when we ran the business. It was confusing having two Dr S Lukars."

"But we borrowed Steve's car, and you were talking just the other night about how happily married you were."

"I've kept the car because I thought mine was about to give up the ghost but it keeps on going. It's true that I was speaking about how happy my marriage had made me, and it is absolutely true. I had a fantastic marriage, and I wouldn't have changed a minute of it, but it's now over, sadly."

Clive was still reeling at the news. He tried to think back to the times that Steve had been in their conversations; she had never thought to say he was dead, and Clive had just built up a clear if misguided picture of Steve as still being around. Clive was beginning to realise that when one starts with a misconception, without very clear evidence to the contrary, it can be easy to fit any new information in to support it. He had assumed Steve was still around, and he took everything Sally had said or done as being proof.

"I'm sorry, Clive," she said. "I had convinced myself that you knew; perhaps I should have been more sensitive to how you spoke of Steve or something. I should have guessed. I didn't mean to shock you."

"I suppose I was so taken up with everything else going on in my life that I just wasn't thinking about the fact that you might have problems," suggested Clive, who was only very slowly coming to terms with the news. The unreality of it all seemed to be compounded by the fact that Sally was apologising to him. Eventually, he collected himself sufficiently to suggest that they might have another cup of coffee; at least it would give him something to do.

As they sat with their drinks, Clive observed, "It certainly goes to support our theory that you can work closely with someone and know nothing about their private life."

"It certainly does that."

"As I was saying before that last bombshell, Pru would love to see you at her place on Sunday. Do you think you might be able to make it?"

Sally smiled and said, "Please tell Pru that I would love to come."

"That's great. She, I mean we, would love to see you there. Oh, and I intend to go down to the Prince William on Wednesday evening at about six. It's one of Council Bill's regular nights down there. He might have some dirt to dish on Hodge. It would be good to see you if you can make it, and we could make arrangements for Pru's do then."

"Well, at least I know that I won't be working. I'll see you there about six then."

Clive was delighted at the fact that he had effectively just made arrangements to meet up with Sally socially, and the anticipation of these proposed meetings reminded him of those days in his youth on the rare occasions that he had plucked up the courage to ask girls out.

It was a very happy Clive who cycled home through the lightest of snow showers, and he noted that during the day the weather hadn't changed, unlike his own state. As far as his personal life was concerned, he felt like an article of washing in a tumble dryer; just as he thought the turmoil might be finishing, life spun him the other way.

When Clive arrived home, he saw Pru's car in the drive, and he calculated that she had probably come over to go through some more of the mail that continued to arrive in considerable quantities. He wasn't surprised to see her in the kitchen sorting through the said junk and being assisted by Nicky.

"Hi Pru, Nicky. I'm pleased to catch you both together. I need to update you on something."

Both the women greeted him, and then Nicky, sensing something important was to be disclosed, asked, "What is it, Dad? What's happened?"

Clive quickly explained about the enforced holiday, to which Pru responded, "Is that all? It's not a problem, darling; you could do with a break after what you've been through."

"It's not just that," said Clive, "it's Sally."

"Is she all right?" asked Nicky. "Has something happened?"

"She's fine, it's just that, well, we were all talking about how happy she was being married to Steve," Clive said hesitantly. "Well, it seems that I had got it all wrong and I learned today that Steve died about four years ago."

This announcement obviously hit the women in much the same way as the news had exploded into Clive's life."

"The poor darling," said Pru.

"I hope we didn't upset her going on about marriage, and she didn't think we were being insensitive," added Nicky.

"I'm sure she didn't. She realises that we, or rather I, didn't know about it, but she assumed that I did. Bless her; she was actually apologising to me because she thought I knew and she ought to have told me. Anyway, you'll both have the chance to see her on Sunday at the party. She was delighted to be asked."

"Great!" exclaimed Pru. "And Nicky's young man says he can attend. The hunk."

"Steady on, Gran, he is my little Bunnykins," declared Nicky, "so don't go frightening him."

It was at that moment that Bunnykins, or Stan as he was known to everyone else, joined them.

"Hi Stan, how's the assignment going?" asked Clive. "Had a good session?"

"Great, thanks, Mr Sullivan, I just have to reference a couple of graphs, and I can hand it in." Despite Clive's repeated attempts to persuade Stan to adopt a less formal way of addressing him, the young man continued to call him thus. Clive was also of the opinion that if that was what Stan wanted, then that was fine. At over six foot six inches tall with closely cropped hair, broad shoulders and a muscular frame that would have suited a comic book superhero, Stan was not the kind of person one would have wanted to disagree with. The truth was that this giant of a man was by nature very gentle and unassuming, not that his opponents on the rugby pitch would have seen him in that light. He was a superb athlete who played hard but never dirty. Stan played fair, brutally fair. While Nicky's name for him of Bunnykins was perhaps going a bit far, he was far from being the great bruiser that his appearance might suggest.

"Isn't he just gorgeous?" exclaimed Pru. "You'd better look after this one, Nicky, or I'll be after him."

Stan knew Pru well enough to appreciate that she was generally harmless, so he just smiled politely at her and said, "I've been trying to persuade Nicky that you are ready and waiting if she chooses not to hang on to me."

"Come on, Bunnykins," urged Nicky. "Let's get that assignment wrapped up so I can get you somewhere safe away from my gran. I may even let you take me out for a drink later."

Nicky led him off by the hand, and Clive was struck by the incongruity of the two figures, his little girl and her enormous boyfriend, like a toddler dragging a huge teddy bear around.

"I wish she'd see sense and settle down with that one," commented Pru. "Far be it from me to suggest that they ought to get married, but they just seem right."

"I like him, and he adores Nicky, but they will no doubt choose their own path."

"I went through your mail again today," said Pru, changing the subject, "and there are a few that I haven't opened that

I thought you might want to look at, including one from a local solicitor."

She sorted through a small pile of letters that had escaped the usual destination in the bin and handed an official-looking envelope to him. He read the name on the front and noted that it had his full initials. At least this one had done their homework a bit better. He opened the envelope and began to read the letter.

"It's from someone claiming to be representing Maureen," he said, before reading out some of the contents, "Notification of intention… petition for divorce... Adultery! Pru, it says that Maureen is going for a divorce on the grounds of my adultery with an unnamed co-respondent. It seems that she wants to let me know her solicitor is doing the initial paperwork to submit to the court. After that we can go to mediation, or we can ask our solicitors to work out terms that are acceptable to both Maureen and I."

"Oh dear, Clive. I was afraid this would happen. Have you any idea what you want to do?"

"I haven't the faintest. It's a pack of lies. Sally and I never… I'm going to ring Maureen now and get this mess sorted out."

Clive walked directly through to the hall, picked up Maureen's card with the contact telephone number on it and dialled it immediately. He heard it ringing for quite a while and was about to put the receiver down when he heard a male voice repeat the number, and he was surprised to recognise that he was speaking to Josslyn.

"Hello, Josslyn? Do you think I could speak to Maureen, please?"

There was a distinct pause before Josslyn replied, "I'm sorry, Clive, she's not available at the moment."

"So when is she likely to be back so I can speak to her?" pressed Clive.

There was a further pause before Josslyn announced, "I'm sorry, but I don't know when it would be convenient. She's been told to... The solicitor suggested that she should communicate through him if she felt it was easier."

Josslyn was obviously very uncomfortable with the situation, so Clive tried another approach.

"Is she there now?" he asked. "I don't want to start a fight over this; I just don't know what she wants."

"She isn't in at the moment, but she's finding all this very difficult. She doesn't know what to do for the best."

"OK. Just tell her I called and would like the chance to talk things through."

Clive walked back into the kitchen to Pru, who was obviously eager to know what had been said.

"That's weird," declared Clive. "She's staying at Josslyn's house. But when we tried to trace the call back to Brussels that day, there had been a call from that same number. Josslyn lives on his own, so who the hell rang us that day? It seems that Maureen has been advised not to talk to me if it makes her feel any better and to communicate through her solicitor."

"Oh dear, Clive. I'm afraid I might know who called from that number. Maureen."

"But she was in Brussels, she called me. It's not the kind of call you forget."

"You took a call, but remember that when we tried to trace the last caller afterwards, it gave what turns out to be Josslyn's number. I'm pretty sure there weren't two calls that day; I've thought about it, and Arkwright normally barks the place down to attract me when the phone rings, so it's highly unlikely that I missed a call. And if Josslyn was supposed to be in Brussels, then who was ringing from his house?"

"So what was she doing ringing from Josslyn's place? Perhaps she was house-sitting for him?"

"I can't see Maureen giving up her time to spend a few days in Josslyn's flat so he can go to Brussels, and why should she lie about going abroad?"

"So you think they were both there?" asked Clive as a very unpalatable truth began to dawn. "They didn't go on a business trip? They were spending the time in his place."

"I've had my doubts about her and the lovely Josslyn for some time," confided Pru. "All those 'trade fairs' and 'conferences'. I once found her passport in her room when she claimed she was attending some bash in Paris. I'm pretty sure that a lot of his camp nature is window dressing for the business, but I've never wanted to admit they were probably having an affair."

"Well, that just about puts the tin hat on it! Maureen petitions for a divorce on the grounds of my adultery while her and Mr Fancy Pants-aren't I-bloody-lovely-Josslyn have been at it like rabbits for years."

"It's not the best time to discuss it," said Pru, raising her eyes in the general direction of Nicky's room. "Perhaps tomorrow, when you've had a chance to think it through?"

CHAPTER TWENTY-TWO

At breakfast the following morning, Clive did not mention the letter from Maureen. He had decided to find out just what she had in mind before he let the children know. Clive's general low spirits contrasted markedly with Nicky, who was her usual bubbly self.

"Stan finally gets to hand in that assignment today," she announced. "It's a big weight off his mind. We thought we might go into town and celebrate with a meal afterwards and then round to his place, so I won't be in tonight."

"Fine. Thanks for letting me know. I'm meeting Sally at the pub tonight, so I may get something to eat there."

"Good for you, Dad. It's about time you put a bit of effort into your social life. Give my love to Sally and say how much we are all looking forward to seeing her on Sunday."

Clive didn't bother trying to explain that his meeting with Sally was for business rather than to promote their non-existent romantic involvement. He just didn't feel like getting into any good-humoured banter with his daughter. After Nicky had gone, Clive was suddenly struck by the fact that he was on holiday but he didn't feel in a holiday mood. He wandered over to the window and looked out at the back garden which was covered in a heavy frost; there was nothing he could do out there at the moment, even in the greenhouse. He decided to make a fresh cafetiere of coffee and to have a couple of hours browsing his poetry books. He tried to settle to some Larkin but found that the tone of many of them only served to make him feel even more down. He remembered

Larkin's appraisal of his own motivation, "Deprivation is for me what daffodils were for Wordsworth." He picked through a number of other books but couldn't settle to any of them; his mind kept coming back to the letter from the solicitor.

Clive was now glad that he hadn't been able to contact Maureen the previous day, particularly after he and Pru had deduced that Maureen and Josslyn shared more than a business relationship. It would have been easy to have said things in the heat of the moment, and that was certainly not his style, but he still felt a bit aggrieved that Maureen had made accusations about him and Sally which were unfounded while Maureen and Josslyn were less than innocent. The day dragged on, and he still couldn't devise a plan of action. He rang Sally in the hope of hearing a friendly voice, but she was out. He spent time preparing an elaborate pasta dish for a late lunch but found he wasn't particularly hungry. Eventually, he looked out of the window and noticed it was getting dark so he went to have a shower and to get ready for his meeting with Sally; at least that was something to look forward to. For the first time in years, he found himself giving serious thought to what he would wear, partly because it filled in the time and partly because he felt it was important to look at his best for the meeting with Sally. Finally he was ready. He looked at himself in the mirror, picked up his wallet and put it in his pocket before checking his watch. It was still only half past four. He still had a good hour to kill, but he couldn't think of much else to do, so he scribbled a note for Sebastian, put on a coat and set off for the pub.

The evening was fine but icily cold, and the snow had evidently given up any hope of making an impression on the road. Clive walked slowly to take up more time, but he soon found himself quickening his pace in order to try and keep warm, and shortly before five he arrived at the Prince William.

Clive was a bit disappointed to find that Council Bill was not standing in his usual place at the bar but then realised that if he were coming in after work, it would be at least half past five before he turned up. Clive greeted the small group at the bar and ordered a pint before warming himself through in front of the fire.

"Bit nippy out there?" asked Beer Bill, quite unnecessarily. "Where's that young friend of yours? Had a tiff?"

"It is a trifle chilly out there, and my colleague will be joining me shortly."

Clive took a serious gulp of his beer and put the glass down with an appreciative sigh.

"That tastes good tonight. Have you been meddling with the barrels again?" asked Clive.

"Cheeky devil! My beer is always first class. I serve the best ale for miles," commented the landlord, holding up a pint he had just pulled for another customer.

"Not unrelated to the fact that you are the only pub for miles," responded Clive. "Unless you count the Pig and Firkin, or whatever they've decided to call it this week, and that's just a glorified youth club. The nearest thing they serve to beer is that Australian lager, and I'm just amazed as to how they get the kangaroos to pee in the barrels."

"Makes you appreciate a proper traditional local pub like this, though, doesn't it? Good beer, convivial company, a range of tasty bar meals at reasonable prices. A little gold mine in the hands of the right owner, and it could be yours for a song," said Beer Bill, looking Clive straight in the eye and smiling.

"Hang on. Hang on just a minute. Lest there be any confusion, I am not in the pub trade, I harbour no secret desire to be in the pub trade, and if I want to do my bit for the pub trade, I will do it from this side of the bar. Thank you. And now to prove the latter point, I would love another pint."

"Please yourself," said the landlord, "but as a valued customer, I just felt you deserved the chance of first refusal."

"Consider the refusal well and truly delivered," said Clive, raising his glass. "If I wanted to make any dodgy investment, I'd put money into one of my son's harebrained schemes, and that's not going to happen."

Clive was soon enjoying his evening. It had been a while since he had joined some of his friends at the pub, and the beer was going down well. After a while, he realised that he had drunk nearly three pints and Sally was not due for another quarter of an hour or so. It was time to slow down. He knew too well that after three pints, he would be relaxed, but after that point his evaluation of his own abilities would become inflated. After four he would think he was witty, after five he would think he could sing and the last time he had six, he had ended up buying Arkwright and taking him home. It was time to slow down.

Shortly after six o'clock, Sally arrived and joined the small group at the bar. "Sorry if I'm late," she said, glancing at the clock behind the bar, "I decided to book a taxi rather than drive."

"Ignore that clock," advised one Bill, "he always keeps it 10 minutes fast in case he wants to close up a bit earlier."

"Very well, as you're not driving," said Clive, "what would you like to drink?"

"I'd really love a vitamin drink," she announced to a bemused Clive.

"What sort of vitamin drink did you have in mind?" asked an equally puzzled Beer Bill.

"I'd love a large vitamin G and vitamin T, please, with ice and lemon."

"A large gin and tonic with ice and a slice, please, Bill," translated Clive.

For a while, the group at the bar chatted genially, and Clive had almost forgotten the original reason for the visit. By now he really didn't care if Council Bill turned up or not. If he didn't, then they could try again the following evening, and in the meantime life was good.

It was almost seven when Council Bill made his belated entrance.

"You're a bit late on parade tonight," commented the landlord, "but never mind. I'll still serve you." He poured out a large whisky, for which Clive insisted upon paying.

"Sorry. I wanted to see a colleague after he'd attended a meeting at the council offices earlier this evening. It's about that matter we were discussing vis-à-vis Dirty Harry, or Sleaze Ball as you quaintly refer to him."

"And did you have any luck?" asked Sally.

"Hodge moves in mysterious ways," continued the council employee. "He passes through the council offices like a shadow, doing the odd deal here and calling in a favour there. He leaves no trail, only a bad smell wherever he goes. He is full of his own self-importance, but he's like a pigeon – he should never be looked up to. As to evidence. As I suggested before, he is a clever weasel, there are lots of bits of rumour about him, gossip, and even vague accusations but no proof."

"Well, thanks for trying," said a rather disappointed Clive. "But surely he can't be so elusive?"

"I might sum up his qualities by recounting a riddle that is going the rounds of the office. What's the difference between Dirty Harry and a haddock? And the answer: one's wet and slippery, and the other's a fish. There have been lots of occasions when he's done the dirty on people, but he tends to bend rules rather than break them. It's no secret that if he was ever found murdered, then everyone at the council offices would be a suspect, and half of them would gladly put their hands up to it if they thought the town was rid of such vermin."

"If they're setting up a hit squad, you can put my name down," offered Sally.

"There is just one, albeit unsubstantiated, rumour that is quite persistent at the offices," continued Council Bill hesitantly. "It would appear that Hodge is looking to expand the family hardware business by opening a DIY store. It would need a reasonably sized site to accommodate car parking. He has tried to get planning permission on a couple of plots that he had earmarked, but the council refused, so he is getting a bit desperate. He has so many enemies on the planning sub-committee that he would be hard-pressed to get permission to erect a tent anywhere in the area. Hodge thinks they all hate him, but that's not true. Some of them haven't met him yet. Unfortunately, they have to work within the law, so if Hodge can get his evil hands on a suitable plot of land, the council couldn't stop him."

"And there just happens to be a sizeable patch of land behind the garden at Kitchener House," observed Sally. "I'll bet he wants to acquire that."

"He might like to," added Council Bill, "but I know the site you are talking about. It backs on to Charlton Road, and the planning department would take the greatest delight in turning down an application on the grounds that access to the site would be difficult. The projected volume of traffic would cause problems. He wouldn't stand a chance of getting it through however much he appealed."

"And he's not an appealing person," observed Sally.

"But if he were to get his hands on the whole Kitchener plot," mused Clive as his beer-softened brain clicked into action, "Would he be able to knock it down and use the area to gain access onto Verona Road in front of it?"

"That would make quite a large plot," calculated Council Bill. "It would depend on a number of factors, though.

I'm pretty sure that the area is not covered by any restrictive covenants. It's not in a conservation area, and Verona Road is quite wide. If the house itself isn't listed, then it is just possible that he could get permission, but there could be any number of reasons that I'm not aware of. You'd need to check carefully through the entire local bylaws and the like at the office."

"I somehow don't think that we would be the first to check that out," surmised Sally. "I rather think that those searches have already been carried out by a councillor who is known to us all. Why else would he be pushing for Kitchener's closure? He will have established that he cannot get by with just buying the plot behind the garden; it's all or nothing."

"The duplicitous heap of slime," observed Clive. "Well, I'm going to do everything I can to foil his plans."

"You'll create lots of friends down at the planning office if you do," declared a smiling Council Bill. "But enough of business, let's celebrate at least the germ of a plan to scupper Dirty Harry."

Clive was very pleased with the way the evening was going. He was so taken up with the fact that they had some idea about how to tackle Hodge that, for a short while, he completely forgot about the troubles with Maureen and the proposed divorce.

"Are you serving food tonight, Bill?" he asked over the bar.

"I can offer most of our enticing items on the menu, or I can provide our usual comprehensive collection of sandwiches or my wife's famous ploughman's supper. Please inspect the range of mouth-watering delights on our traditional pub menu," suggested Beer Bill, handing a card to Clive.

"For the last time, Bill, I don't want to buy the pub, just a bite to eat. How about you, Sally? Would you like to risk something on here," he said, offering her a menu.

"That makes sense. Thank you. It will mean I won't have to cook when I get home."

"I know what you mean. Cooking for one can seem such a lot of effort," commented Clive, before feeling that this was perhaps a bit insensitive, given her recent disclosure about Steve.

"I mean, I often find myself cooking for myself, like at lunchtime today, and it can seem a lot of work."

"I know exactly what you mean, Clive. Don't worry." She smiled, and he felt a bit better.

They ordered their meals and wandered over to the table by the fire. Having broken from the cocoon of conversation at the bar, there was a moment of quiet, and Clive felt it was possibly appropriate to let Sally know about Maureen. To be honest, he hoped she might be able to give him some advice. He hadn't bothered to rehearse his announcement as he knew that never worked in such circumstances, so he just started to tell her.

"I had a message from Maureen, or rather her solicitor, yesterday, and it seems she wants to get a divorce."

"Oh Clive, I'm so sorry to hear that," she said, resting her hand on his arm. "And I guess it's not unrelated to the newspaper report? I'm so sorry."

"I'm beginning to see now that the Hull episode was just a rather convenient excuse for Maureen. Any idiot would have known years ago that our marriage wasn't working, but this idiot didn't. Even Nicky and Pru have been trying to open my eyes to the situation, but there's none as blind as those that don't want to see, as my old mother used to say. I still can't understand why Maureen didn't just come round and discuss it with me face to face instead of that letter. I don't want to communicate through solicitors. I remember my dad used to hate doing divorce work. He would say that divorce was traumatic enough without bringing in others to speak for you. The minute you bring in third parties communicating through letters, there is more scope for misunderstanding and then accusations and recriminations. And, whatever people say, Maureen is not a vindictive person, sure she's self-centred, vain and obsessed with material things, but she does love the children, and she does care about me. So why is she acting this way?"

Clive realised that he had been going on a bit, and he'd said far more than he intended to. Sally was such a good listener. He had thought that it was just part of her training, but he was coming to realise that it was also related to the fact that she genuinely cared for people.

"Why do you think she might be doing it?" asked Sally.

Clive recognised it as one of those open-ended questions that necessitated a considered response, and after a moment he replied, "It must have been a shock reading about the whole thing in the paper that way, the money and the police and us. Even though there wasn't an 'us' in that sense."

"But what do you think might have triggered the response she has shown? Was it the money, the police or 'us'?"

"Money has always been important to her, or rather the prestige of having money and being able to show off her lifestyle to those she classes as her friends. Yes, she would have been concerned about the money. But on the other hand, she would know that it wasn't something I could have really kept a secret from her. All things being equal, I think the mention of the money would have rather pleased her. Twenty million indeed! She wouldn't have liked the mention of the police, that wouldn't have been something she would want parading in front of her friends, but she would have quite enjoyed presenting her version of the incident to those she chose to share it with. No, I can't see any of that causing the explosive outburst on the phone or this refusal to discuss the matter with me."

"If that's right, and you should certainly know what makes Maureen tick, that only leaves 'us' then. How do you think she would feel about that?"

"Well, that's not really an issue because it's just not true. There was the money and the police, which were sort of true, if somewhat exaggerated, but the romantic love nest was rubbish, pure fabrication. No one in their right mind would think that was true," protested Clive.

"I wonder how Maureen saw it when she read her paper that morning," prompted Sally.

"I guess the photograph looked incriminating; that can't have helped, seeing me with you like that and you being described as my attractive young girlfriend. The photo certainly made it look as if we were having a good time, particularly with my hand as it appeared on the photo."

"We were having a good time."

"Yes, but not in the way that they suggest. It was good, but not that good."

"But what would Maureen gather from the picture? What would she see?"

"It would be me with an attractive young woman in a bar enjoying ourselves." Clive paused for a moment before adding thoughtfully, "I suppose that much is true. Me, you an attractive young woman, enjoying an evening together."

Clive realised that he had inadvertently complimented Sally, and for a moment he was a little embarrassed, but he pressed on, "Maureen wouldn't have liked that. She is so particular about her looks and not looking her age. The thought of me being stolen from her by a younger woman and one that looks as good as you would be unbearable."

"Thank you," said Sally, "I don't know what they put in the beer here, but it certainly fires you up."

"But that's what Maureen would see, and it would really hurt her. It's one thing for her to have her young lover, but she wouldn't want to face up to the fact that she has lost out to a younger woman."

"Young lover?" queried Sally.

Clive knew he had said too much. He had never intended to mention his wife's relationship with Josslyn; he hadn't really intended to mention much of what he had said, but the combination of a few good beers and an even better listener had led to the whole story coming out. He began to explain this latest complication in his life.

"It seems that Maureen has been spending a lot of time with her partner or whatever he is. There was a mix-up over some telephone number, and we found that Maureen was with Josslyn in his place when she said they were on a business trip to Brussels. And Pru has noticed other inconsistencies in the reports that Maureen has given of other events. Looking back, it is easy to see that this has been going on for some years, but I never guessed."

"No, you wouldn't. You never question people's behaviour, too trusting by half, but that's part of your charm. But tell me, how do you feel about Maureen having such a relationship?"

"At first, I was livid. How could she accuse me of adultery when she and Josslyn were 'involved' with each other? But when I started to think about it, I realised that it hadn't traumatised me too much Yes, it was two-faced, and that's what really annoyed me, but if that's what had happened, then I just hoped Maureen was happy. The bottom line is that I was never the right man for her; I should have seen it years ago, but life was comfortable, and things just went on. As for the lovely Josslyn, I never really got on with him, but he was pleasant enough, and Arkwright likes him."

"Well, that's OK then."

Their conversation was interrupted by the arrival of the landlord with their meals.

"There we are, sir and madam, compliments of Mrs Beer Bill. I trust you will enjoy your meals in the romantic ambience of this welcoming and thriving gastropub, and if we can do anything further to increase your enjoyment of this particularly fine traditional pub environment, then please do not hesitate to call us," oozed the landlord in a particularly obsequious manner.

"It would greatly increase my enjoyment if you stopped trying to sell me the place, thanks," replied Clive.

Having finished their meals, the couple sat back and stared contentedly at the fire.

"How are you getting home tonight?" he asked after a while.

"I said I'd ring the taxi company. He's a friend of mine, and he said he could get here within a few minutes as business is quiet mid-week. Come to think of it, I could ring him now and ask him to pick me up in half an hour. Does that seem OK?"

"Fine. It seems a shame to draw the evening to a close, but if I drink any more I could start dancing, and this place isn't ready for that."

While Sally arranged her transport, Clive returned the plates to the bar and settled the bill before returning to their table.

"I've really enjoyed this evening, Sally, and thanks a lot for the advice."

"What advice? I didn't give you any advice."

"About Maureen and that. You cleared up a lot of what was on my mind. I don't know exactly what I intend to do, but I'm not going to create a big scene. You helped me to see it from her point of view. I needed some answers, and you provided them, thanks."

"That's kind of you, but you provided the answers. All I did was ask a few questions."

"You are a very clever woman, Doctor Livingstone," he added with a smile as he leant forward and kissed her lightly on the cheek.

As Clive leant back in his seat, he was aware of a silence in the room and, turning to the bar, noticed that the entire, if small clientele were looking in his direction. It had been one of the few impulsive acts of his life, and now it seemed the world had been watching. The group at the bar smiled and then got on with their respective conversations. Sally smiled and then giggled before saying, "If the beer's going to have any effect on you, I think that is rather more discreet than dancing."

All too soon, the taxi arrived and the couple bid farewell to the people at the bar and went out to the car park.

"Do you want the taxi to drop you off on the way?" asked Sally.

"No thanks, I rather feel the walk will do me good; I can burn off some of the meal and the beer on the way."

"Thanks for a lovely meal and a most enjoyable evening. Life's never dull with you around," she said before kissing him on the cheek and getting into the taxi.

Clive felt sure that everyone in the pub must have been looking out of the window at the time, but he refused to look and see. Instead, he waved after the taxi in what he hoped would look like a nonchalant fashion, and he set off on the short walk home.

CHAPTER TWENTY-THREE

As he walked home, Clive was aware that the temperature had dropped further and a biting wind made him regret turning down the offer of the lift. He was pleased to see Pru's car on the drive when he got home; he knew that meant she would have lit the gas fire in the lounge, and he needed that fire at the moment. Arkwright rushed over to see him when he entered the kitchen before scurrying back into the lounge. As Clive had hoped, Pru was sitting in front of the fire and the whole room was cosy.

"I've just made a pot of tea. Would you like some?" she asked.

"That sounds terrific, I'll get myself a cup," he replied before going into the kitchen to get one.

"It's bitterly cold out there tonight, Pru, this is very welcome."

"Good," she replied, "I just thought I would drop in to update you on a couple of things."

"Oh yes. So what's been going on now?"

"I decided to go to the factory and try to have a word with Maureen. I don't want to seem to be interfering, but I just wanted to try and persuade her to at least talk to you over the solicitor's letter rather than going through all the turmoil and expense of setting solicitors against each other."

Clive was a little surprised at the news but assured Pru, "I wouldn't ever see you as an interfering person, Pru. After all she is your daughter; she may take some notice of what you have to say. So how is she?"

"Frankly, she looked terrible. She just seemed so down. She appears to have taken the newspaper business very badly."

"In what way?"

"It just looks as if she was shaken by the whole thing. We talked for a while, but she hadn't got any of her old sparkle. I had expected to see her all fired up and eager to make a good fight of it but, on the contrary, she looked as if she had given up; not at all like the Maureen of old who would have loved the challenge. We spoke for a while, and I'm pretty sure that she realises the article about you and Sally wasn't true, but it has still rocked her world somehow."

"Perhaps," suggested Clive, "she was threatened by the thought of me going off with a younger woman; perhaps it hit her ego a bit?"

"I hadn't thought of that but it would make a lot of sense, knowing her fear of looking her age. Well, she certainly looked it today, poor thing."

"The paper going on about my young, attractive girlfriend would have been rubbing her nose in it a bit," added Clive, thinking back to his conversation with Sally.

"I think it came at a bad time in her life as well because the business is not doing very well. It was obvious that the factory was very quiet, particularly in what should be the hectic run-up to Christmas, and when I commented on it she explained her worries. Sales have been very slow after some negative reviews in the papers about some of the products she stocks. She knows that will pass, but she had wildly over-stretched her finances to buy in raw materials so the company is strapped for ready cash. Maureen is worried sick about having to lay off staff, particularly so near to Christmas, but it seems inevitable."

"So Maureen is no longer a leading entrepreneur, and her husband is alleged to have run off with a younger woman. No wonder she is taking it badly; her whole self-image is under attack."

"The one good thing in her life is Josslyn. He is obviously very concerned about her," added Pru.

"And what did she say about her relationship with Josslyn? Did you challenge her on it?"

"There was no need; she came straight out with it. She said it was the one thing in her life at the moment that kept her sane. I must admit that I had always assumed that Josslyn was not exactly a lady's man, but as we suspected they have been 'an item' for a few years. It started while they were attending a convention in Paris together and just sort of grew. They took every opportunity to attend as many trade fairs and the like all over Europe, but when the money was tight they would just stay at his house and invent venues they could claim to have visited. She wasn't proud of it, and I'm sure she's glad it's out in the open."

"I just wish she'd said earlier," remarked Clive. "Why go on living that charade?"

"To start with, I think she honestly thought you needed someone to look after you, and then there were the children and the effect any split would have on them."

"So what does she intend to do now? Did she say?"

"She's not sure what's going on in her life at the moment, but I did convince her that an acrimonious divorce was in no one's interest, and she was quick to admit that it wasn't what she wanted. She needs time to get it all straight in her head. I know that doesn't sort anything out for you, but at least you know that crisis can be left for a little while."

"Thanks, Pru. I wish life had a pause button so you could take time out to settle one thing before the next problem comes charging in. Still, at least I don't have to expect to find a snotty solicitor's letter on the mat in the run-up to Christmas. Speaking of which, how is my fan mail coming along?"

"The initial rush has died down a little but they're still turning up," answered Pru. "And you appear to have rather a lot of Christmas cards this year. I'm keeping a separate pile for them. I've taken the liberty of binning all those from double-glazing companies and the like, but I'm sure you will feel all warm and cosy inside to know that they send their heartfelt and sincere wishes for the season. I did have another category for 'dear valued customer'. You have no idea how many companies see you in that light, and some of them are providing goods and services that I'm sure you would never have wanted."

"Thanks, Pru. I guess I'd better try and weed out the rubbish from those that are left," said Clive, taking a large handful of cards from a sack. He methodically read through some of them and noticed a large number that he didn't recognise, most of which appeared to be directed to him rather than to Maureen and himself.

"From Pam and Jack and all at number 36. Who the hell are they? And here's one with a lengthy letter from Felicity and Colin; we haven't heard from them since we left Hull. It appears that their daughter has just finished an economics degree, and she is prepared to act as my financial adviser."

"That card could also go in the sack with all the others who are offering you the benefit of their financial advice with the prospect of magnificent returns. The only way many of those groups could make you a small fortune would be if you initially gave them a large fortune."

"It's a pity," said Clive, "that you can't be sure which companies are the reliable ones. I'm sure they're not all crooks, and I could do with some good advice as to what to do with the money, but where do I turn?"

Clive looked through some more of the mail, and eventually he was sitting on the rug surrounded by heaps of brightly coloured Christmas cards. "This is hopeless, Pru. I don't know who most of these people are. They may be Maureen's friends. I can't just throw them all away."

Clive thought for a moment before declaring, "Do you think you could persuade Maureen to come round and go through them? I could arrange to be out so as not to embarrass her, perhaps on Saturday? I could go to the rugby with Stan if I can prise him away from Nicky for a while, and then go to the pub. I'm sure we could fix it so that I'm gone for most of the afternoon."

"I should think she would be glad of the excuse to be here," replied Pru. "I'll give her a call tomorrow and see what I can do. I must go now, but I'll be round in the morning to see what I can do with some of the other mail. A bonfire would probably be the answer but you just can't be sure."

The following day Clive decided he would do his own research at the town hall to determine what the prospects might be of getting planning permission to develop the Kitchener House site. Like most people, he had never visited his local town hall, and he was dismayed to enter the cavernous reception hall to be faced with a board indicating the location of the different departments. It was made up of small white plastic letters that fitted into a large blackboard full of holes. Most of it seemed to be self-explanatory, but someone had obviously had fun rearranging one or two of the letters. Clive deduced that he wanted the 'Planting Department', and set off to find the appropriate lift to get him there. He got out of the lift at what he took to be the correct floor, walked up and down a couple of corridors, reading the small signs on a series of heavy oak doors before deciding he was in the wrong area. After a while, he retraced his steps to the reception hall and did that most unmanly thing of asking for directions. He approached a young woman at the reception desk and announced, "Excuse me, but could you direct me to the planning department, please?"

The young woman looked up, smiled at him politely and said, "I certainly could, but then we'd probably have to send a search party looking for you after an hour or so; we lose dozens of visitors a year up on the fourth floor. Hang on a minute, I'll get someone to show you the way; it's quicker in the long run."

A young girl who looked barely old enough to be out of school was summoned and she led Clive off on his quest.

"I've got a friend who works here," announced Clive in an attempt to start up a conversation.

"Oh, who's that?" she asked. "There are hundreds of people who work here, and I've only been here a few weeks, but I may know your friend."

"It's Council Bill. That's not his real name, it's just what we call him at the pub. I think his name is Henry or maybe Harry, but I'm not certain. He drinks whisky. I'm pretty sure he's married or was at some time." Clive suddenly realised that he had no idea what Council Bill was really called.

"It's not ringing any bells with me," said his perplexed young guide. The rest of the journey through countless corridors, pushing through numerous fire doors and ascending a number of flights of stairs was conducted in silence. At last he came to a door clearly marked as the planning department.

"Here you are, sir," announced the girl. "And if I were you, I'd ask for someone to see you down to reception when you've finished unless you've got half a day to spare."

Clive had half expected to see a large room full of people working at big desks, but the planning department that day was made up of just one man who was busily transferring information onto a large map.

"Good morning," said Clive. "I'm trying to get some information about a possible planning application."

"Then you couldn't have come to a better place. What area was it in?" replied the man as he walked over to a large shelf full of files.

"It's between Verona Road and Charlton Road."

"Kitchener House?" asked the official.

"Yes. That's brilliant, but how did you know?"

"Supreme efficiency on the part of the office here and the fact that we've had someone else looking into the site."

"Oh, and who's that?" asked Clive, attempting to look as though he wasn't particularly interested.

"I am not at liberty to divulge the identity of such individuals; we have a particularly strict code of conduct here in planning."

Backing a hunch, Clive decided to try another approach. "I suppose you wouldn't be able to confirm that it was Dirty Harry up to his tricks?" The mention of Councillor Hodge's nickname within the office was like using a magic key.

"I gather you are not one of the said gentleman's friends?" asked the planner, leaning forward conspiratorially.

"Hodge has no friends, as far as I'm aware."

"You will understand, sir, that I cannot confirm that any particular piece of human detritus was showing an interest in a particular plot such as that between Verona Road and Charlton Road. Nor can I let you know if that said low-life was asking about the possibility of permission ever being granted for the development of a DIY store on the site. It would be more than my job's worth to tell you the feeling of sadness I might have experienced if I had found it necessary to tell him that I can see no obvious reason why planning permission could be withheld. I have since searched through every file in our records and can say that I have found no reason to object to a planning proposal from him except on the grounds of him being an offensive heap of slime, and the legal department couldn't sanction that response."

"So, hypothetically, if Hodge could get the plot, he could knock the house down and redevelop the whole site?"

"The way he was talking, he already owned the site. Believe me, sir, if we could find any reason at all to stop him, we would. We might be able to slow things down a bit if his plans are not perfect, but he's a clever devil and he has a pretty fair grasp of the building regulations. It's a shame because it would spoil the area in Verona Road, but then good taste often counts for nothing in town planning."

"Thank you so much for your lack of information," concluded Clive. "It's such a pity you weren't able to give me any information about any proposed development."

Clive managed to persuade his confidant to escort him back to the reception area, and as they parted company, the official announced loudly, "I'm so sorry we weren't able to be of any real help to you, sir."

Clive walked out of the town hall feeling pleased that at least he knew what Hodge was up to. All they had to do now was find a way to stop him.

As Clive unlocked the kitchen door at home he heard the phone ringing, so he rushed through to answer it.

"Hi Clive, I was beginning to think you weren't in," said Pru as he answered the phone.

"Yes. I've just got in from town. How are things with you?"

"Fine. I managed to get hold of Maureen and she has agreed to come over on Saturday to help with the mail and to pick up some more of her things. She evidently had no idea about all the junk you've been getting. If it's still OK, she will come round and meet me at about midday on Saturday. She said she didn't want to drive you out but agrees that at the moment it might make it easier for her if you weren't there. To be frank, I think she is rather embarrassed about the whole thing."

"That's fine. I've arranged to go to the match with Stan on Saturday; it will be good to spend a bit of time with a possible son-in-law."

"OK, darling, I'll let Maureen know of the plan. See you later."

Clive found himself holding the receiver and thought that he had better contact Sally to let her know of his morning's findings.

"Hi Sally, Clive here," he announced when she answered. "I just thought I'd let you know what is going on with Hodge and Kitchener House."

"Hello, Clive. Nice to hear from you; so what have you been finding out now?"

"It was as you suspected; Hodge has been making enquiries about the site, and it would appear that, if he gets it, there is nothing to stop him from knocking it down and developing the entire site for his proposed DIY store. The guy in planning made it clear that he had explored every avenue to find a legitimate objection, but sleaze ball seems to be sitting pretty."

"He would be," suggested Sally. "If he owned the site, and he is doing all he can to make that purchase with minimal financial outlay. June phoned earlier to let me know that Hodge has called the next meeting of the steering committee for Friday the twenty-first at seven in the evening. We stipulated that it had to be after two weeks had elapsed and he's gone for the first possible date. He's probably hoping that as it's so near Christmas many people won't attend, so he can bulldozer it through the steering committee and present it to the full committee as a done deal. He can then sit back until Kitchener House is put on the market and snap it up at a very reasonable price."

"Have you received official notification of the meeting, Sally?"

"Not a word, other than June's informative telephone call. How about you?"

"Nothing as yet. Welcome to the persona non grata club. It doesn't matter how much he tries, he can't stop us attending, but I think it will be in our interest to let him believe that we don't know anything about it. In the meantime, I have an idea how we might be able to make things rather difficult for him."

"Clive, you sound almost Machiavellian," said Sally with a suggestion of admiration in her voice. "This is a side of the mild-mannered Clive Sullivan that I haven't seen before, so what have you got in mind?"

"I don't want to discuss it now in case I can't fix it, but suffice it to say that I have to contact a couple of people to see if I can swing it."

"Intriguing," said Sally, "and rather exciting. I look forward to seeing what comes of it."

"All in good time. But, far more pressing, I've had a word with Nicky's boyfriend Stan, and if you don't mind, they will drive over and pick you up on Sunday for Pru's Christmas do. Pru likes to impress with her range of cocktails, and we tend not to drive afterwards. Stan rarely drinks anything, and he's mad keen to drive the Rolls, it will make quite a change from his ancient Land Rover, so he would love to pick you up and get you home safely."

"Sounds like quite a party!" observed Sally, "I'm not sure I could cope with such revelry but I think I'll give it a go. Tell Stan and Nicky I'll look forward to seeing them. What time?"

"About half past twelve. We never fix a finish time; people just leave when they are ready. I look forward to seeing you at the party."

CHAPTER TWENTY-FOUR

On the following Saturday morning, Clive was just finishing his breakfast when Pru arrived. "Morning, darling," she greeted him. "I thought I'd get over early and sort out the letters and cards that you wanted Maureen to check over."

"No need," replied Clive, "I've put all the ones I'm not sure of on the kitchen table. She's welcome to go through any of the junk that arrives today just in case there is anything that is genuine. Stan is picking me up about 10, and then we'll grab lunch somewhere before the game. We might even do a bit of Christmas shopping, although it's a bit early by my standards. I might be able to drop in at the fire station and see if they're doing a two-for-one offer on firemen for you."

"Thank you, darling, but please get me a couple of fit ones – I do have my standards to keep up you know."

"Only the best for you. Tell Maureen that we won't be back before six, not that she has to vacate the building, but she might like to be out of the way. She's welcome to stay on if she likes."

"I'll tell her. I'm sure she will appreciate the gesture, but I don't know how she will respond; as I said before, she seems to be embarrassed by the whole thing. She feels she's made a bit of a fool of herself and is reluctant to face you."

"If I stopped seeing people after every time I'd made a fool of myself, I'd never leave the house," confided Clive. "She was just a bit hasty, that's all."

Stan arrived promptly, and Clive made sure he was ready to leave. The two men had an enjoyable time in town. After an hour's shopping, they had bought most of what they wanted so they adjourned to a pub for lunch before going on to the match. They arrived home at half past six and after Stan had dropped him off, he went in to find Pru was on her own.

"Hi Pru," said Clive, looking at the much-reduced pile of cards on the table, "I see that Maureen has had a good go at those."

"Yes. She was obviously a bit uncomfortable about being here at first but she got over it. She has left that pile of cards from people that you both know, but she did comment that some of them hadn't been in touch for years, and she wouldn't particularly wish to contact some of them again. She did leave that small group of cards from friends who seem genuinely pleased that you have done well."

"It's nice to see there are people who are pleased for us and not just trying to make something out of it for themselves. Thanks for organising today, Pru, I know you must have been busy arranging tomorrow's party. It was good of you to take the time."

"Nonsense!" exclaimed Pru, "my little gatherings almost organise themselves; I provide a few drinks and the odd bite to eat and the party takes care of itself."

"If I believed that, I'd believe in Santa Claus. It was very good of you to come round, Pru, but you really must get off home now and weave your party magic."

Clive was up relatively early the next day, and he spent some time preparing himself for the party. Usually he would glance into his wardrobe and pick something from the smart end of the rail, select a pair of shoes and hope the general ensemble more or less went together. Today he took out two suits and a variety of shirts and ties and placed them alongside each other systematically until he had the combination he felt looked best. His total lack of dress sense meant that he might as well have taken the first articles out of the wardrobe and thrown them together, but he felt as though he had made the effort. He even went as far as to apply a more than liberal dousing of the expensive aftershave that Maureen had brought back from one of her trips. He looked in the hall mirror, generally distorted his face, pulled in his stomach, but decided the whole image was not so much beefcake as beef dripping. He practised his nonchalant smile, realised he was wasting his time trying to look good and went to sit down in the kitchen. A knock on the door announced Stan's arrival and Clive let him in, by which time Nicky was in the kitchen and obviously dressed ready to go out.

"Morning, Bunnykins," she greeted him. "All ready to go?"

Stan did an elaborate twirl and said, "So what do you think? Do I look ready to go?"

"I know Gran's parties are smart events, but I don't think a full dinner jacket was necessary, you doughnut."

"Nothing is too good for you, my princess. If I'm to transport you away in a beautiful car, I need to dress the part. Anyway, I didn't have an ordinary suit and this whole rig only cost 20 pounds in the charity shop. It appears that they don't shift many dinner jackets in my size. They were relieved to get rid of it."

"Well, you do look rather smart," she conceded, straining up to kiss him. "So let's go and paint the town or something."

"Aren't you a little early to pick up Sally?" queried Clive. "You're not supposed to be there until half past twelve."

"We thought we might go for a little run, just to get used to the car," replied Nicky.

Clive sorted out the keys for the Rolls, and within minutes the couple were gone.

Sebastian was looking less than perky when he came downstairs, having returned home very late the previous night after a series of meetings in one or two pubs.

"Morning, Dad. What's that smell?"

"Probably my aftershave," he replied before explaining, "I'm going to your gran's for her party, remember?"

"I don't think I'm up to one of her parties, dad. It took me two days to get over the last one, and on top of that, I think I've got a bit of a cold."

"Obviously. Chilly places some of those pubs."

"It's Christmas, Dad. It's only once a year. In business you have to be sociable, to make contacts, to network."

"Yes, I heard you networking to the toilet last night when you got back. I'm not sure who you were trying to be sociable with, sounded like Hughie."

"Probably a dodgy burger," suggested Sebastian weakly.

"Undoubtedly," was the less than convinced reply. "Well, I'm going to your gran's for about half past eleven; you're welcome to walk over there with me if you change your mind. She'll be disappointed if you don't go."

"I think I'll just nip back to bed for a while and see how I feel later, Dad. I don't think I'll bother with breakfast just yet."

Clive toyed with the idea of giving Sebastian some advice on the problems of over-indulging, but his son was suffering enough at the moment. As Clive suspected, Sebastian did not emerge in time to go to Pru's with him, so he set off on his own. It was typical Christmas weather, being very overcast and with a slight drizzle in the air. At that time of year, the early morning gloom seemed to merge into the evening murkiness with very little distinct daylight in between. Clive's spirits were not dampened by the weather, and as he walked along he felt increasingly cheerful at the prospect of spending the afternoon with a few friends, and he knew Pru's cocktail sessions never failed to entertain. There would no doubt be the usual gang of her friends, including two elderly neighbours called

Sarah and Clara, and both had the honorary title of Aunty. Aunty Sarah was a small, cheerful woman whose cheerfulness on such days was not unrelated to the amount of gin she managed to consume in a number of cocktails. Aunty Clara was generally more reserved but also became remarkably gregarious after a single glass of her annual cocktail.

Clive was early when he arrived at Pru's house, but there were already a few guests. It was always very informal on such occasions, and Clive noted that, despite her hostess duties, Pru was always perfectly at ease. One of her gentleman friends had obviously been allocated the job of barman and stood beside an extensive array of drinks, ice and assorted fruit.

"Hello, darling," said Pru, kissing Clive warmly. "Get Charles to make you up a drink. If you can't decide what you want, then look in the bible."

"Thanks, Pru," he replied, "I think I'll just stick to something simple. I may resort to the bible later."

The 'bible' was an illustrated recipe book for cocktails from which the guests could choose whatever they fancied. All the recipes were listed and made up with exact measures so the precise nature and strength of the finished article would be known. This did not stop the odd miscalculation of the effect a particular drink might have. Aunty Clara was already sipping at her drink. It looked innocent enough, but its appearance as an attractive glass of orange juice concealed two measures of gin, but the glass would probably last her the entire afternoon. Aunty Sarah was less conservative in her selection of drinks; as long as it was based on gin she was happy, and sometimes she became very happy.

"Help yourself to food, darling," suggested Pru. "There's plenty of reserves in the kitchen."

"Thanks," replied Clive. "It all seems to be going well already. I see Aunty Sarah is enjoying herself."

"Yes. She did say she was going to take it easy this year as she admits she was a 'little tiddly' last year. I remember she did very well in the karaoke session."

"But there wasn't a karaoke session."

"I know, but after most of the guests had gone, she treated us to a couple of numbers. Including a particularly raunchy rendition of 'Simply the Best'. Tina Turner doesn't need to worry about the competition."

Clive sipped his drink and helped himself to some of the delicious buffet as he circulated among the guests. Each time the doorbell rang to announce the arrival of new guests, Clive would look up to check who it was. At last Stan and his little party arrived and, extricating himself from a conversation with a group of Pru's friends, Clive moved over to greet them. The trio were all in quite high spirits and appeared to have been sharing a joke when they came in.

"Hi Dad," said Nicky. "Been here long?"

"An hour or so, but this is my first one," he answered, holding up his glass. "You can't be too careful with some of these cocktails." He turned to Sally, who was wearing an elegant black dress, and said, "You look lovely, Sally."

"Thank you," she said, before adding, "Are you sure that's your first one?"

Pru was busy with another couple who had just arrived, so Clive took over the less than onerous duty of acting as personal host for the trio, and he had soon arranged drinks for them. Nicky and Stan wandered off to socialise, leaving Clive and Sally to chat.

"I must admit I wasn't expecting such a smart chauffeur, Clive," said Sally pointing at Stan in his dinner jacket. "And he's so big; he almost fits the car."

"Yes, he's a big boy, our Stan," observed Clive.

"And what a driver! I didn't know that a Rolls Royce could achieve such speeds, and on minor roads as well. I had complete confidence in him, though; you wouldn't have thought we were doing 90. I think he was overdoing it a bit with the hand break turn outside Pru's, but he didn't hit anything."

Clive looked at her and smiled before commenting, "And I suppose I'm expected to trust you because you're a doctor?"

"Perhaps I was exaggerating a little. The truth is, he's a fantastic driver. He drove so carefully that Nicky and I in the back were hardly aware the car was moving and we had chance to have a very long chat. You'd be amazed at what she's been telling me."

Clive felt distinctly uneasy at this news. Women seemed to have an ability to quickly get on to discussing matters of an uncomfortably private nature, particularly by his reserved standards.

"You don't want to believe everything she says," said Clive defensively, "and particularly anything she might have said about me."

"That's a shame; she was highly complimentary about you. She obviously loves you very much."

"She's a great daughter, and I love her madly, but she does tend to try and arrange my life for me."

Sally giggled. Clive loved that giggle, even when it was at his expense, but he had to ask her,

"OK, so what's so funny?"

"It's just that, well, I get invited to a lot of social events where people are trying, with the best possible intentions, to sort out my life for me. As a single woman, I often find I have been invited to things where there just happens to be an eligible bachelor who just happens to end up seated next to me. Women friends in particular are always trying to make me happy by acting as matchmakers. You can almost see their thinking.

'Poor Sally, all on her own, doesn't look bad for her age, has all her own teeth, knows how to behave in public, must need a man in her life. Who can we fix her up with?' They mean well, but I like to make my own decisions in my life."

"It must be annoying for you," commented Clive.

"Not really. As I say people mean well, but it puts pressure on me and the poor guy who's been selected as my partner. If we don't hit it off, then it's almost like letting our friends down. But today is very different."

"Different?" prompted a bemused Clive.

"Yes," said Sally, barely suppressing a giggle. "This is the first time I've been invited to a social event where my partner has been set up by his daughter and mother-in-law."

Clive was mortified. Sally obviously found the whole thing amusing, so he tried to pretend it wasn't the major embarrassment that it clearly was for him. He wanted to nonchalantly make light of the situation but lacked the social skills to be convincing.

"So what exactly have they been up to?" asked Clive, as calmly as he could manage.

"Nothing devious, I assure you, but it is quite clear that Nicky is very concerned about your happiness, and she seems to see me as someone to fill a place in your life. I get on very well with her and with Pru, and I think we make a great little group. It appears that when they found out that I wasn't married, and knowing your marital difficulties, they came up with their own solution."

"But when Pru invited you to this do, she didn't know about your single status," Clive pointed out.

"No, that's true," admitted Sally. "But even at that time, she could see that you needed someone else in your life, if only as a friend."

"And you picked up all this in a conversation with Nicky on the way over here?"

"I've been sort of aware of Nicky's views since we first met, and then it's simply a matter of listening to what is going on and observing people. I suppose it's a by-product of my job skills. Nicky is a very open, warm person who makes no secret of her feelings, and it's obvious that she feels very disappointed by her mother's treatment of you over the years. She loves you and wants you to be happy."

"I'm sorry about all this, Sally. I had no idea."

"I know, and please don't apologise. I think it is rather sweet that they are concerned for your happiness, and anyway, I enjoy meeting up with you all. Now, let's enjoy the party," she said, holding up her glass,"

The party went well, despite the fact that Clive felt he had been manipulated. He wasn't pleased that Nicky and Pru were trying to promote a deeper relationship between Sally and him, but above all, he was disappointed at the thought that Sally might have turned up merely in response to coercion from the others. He found himself glancing at her throughout the afternoon; she certainly seemed to be enjoying herself, but was she just being polite? After a couple more cocktails, Clive was seeing the world in a more positive light. He felt it was obvious that Sally was there because she wanted to be there. She enjoyed his company, despite the pressures from his family, and so he felt bold enough to suggest something to her. Having manoeuvred to get her on her own, he started with his prepared proposal.

"I've got a bit of business in Hull tomorrow, and I thought we might drive up together if you liked," he said before adding, "I can't promise you another wild night at our little love nest; it's just a matter of going up for the day to see old Pearson about a couple of issues. Perhaps we could have a meal?"

"I'm terribly sorry, Clive," she replied, "but I've agreed to go out for lunch with an old university friend tomorrow.

I do wish I'd known, but it's all arranged now. Perhaps we can do it some other time?"

Clive felt completely deflated; it had all been going so well, and now he felt Sally was rejecting him while trying to spare his feelings. "Yes, sure," he said. "It's only a quick trip to Hull; it would have been nice to have a bit of company for the drive. As you say, perhaps we can have a trip out some other time."

It had been a good party; it started very well but never lived up to Clive's expectations, not that he was really sure what his expectations had been.

CHAPTER TWENTY-FIVE

As Clive drove to Hull the next day, he reflected on Sally's comments at the party. She seemed to be able to understand what people were really like. She understood what was going on in other people's heads. As far as he was concerned, life was a mystery, and people kept surprising him. She was in control of her life while he was just constantly being buffeted by whatever life threw at him, and he was getting a little fed up with it all. As the great bard of Humber had said, "Life has a practice of living you if you don't live it." It was time to take life by the throat and take control, but he had no idea how to do it. He resolved that he would concentrate on what he was good at, and his area of expertise did not include people skills; he had been good in his job at the paint plant where he worked with projects on paper. His life had to become a business, and then he might have a chance of making it work.

The meeting at the solicitors went well because it involved Clive Sullivan, the businessman who could deal with such things, and as he drove home he began to make plans for the rest of the week. He was developing a business plan. There were two projects that he needed to sort out: his relationship with Maureen and the future of Kitchener House. He was fully aware that his relationship with Sally fell into the fuzzy 'people' area that he knew nothing about, so that issue could not be resolved by any planning on his part. He had a very full week ahead of him, and he needed to get on the phone as soon as he got home to arrange a couple of further meetings. The steering committee met on Friday, and things needed to be in place before that, or Hodge was in danger of buying up and demolishing Kitchener House.

Clive put the first part of his plan into action by phoning Maureen's factory. The phone only rang for a very short time before it was answered. It was Maureen herself, and she was obviously very surprised to hear Clive's voice. He was polite but businesslike as he announced, "Hello, Maureen, I've been giving a lot of thought to your position and feel that it is very important that we meet very soon to resolve certain issues."

"Err, we are very busy at the moment, Clive. I'm not sure if it's possible to get anything fixed up before Christmas."

"Maureen, I have been hearing about your business, and if you don't get something sorted out very soon, you won't have a business after Christmas. Shall we say 10 tomorrow morning in your office? I expect that you will need to have the appropriate staff there with you, but I suggest we restrict it to your senior team only."

There was a pause before Maureen said, "Excuse me a minute. I need to consult with a colleague."

"Tell Josslyn that it would be in the company's interest to resolve this matter immediately," added Clive, suspecting who the other colleague was with Maureen.

After a few minutes, Maureen announced, "We think we can make that slot. How many will be attending in your party?"

"Just me," answered Clive. "I'll look forward to that then, 10 o'clock at your place. See you then." Clive hung up. The call had gone well, and Maureen had been unprepared and therefore had not been able to think of any excuse not to meet.

The following day, Clive's Rolls Royce drew up in front of Maureen's factory and he stepped out. He was wearing a smart suit and carrying an impressive leather document case. He caused quite a stir among some of the workforce who were huddled outside having a cigarette break. Maureen met him in the reception area. She had obviously made an effort to look her best, but she did not look the same self-assured woman he had been used to.

"Hello, Clive," she greeted him. "Shall we go straight through to the office? I've ordered some coffee for us."

Clive was led through the dispatch area and into Maureen's office, where a rather sheepish-looking Josslyn was waiting. "Morning, Clive. Coffee?" he asked.

"Not at the moment, thanks. I'd rather get straight down to business," answered Clive, taking a seat at the small table and opening his document case, from which he drew a few sheets of paper.

"Look, Clive," said Josslyn, "I'm sorry about the way everything has turned out. We didn't mean to… it just happened… we should have come clean years ago."

"I think we need to clarify something," announced Clive. "I am not here to delve into your relationship or to start any recriminations. I am here to propose the outlines of a rescue plan for your business. Before you start to deny it, I would inform you that I know your unit here is in a poor financial state. Even a preliminary glance on the way in would be sufficient to convince me that this is not the thriving setup it should be at this time of year. Your dispatch area is admirably clean and tidy, but there is little sign that any great amount of work has been going on. From what Pru has said and from some personal investigations I have carried out, it is obvious that without a cash injection this place is going to close down. You have the classic cash flow problem, and you need to sort it now." Clive held up the papers he had taken from his case as if to show evidence of his findings about the company.

"And, just supposing this place was in such dire straits, and I'm not admitting it is, what do you think we should do about it?" asked Maureen.

"I have a pretty fair idea about how this place should be performing. I have obviously seen your more than competent handling of the business over the years, and so I am absolutely convinced that essentially the place is worth rescuing."

"Rescuing?" said Josslyn defensively. "The business is fine, and it's just a slow patch."

"Self-delusion won't help," argued Clive. "You have a mass of raw materials which have not been paid for but no immediate orders. Your first option is to lay off staff, but if you do that you won't have the capacity to keep going when things pick up. The scare stories in the press are unfounded, and we all know how the press can get things wrong. In a couple of months, the shops will be crying out for your products, but this business won't be in any state to meet that demand. So, in answer to your question, Maureen, I intend to ensure that you have the funds."

"You want to invest in the company? To lend us money?" she asked.

"Yes and no. I want to invest in the company, but I do not intend to offer you any loan. Let's look at the bigger picture. You need money for the business, Maureen, and you also seek a divorce. Is that correct?"

"I thought this was all about the business?"

"It is, but by sorting out one issue, we may partly resolve another. I would make it clear that I am delighted that you decided not to negotiate the divorce through a solicitor, and I am sure that we can come to some arrangement that more or less satisfies everyone. I was talking to my solicitor yesterday, not about fighting a divorce, I must add, but in order to see how we might find a mutually beneficial course of action. He has suggested that I might put a certain proposal to you that you might in turn check out with your solicitor to see if it is acceptable."

"So what is this master plan?" asked an intrigued Maureen.

"I have made arrangements for seven hundred and fifty thousand pounds to be made available for your business, which I calculate should be more than enough to cover your immediate shortfall. At the end of next year, when the final instalment of my inheritance comes through, I propose that I pay you a further one million five hundred pounds, which I suggest is a reasonable total for you to accept as full settlement for the divorce, which I obviously do not intend to contest. In return, I would keep the house and would expect you to forfeit any rights to my pension."

There was a stunned silence from Maureen. Clive waited for a few seconds before continuing.

"I realise that this may seem a lot to take in, and I would stress that you ought to consult your solicitor, but I should inform you that my legal adviser calculates that with this deal, you will be acquiring about 50 percent of my money which may be seen as fair by most courts. I am sure that neither of us wishes to get into a protracted and acrimonious legal fight which will only benefit our solicitors and during which your relationship with Josslyn would unfortunately be exposed."

"It all seems very reasonable, but I must have time to think it through, as I'm sure you will understand," replied Maureen, who was still apparently in a slight state of shock at this proposal.

"That's fine," agreed Clive. "There is no great rush, except over the matter of the cash injection for the company, which I intend to pay immediately without prejudice."

"But why would you do that? What happens if I didn't want to accept your offer?" asked a very confused Maureen.

"It's by way of being an investment," he replied.

"So you want some sort of controlling interest in the company?"

"No."

"So it is a loan?"

"No, it's a gift."

"So where's the investment element?"

"I'm investing in you for the sake of our children. You are a good businesswoman who has just been very unlucky. When you get over this bad patch, the company will return to doing well, and ultimately the wealth of the company will presumably benefit our children," explained Clive.

"Yes, of course, I've always tried to ensure that they were provided for. But why are you being so reasonable?" asked Maureen.

For a moment, Clive could see this conversation moving away from the businesslike exchange he had intended, so he tried to explain his relationship with her in a logical way.

"We have been married for a long time, and we both see now that it hasn't been perfect, largely because we had different ambitions for our partnership, but it's been a long association, and I recognise what you have contributed. We have children that we share, and we both want what is best for them. It makes more sense to dissolve the partnership equitably rather than to fight over the assets."

By seeing their marriage as a business concern, Clive could briefly achieve a level of objectivity in discussing it. Maureen knew him well enough to know that he was a fair person, not prone to deviousness, so she recognised the offer as genuine.

"As you suggest, I will have to ask my solicitor to check it over, but I can say that it all seems very satisfactory, even generous, and I shall be informing him that I am inclined to accept," she said.

"Good. Here's my solicitor's card; if we let them settle the fine details and sort out the appropriate paperwork, we can sign it and get the matter resolved. And now, if you will excuse me, I have further business to conduct elsewhere," concluded Clive, replacing the papers in his document case and turning to leave.

"Thank you," said Maureen. "Thank you very much for being like this."

"Thank you, Maureen, and by the way, you know you are welcome back at home. The children, we, would be pleased to see you. That goes for you as well, Josslyn. Arkwright misses you."

Clive strode out to his car and placed his document case on the passenger seat. He reflected that, as a business meeting, it had gone very well, but he felt little sense of achievement, rather a sense of failure that they had been unable to make their marriage work. It had all been very civilised, very grown up, but still an acknowledgement of failure. By the time he had driven home, he felt a little better; he had more business to conduct and this time he was looking forward to it. He had a lot to arrange before the steering committee meeting on Friday evening, and he had to find the best way of telling the family of the situation with Maureen and the divorce. As regards the latter issue, he need not have worried about how to break the news. Nicky and Pru were a little upset at the finality of the arrangement, although they had both realised long since that the marriage was not a strong one, and they were soon reconciled to the possibility of different domestic arrangements at home. Sebastian just accepted the matter; it had few financial implications for him, so it was no big deal.

CHAPTER TWENTY-SIX

On Friday evening, Clive was ready for the steering committee in plenty of time. The plan was a simple one; he would leave home at half past six and drive round to Sally's house so he could give her a lift to the meeting. Nicky was being picked up by Stan to go to a party that evening, so she was taking one of her lengthy baths.

Clive checked his watch and found he still had over an hour before he had to leave. With no Nicky to chat with, he chose to use the time to go over his plans for the meeting, so he went through to the lounge with a cup of coffee and his notes. It was starting to snow a bit outside, those inconsequential indecisive flakes that drift down and make little impression on the ground. In the light from the window, he could see the front drive with a faint suggestion of snow on it. He pulled the curtains and went to sit by the fire with his drink. He silently rehearsed what he was going to say at the meeting until he had it all prepared. He felt content and warm, but he failed to see that he also felt tired, and he was soon sleeping peacefully.

"Dad, it's nearly half past six. You'll be late for your meeting," said Nicky, shaking his arm gently.

Clive stretched slowly and smiled at her as he said, "No problems, it won't take me long to get to Sally's. I must say I feel completely refreshed after that nap. I've never looked forward to a meeting so much in my entire life. Bring on Sleaze Ball Hodge!"

The headlights shining through the closed curtains announced the arrival of a visitor.

"That must be Stan," observed Nicky. "He's early, bless him."

Nicky quickly made her way through to the kitchen to meet Stan, and Clive, having picked up his papers and his empty mug, followed her. In the kitchen, Clive was surprised to see Stan dusting copious amounts of snow off his dinner jacket and stamping his feet to dislodge further snow from his shoes onto the doormat.

"Evening, Mr Sullivan. Your garden is looking rather pretty now," commented Stan.

"Evening, Stan. Yes, I noticed it was trying to snow earlier."

"Well, I think it's trying a bit too hard at the moment," replied the young man, pointing towards the window that overlooked the lawn. "Some of the minor roads are getting clogged already."

Clive went over to the window and peered out. Through the mass of large falling flakes, he could see the series of white mounds that had previously been his garden. He estimated it at three inches deep and still falling heavily. Clive felt a slight panic setting in. He knew that even slight flurries of snow could soon make some of the local minor roads very difficult, and this was considerably more than a flurry. The prospect of taking out the Rolls in such conditions and the possibility of the roads getting worse as more snow fell caused Clive to feel distinctly apprehensive.

"How are Sally and I going to get to the meeting now?" he moaned. "If we can't get there, Hodge will assume he can just push his plan through."

"No problem, Mr Sullivan, I can get you there in the Land Rover if you like. How long is the meeting likely to last?"

"We should start at half past seven, and I calculate the business will be concluded by a quarter to eight at the very latest," replied Clive as his hopes of avoiding a disaster rose slightly.

"Easy. If we set off now, we can pick up Sally from her place, we can get there in plenty of time, and I can wait to pick you up afterwards," suggested Stan.

"Bunnykins, you are a hero; if Nicky won't marry you, I might," enthused Clive. "Just wait while I get my coat."

Clive clambered into the front of the Land Rover alongside Stan, and they were soon making steady progress. In most of the side roads, there was little evidence of traffic tracks in the snow, and the Land Rover coped easily with it. Sally was more than a little surprised when her transport arrived, but she was relieved to see that Clive had managed to get through. The snow continued to fall heavily, and the elementary windscreen wipers did well to enable Stan to see what was ahead. The town was relatively quiet near the meeting room, and Stan was able to pull up and park within a few yards of the door, and they still had five minutes to spare.

"We shouldn't be long, Stan," said Clive. "We'll be out as soon as we can. It will be a bit cold sitting around out here; you could have done with a coat over that dinner jacket."

"That's OK, Mr Sullivan, I'll be fine. Smart suit this, wouldn't do to cover it up with my old coat."

"If it gets too cold, you could stand inside the foyer," suggested Sally. "At least it will be a little warmer."

Sally and Clive gingerly made their way through the snow to the door of the Co-op building where they turned and waved to Stan. In the tiny foyer, they were surprised to be confronted by Councillor Hodge in person, who was standing on the bottom step of the stairs that went up to the meeting room and next to him was Mr Tennett. Between them, they were effectively barring access to the meeting.

"I rather guessed that you two would be turning up," announced the offensive councillor. "Well, you've got a nerve, and you've wasted your time because you're not allowed to attend the meeting, so I'll bid you goodnight."

"An interesting, if incorrect, interpretation of the situation," observed Clive. "But tell me, why exactly do you feel you have the right to deny us entry?"

"The pair of you cannot legitimately attend a meeting as employees because you are suspended," explained a defiant Hodge with more than a suggestion of triumph in his voice.

"Just one little point of order, Mr Chairman," announced Clive. "We are not suspended; we decided to take some of our annual holiday."

Hodge was beginning to look a little flustered, but he was not prepared to give way. He still felt he had the upper hand, and he certainly had the upper step. "That may be your interpretation of the situation, but as chairman I can decide who attends the meetings, and I've decided you don't."

"I am sure you will concede that you cannot overrule a motion passed by the steering committee at their last meeting," interjected Sally. "And I quote, 'the said report should then be discussed in full at a meeting of the same members here present at a date and time to be decided by the chairman but not before two weeks has elapsed.' We were present at the last meeting, and we are back again after the elapsed period to discuss the report, so if you'll excuse us."

Sally made to ascend the stairs to the meeting room, but Hodge moved to block her. There was a farcical episode where the four people stepped from side to side as Sally and Clive tried to get up the stairs while Hodge and Tennett did all they could to stop them. This little dance might have gone on longer but for the arrival of Stan, who had decided that the foyer might indeed be warmer than the Land Rover.

"Is there a problem, Mr Sullivan?" asked Stan.

Hodge observed this latest arrival. With his enormous frame in a dinner jacket, Stan could easily have been taken for the doorman at a night club, and that is more or less what Hodge took him to be. Convinced that Clive had brought his own 'heavy', Hodge decided to concede ground, and he and Tennett turned to go upstairs.

"No problem, Stan," answered Clive, having seen Hodge's reaction. "Just hang about here if you would. We won't be long."

By the time Clive and Sally arrived in the meeting room, the committee was about ready to start the meeting. Despite the weather, there had been a good turnout. June was ready with her minute book, and she gave Clive a knowing smile when he took his seat.

"Ladies and gentlemen," started Hodge, "I am sure none of you wish to stay out long on an evening such as this. Fortunately, there is only one item on the agenda. The sole purpose of this evening's meeting is to ratify the report presented at the last meeting."

"Mr Chairman, with your permission, it's to 'discuss' the report, isn't that right, madam secretary?" asked Sally.

Before the obnoxious councillor could object, June read out the motion from the previous meeting, which supported Sally's correction. Hodge was aware that the meeting was slipping out of control, so he decided to try and reassert his authority.

"I stand corrected, Doctor Livingstone, but I am convinced that anyone who has taken the time to read the report in depth will be under no illusion as to its value."

"I think its value is beyond question," remarked Clive. "Indeed, I would go so far as to say it is very clear in what it is proposing. With your indulgence, Mr Chairman, I would like to make a comment on the report that I am sure the committee will value."

The chairman hesitated and then mumbled something to Tennett. Clive took his opportunity and continued.

"As you are personally aware, Mr Chairman, I have other business, and I am keeping a friend waiting," he said while casting his eyes in the direction of the door. Hodge knew exactly who was in the foyer downstairs, and he was more than prepared to be lenient with Clive, if only so he would leave quickly and take his minder with him.

"Very well, Mr Sullivan, but please be brief."

"Thank you, Mr Chairman. The report suggests that the association is in a dire financial situation. Despite any absolute proof of this assertion, we must allow for the possibility that it is true. The course of action suggested by the report is that Kitchener House should be sold off to free up funds. An apparently logical solution."

Hodge nodded and then tried to force what he would like to have been seen as a benign smile.

"There is however another possible way forward," continued Clive, "and it's one that I have discussed with our president, Sir Jack Stamp. Sir Jack wishes me to convey his thanks to Councillor Hodge and Mr Tennett for their illuminating work done in the report to awaken us all to the financial problems we face. He notes that the report places a suggested value of two hundred thousand pounds on Kitchener House, and he did admit that this didn't seem like a lot for such a large property in such a pleasant area. He is mindful of the fact that Councillor Hodge has connections in the business world and at the town hall, so he could see no reason to question the valuation."

Hodge was almost beaming with a sense of satisfaction and pride; he could see his plan falling neatly into place, but his moment of triumph was short-lived.

"Sir Jack acknowledges his responsibility to ensure the financial stability of the association, so he has agreed, having obtained the necessary authorisation from the full committee, to sell Kitchener House for the said price." Clive paused for a moment before dramatically concluding, "To me."

Hodge was in a state of utter consternation and had some difficulty in thinking of any response, so Clive continued.

"It would not be unreasonable to suggest that two hundred thousand pounds is a paltry sum to pay for such a lovely house, and I am sure I'm not alone in feeling that none of us here would wish to take advantage of the association by paying a price that is so obviously below its true market value. So, having bought the property, I intend to lease it back to the association at an annual rent of one pound on an indefinite lease."

There was a spontaneous ripple of applause from those around the table. Sally leant over and said very quietly, "You certainly kept that quiet, you dark horse."

As if to respond to her comment, Clive addressed the meeting again. "I am sorry to have to spring this on you all in this way, but I only received confirmation that the deal had been agreed a short time ago. I am sure that we are all feeling a lot happier knowing that the future of Kitchener House is assured. Thank you for your attention, and now, if you would excuse my colleague and I, we have another meeting to attend."

Sally and Clive left the room with the goodwill wishes of most of those present, and they rejoined Stan in the foyer.

"That was quick," observed Stan. "Good meeting?"

"Bloody brilliant!" answered Sally. "Thanks to this darling of a man. He's just considerably reduced the chances of the Sleaze Ball Hodge having a good Christmas. So how did you set it all up, Clive?"

"I'll explain it all when we can find somewhere a little warmer. But that depends a lot on Stan," answered Clive before asking Stan, "Could you possibly run us back to my place, Stan, and then drop Sally off later on your way out to your party?"

"That's not a problem. It's still not eight, and we don't want to arrive too early anyway."

As the Land Rover and its occupants made their way through the relatively quiet streets, Clive knew that Sally was longing to find out what he had been up to, and he rather enjoyed keeping her in suspense. The snow had stopped by the time they got home and made their way into the kitchen, where Nicky was surprised to see them back so early. No sooner had they got into the house than Sally said, "Hi Nicky, you are about to hear how your wonderful, adorable father has managed to stitch up Hodge."

"Steady on, Sally, it was only a business deal that I managed to negotiate," declared Clive modestly.

"So why don't we each take a glass of wine through to the lounge and find out just how my adorable father managed it?" suggested Nicky.

A few minutes later, the group were settled in the lounge, awaiting Clive's explanation as to how he had achieved his masterstroke.

"To put you in the picture," started Clive, "I had a meeting with old Pearson in Hull about the financial settlement for your mother, and while I was there, I discussed the possibility of purchasing Kitchener House and then leasing it back to the association for a peppercorn rent.

"I then met up with Sir Jack Stamp and outlined the benefits to the association, who would gain two hundred thousand pounds, but they are guaranteed the lease on the place for one pound a year in perpetuity. The arrangement stipulates that the association are responsible for the upkeep of the building and for all the rates and service charges. Sir Jack obviously had to get the OK from the rest of the committee, and he told me this morning that it is all settled."

"That's extremely generous of you, Dad. In effect, you give them the money, and all you get back is a token one pound per year," observed Nicky.

"As I explained to Sir Jack, the association rent the house and the ground it is set in, but I have purchased all that plus the plot behind Kitchener's rear garden that backs onto Charlton Road. That plot of land is mine, and in time I could, possibly, get a reasonable return on it."

"So why didn't you just buy the plot of land?" asked Sally. "And then the association would still have had some cash, and it would have thwarted Hodge."

"True," conceded Clive. "But Pearson explained that by setting up the proposed lease as a form of trust it will make the future purchase of Kitchener House more complicated and thus less attractive to people like Hodge. Sir Jack knows that hell would freeze over before I sold the other plot of land to Hodge, and Sir Jack would do just about anything to thwart him. To further annoy the sleazy councillor, Sir Jack has persuaded the rest of his committee that he can see little point in going ahead with the disciplinary meeting next week. He argued that it was inappropriate to press ahead with such unsubstantiated allegations, particularly with someone who wishes to be a benefactor."

"So we don't need to go to the silly meeting?" asked Sally.

"No, and I think Sir Jack is looking forward to communicating the information to Hodge along with a suggestion that Sleaze Ball might wish to stand down from the chairmanship. Sir Jack will point out to Hodge that there is nothing to be gained by being on the committee now that the scheme to close Kitchener has been exposed."

The group sat and chatted for a while, during which Clive had felt obliged to outline to Sally the arrangement he had made with Maureen. He hadn't intended to do so, but Nicky made a point of bringing the matter into the conversation. Clive recognised that this was a subtle attempt to match him up with Sally, but he still had to give some account of what he had done.

Sally had expressed genuine sorrow for his situation, and then the issue had thankfully been dropped. It was Stan who recognised that he and Nicky ought to be going to the party, so he announced, "Sorry to break this up, but we have to go. So if you want to grab your coat, Sally, we'll get you home."

"Why doesn't Sally stay over here tonight, Dad?" asked Nicky before adding, "She could sleep in the spare room, and then we could have time for a good long chat over breakfast."

Clive immediately saw through her plans to engineer a situation where he was alone with Sally, and he was mindful of Sally's comments about the way people were intent upon trying to find partners for her, so he quickly replied, "I'm sure that Sally would like to get back to her own place, and anyway I'm not going to be good company tonight. It's been a long, eventful, and tiring day, and I'm bushed."

Sally picked up on his reluctance to try and persuade her to stay and simply said, "Your dad's right, and we've got a big social event tomorrow at the pub. The Kitchener House Christmas party."

Sally rose quickly, kissed Clive on the cheek and said, "It's been a fantastic day, Clive, thank you. I'll see you at the Prince William tomorrow night. I'm really in the Christmas mood now."

When the others had left, Clive sat down to finish his glass of wine. It had indeed been an eventful day and one that he had enjoyed. In his mind, he replayed his demolition of Hodge's plans to close Kitchener House. It had been a well-implemented ploy that had gone well, so why did he have the feeling that the day had not gone quite as well as it might? He had neatly managed to foil Nicky's attempt to arrange for Sally to stay over, but he wouldn't have minded at all if Sally had appeared a little more willing to be persuaded to stay. On the other hand, she had made it quite clear that she didn't like people trying to match her up with every available male in the area. It was this thought that reminded Clive that he was now, or soon would be, a single person again. He contemplated what difference this made to his life. Did he intend to stay a single unit, or was he going to make himself available for some lucky woman? He thought about his track record for attracting women when he was single; it wasn't good. As a young man, he had never been good at the romance thing; he'd had a couple of girlfriends when he was at school but the truth was that they had picked him up, as had Maureen. In those days, he had been in reasonable shape with good job prospects, but now all he had was a lot of money, and he had discovered that this didn't necessarily attract the kind of attention that he wanted. Once again, Clive realised that he was quite good at the business side of life, but when it came to the personal side he was less than proficient.

CHAPTER TWENTY-SEVEN

Clive didn't sleep well that night. He found himself trying to sort out his elusive life plan. He didn't expect to get it all mapped out in a few hours, but it would help if he had some rudimentary plan of action, but he hadn't. The following morning, he had been up and had finished breakfast before Nicky came down.

"Morning, Dad. Sleep well?"

"Morning. Not that well, I'm afraid. I seem to have a lot on my mind, but I'm steadily getting things sorted. How was the party?"

"It was OK, but a lot of people from university couldn't make it because of the weather. It was a shame because it was already starting to thaw by the time we left.

"It was very kind of Stan to give us a lift to the meeting. His presence in the building really intimidated Hodge, who obviously thought I'd brought a bit of extra muscle in case things turned nasty. I suppose I should have made it clear that Stan is a really nice guy and not one for throwing his weight around, but somehow it slipped my mind."

"You don't mean you used dear Bunnykins to frighten the councillor? That's a bit naughty, Dad."

"I know, but I've learned to live with the guilt."

"It's a pity Sally couldn't stay over," commented Nicky. "You could have had a chance to get to know each other better, away from work."

"Nicky, I can see what you are trying to do, and so can Sally. She, or rather we, don't want to be coerced into anything by other people. We are friends; we get on very well, but please don't try and make anything more of it."

"Sorry, Dad. It's just that you obviously get on so well with Sally. You seem so comfortable in each other's company."

"I know you don't mean to interfere, Nicky, but consider how you would feel if I was pressuring you to marry Stan. You get on well with him, and you are both 'comfortable in each other's company', so why not marry him? If I ever intend to become romantically attached to anyone, then I will go about it in my own way and in my own time and with the person of my choice."

"I know you're right, Dad, but you're not exactly good at that sort of thing. Sometimes you need a bit of encouragement, a bit of a shove."

"I admit I'm a bit out of practice, but sometimes we just have to learn through experience."

Nicky realised that she couldn't arrange her father's life for him, so she kissed him on the cheek and said teasingly, "You're right, Dad. So do you mean, if I marry Stan, you will see more of Sally?"

"Nicky!" he replied with mock severity before adding, "Perhaps I would promise to ask Sally to accompany me to your wedding in the unlikely event of your marrying him, but in the meantime, do we agree not to try and run each other's lives?"

"It's a deal, Dad."

Sebastian was later than usual coming down to breakfast. He tried to be at the showrooms early on Saturdays as it was usually the peak selling day, but in the run-up to Christmas the trade was very slow.

"Morning, Dad, Nicky. It was a bit tricky getting home last night in the snow, but it's virtually cleared now," he said, before adding, I've got a car lined up for my Christmas present, Dad, if it's OK with you?"

"So what is it this time?" asked Clive, preparing himself for the worst.

"Nothing flash or too speedy. It's an Audi. It is a standard car, not customised or altered in any way. It is rather smart, and it will go fast in the wrong hands, but it is basically a very smart, classy car."

"Sounds good," commented Clive warily, "but it doesn't sound like your usual model of choice. Why that particular car?"

"To be honest, it's just too good a deal to miss. Someone traded it in against a new car. The trade is so flat that they didn't get a great deal on it, and I have the chance to get it, at trade, almost three thousand below list price. It's a quality car, smart and comfortable with low mileage. What do you think, Dad?"

"Sounds very reasonable, but don't expect me to gift wrap it," replied Clive. "You'd better get it organised."

"Thanks, Dad, I'm on my way," said an elated Sebastian before kissing his sister on the cheek and rushing off to close the deal.

A rather bemused Nicky watched him depart before commenting, "He's a happy soul this morning."

"Yes, and I think it could be a good day all round; it's the big party tonight. Speaking of which, I have to get down to the pub at lunchtime to arrange a few details for this evening. What have you got planned for today?"

"Not a lot. I thought I might nip over to Stan's place and ask him to marry me."

"Best of luck. When I offered to marry him last night, he didn't seem too keen. On a more practical level, I would be grateful if you could give some thought as to the arrangements for Christmas. I suspect your mum will feel more comfortable staying at Josslyn's, but we need to have something planned for us."

"With everything else going on, I had almost lost sight of the fact that it's nearly Christmas. I'll talk it over with Bunnykins."

"Great, and now if you'll excuse me, I have to get to the Prince William."

Clive looked out at the garden and noticed that the snow had largely gone, so he decided to risk taking his bike to the pub. He packed his shoulder bag with a few presents for the pub raffle, bid goodbye to Nicky and set off.

The Prince William had undergone its annual transformation with an assortment of Christmas decorations and a rather large tree, which Mrs Beer Bill was in the process of dressing as Clive arrived.

"This is all looking rather festive," observed Clive, looking around the room, "I must say I like the fact that your decorations never go up too early."

"It's policy," said the landlord's wife. "I can't stand it when the shops try to persuade you to start Christmas shopping by playing carols over the sound system in October. It's just not right. Christmas is special, and any attempt to spread it over a few months only dilutes the magic. Are you all set for the party tonight?"

"Yes. I've brought a couple of extra prizes that we can arrange to be 'won' tonight. I've wrapped them and attached special raffle tickets to them so we will know which the extras are."

"Fair enough. Just pop them behind the bar next to the till, and Bernard will keep an eye on them until the draw."

Clive felt it strange to hear the landlord being referred to by his real name but dutifully placed the extra prizes as directed.

"Is there anything else that I can help out with?" asked Clive.

"You could give Bernard a hand to rearrange the tables for tonight," replied the landlady. "We need somewhere to stack the prizes and somewhere to put the raffle drum. If you can do that, I can sort out the table for our special party. How many of you will there be tonight?"

"The three VIP guests, June, who will technically be with them as staff, plus me and Sally."

"That lovely young girl you went to Hull with? That's nice! So, that's six to dine?"

Clive was a bit dismayed to hear Sally still being viewed as his girlfriend but didn't bother to correct the misapprehension.

"That would be great, thank you. I bet the family are looking forward to it as we speak; it's a central part of their Christmas. Conrad will be sitting there already, dressed like something out of a tailor's window. Len will no doubt be having a nap in front of the fire, and Minnie will be bustling about with her pinny over one of her posher frocks, doing no end of little bits of preparation and achieving nothing."

"I've been meaning to ask," started Sheila. "Would you like us to make it possible for Conrad to have tea with his meal? We can always get a pot set up for him."

"That's a very kind thought, but despite his repeated announcements, Conrad never drinks the stuff!"

The landlord appeared from a door behind the bar and under his wife's directions, he and Clive set about arranging the tables for the party.

"Thanks a lot for that," said the landlord when the tables and chairs had been arranged for the evening. "Would you like a drink now?"

Without waiting for a reply, Beer Bill had drawn a pint and stood it on the bar. Clive went to his pocket to pay, but the landlord stopped him. "No. This is on the house, and I may join you. How about you, Sheila?"

His wife looked up from placing Christmas crackers on the table and said, "Go on then, I'm nearly finished."

"Bernard was telling me that there are plans to sell off the place where you work. We'll miss having the family in. It doesn't seem right to sell off their home," commented Sheila.

"I think we can safely say that those plans have been revised," said Clive. "The place is going to be sold but it won't be closing, and the family love coming down here. As your dear husband points out, this is the best pub in the area."

"I'm really looking forward to the do tonight," added the landlady. "It really is the high point of our Christmas. All the regulars love seeing the family enjoying the festivities. I might suggest it puts a bit of magic into the lives of all our regular idiots. Mind you, most of them still believe in Santa Clause anyway."

"You've got a great little caring pub here. You should be proud of the service you offer, and we idiots appreciate what you do."

"And the whole concern is available at a very reasonable price," offered the landlord.

"I'd love to discuss terms with you, but I've got to go and get ready for the big party. I'll be in at about six, and the main guests should be here about seven." With this, he finished off his pint, took one last look around the decorations in the bar and set off home.

Clive was more of a shower person than one for taking baths, but today he decided that he would pamper himself a little. He methodically set about collecting together his bathtime luxuries. His transistor radio, the bottle of expensive bubble bath that he had received three Christmases ago and a generous glass of whisky. He toyed with the idea of taking one of his poetry books, but he had always found it hard to hold a book comfortably in the bath without risking it getting rather damp. He was ready for luxury. As the water ran into the bath, Clive poured a rather generous amount of the bubble bath in. He wasn't sure exactly how much he should put in, but as he whisked at the water with his hand, he deduced that he may have overdone it. He soon had a dense mass of bubbles, but it smelt very nice. Clive moved some of the suds as best he could, just to check how much water was actually in the bath; there seemed to be sufficient. He switched on his radio, selected a music channel playing Christmas favourites, and put the set on the window sill. He lowered himself into the tub, sipped his whisky and enjoyed the music.

His bathtime bliss was disturbed by a knock on the door. Clive knew it was Nicky, but he couldn't hear exactly what she was saying for the music. Checking that the bubbles made an effective modesty blanket, he called for her to come in.

"Hi Dad, that smells nice. I saw Mum in the supermarket, and she asked me if I would get her black dress out for her and drop it round at Gran's place before Monday."

"Help yourself. I'm not exactly dressed to search it out myself," replied Clive, taking another sip on his whisky.

"How was your mum, by the way?"

Nicky walked over, switched off the radio and put the seat down on the toilet before sitting on it and continuing, "She seemed OK. She was in the shop to buy one or two things for the little party she is putting on for her staff on Monday. I think it's a bit of a thank you to them for sticking by her during her recent financial problems. She was telling me how much she appreciated your help recently. I know it may sound silly, but she actually looked quite happy."

"I'm pleased. Perhaps as she starts to feel more comfortable with the situation, she will be able to come round and see us all."

"I'm sure she will in time. She even hinted that she and Josslyn might drop by in the New Year."

Their conversation was interrupted by the sound of voices on the stairs and then by the sight of Sebastian and Pru in the open doorway.

"Hello, Clive darling, please don't get up," Pru greeted him cheerfully before perching on the side of the bath. "I just had a call from Maureen and she said she'd asked Nicky to deliver her black dress, so I thought I might as well save her the journey and pick it up myself. That smells lovely, what is it?" Pru picked up the bottle of bubble bath and read the label.

"Very nice. French. I thought it didn't smell like one of those that Maureen churns out," she said, putting the bottle down.

"It does smell good, Dad," added Sebastian. "It's certainly better than your usual stuff that smells like Dettol."

"I might venture to say," said Clive, "that I am delighted to hear your fulsome praise for my bubble bath. But perhaps you might like to ask some of the neighbours if they would care to come in and give their evaluation of it? That is, if they can find space in what is fast becoming the most crowded bathroom in town?"

"I can do it later if you like, Dad," continued Sebastian, ignoring his father's sarcasm. "But I just wanted to tell you that I've brought that car around to show you. It's parked outside."

"I won't come down and see it right now," answered Clive. "It's just that it's a little cold at this time of year to venture out in my current outfit."

"Perhaps we could leave you to get dressed?" suggested Nicky.

"Good idea," agreed Pru, before looking at Clive and adding, "I would get in there with you, darling, but I'm sure that perfume would clash with my Chanel."

When Clive was finally left in peace, he realised that his relaxing bath was just not going to happen, so he dried himself and put on his dressing gown before going down to meet his tormentors.

By the time he got downstairs, there was a cup of coffee waiting for him, but before he could risk a sip, Sebastian was ushering him out to look at the car he hoped to purchase.

Clive's dressing gown gave little protection from the cold, but he knew he would have to show interest.

"It actually looks like a normal car," observed Clive. "No silly spoiler on the back, no huge exhaust pipe, no go-faster stripes or anything. I must say I'm pleasantly surprised. I suspect that it could still achieve quite a turn of speed, but I'm sure that you would never want to push it too hard?"

"Of course not, Dad," replied his son in an almost believable tone. "This is the new, more mature Sebastian."

"Let's hope so. Anyway, you'd better get off and sort out the paperwork."

"Thanks, Dad, I'll look after it, promise."

"Just look after yourself. Now get on your way before I freeze to death out here."

Sebastian was delighted, and he cheerfully got into the car and, driving very sedately, he set off for the showroom to complete the deal. Clive watched his son drive off and couldn't help but wonder if the careful driving display was for his benefit; he was pretty sure it was, but he was freezing and hadn't time to worry about such things. Returning to the kitchen, Clive warmed his hands on his coffee mug and asked Nicky, "Do you and Stan have any plans for this evening?"

"We are going over to visit Stan's parents but we should be back later. It's your big Christmas raffle party tonight at the pub, isn't it? Give my love to Sally."

"Yes," added Pru. "Give her our love; she's such a nice young woman."

Clive was aware of the pressure being discreetly applied to encourage him to take more interest in Sally, and he was tempted to tell them what she had said about feeling pressured into relationships by well-meaning friends, but he didn't want to hurt them by suggesting that Sally might resent their interference.

He restricted himself to commenting, "Yes, I really enjoy working with her."

Clive was in no doubt that evening that he was not going to drive to the pub. He had been to a number of these annual events, and he knew he was likely to be having a drink. He toyed with the idea of taking his bike, but somehow even he felt that he was over-dressed for such transport. He had taken considerable care in selecting his clothes for the evening, this was becoming a habit, and he felt the overall effect wasn't too bad. He had chosen one of his better dark suits, which he wore over a new white shirt – unimaginative but smart – and he had picked out one of his special Christmas ties that he had been given by one of the girls in the paint plant. The tie wasn't one of his better decisions, but with its reindeer motif, it was seasonal even if it was unfashionably wide. In its favour was the fact that the battery in it had long since died, so it no longer emitted the strains of jingle bells when squeezed. The necessity of wearing a heavy overcoat in the cold weather meant that much of the impact of the tie was diluted, so Clive looked quite smart as he walked to the Prince William.

CHAPTER TWENTY-EIGHT

The interior of the pub looked wonderful. As well as the tree that the landlady had been decorating earlier, there were decorative streamers and countless yards of tinsel. The effect was enhanced by the fact that some of the bulbs in the wall lights had been replaced by red ones. Purists would no doubt have said there were just too many decorations, but the jumble of colour and sparkle was almost magical. Clive felt that Christmas was really here, and the power of the season to evoke memories took him back to his own childhood. As the only child of a professional couple who had married relatively late in life, he had enjoyed a comfortable childhood, and Christmases had been wonderful. These happy memories stood alongside the recollection of the Christmas Eve that his father had returned home late from the office, loosened his tie, sat down in front of a welcoming fire, dropped off to sleep and never woken up. He was the man that had often told his son, "Remember, lad, there are no pockets in a shroud," but still he had laboured on to provide for his family, and he died in harness when he could have retired years previously; the Toad of work had done for him.

Clive was unable to ignore another Christmas memory of that time in the Conservative club when he had first seen a beautiful young girl behind the bar. She was new to the job and obviously lacking in confidence as she tried to cope with the mild lechery displayed by some of the more inebriated customers. It was perhaps her air of endangered innocence that had made him feel sorry for her and gave him the courage to chat to her. In making her feel more comfortable, he had become more at ease himself and, much to his delight and surprise, she had agreed to see him again. Within months they had married, and Clive was blissfully happy. They had been good days.

Clive's nostalgic reminiscences were interrupted by the landlord asking, "So what do you think of it then?"

"It is absolutely lovely," observed Clive. "This is what pubs should be like at Christmas. It's not enough to scrawl Christmas greetings on the dartboard, wrap some tinsel round the pumps and throw up a string of fairy lights in early December. You and Sheila have done the place proud; I might even be feeling sufficiently nostalgic to buy you a drink."

The room was relatively empty. The usual early crowd would no doubt be turning up a little later as the raffle wouldn't be drawn until after eight.

"I've got your sound system linked up for the raffle," said the landlord, pointing towards a microphone standing next to a large speaker. "And I think that this year we may actually have got one that works."

Clive had somehow become the regular raffle caller and general master of ceremonies at these events and, over the years, had often had to revert to shouting as the various sound systems had whistled, crackled or just refused to work at all. He walked over to the microphone and picked it up. He switched on the amplifier unit and was pleasantly surprised that there was no scream of feedback. He held the microphone near to his mouth and tried it out. "Welcome to the seventy-seventh annual Prince William turnip raffle with plenty of pretty prizes." It was nonsense, but in the past the sounds 'S', 'T' and 'P' had proved difficult for some of the cheap systems they had used. "How's that sound, Bar Bill?"

The landlord raised a thumb in Clive's direction; for once the system seemed to work, so Clive switched it off and set about checking that the rest of the equipment for the evening was ready. He had just finished sorting the prizes and ensuring they were all accounted for and settled for a well-earned pint when the Kitchener party arrived.

It was quite clear that the group had made a great effort to dress up for the occasion. Conrad was in his best suit with a perfectly matching shirt and tie, Minnie had selected a rather smart flowery frock and even Len was wearing a suit, although he didn't look particularly comfortable in it, and he gave the impression that he was wearing it under duress, which he probably was. Sally and June had also obviously taken some time to prepare for the evening, and both of them were elegantly dressed and with make-up that went far beyond the quick application of lippy and eye shadow. Clive honestly felt that if they hadn't turned up with the Kitchener group, then he wouldn't have recognised them. Clive was pleased that he had made the effort to dress for the evening, but even he would concede that he wasn't in their class.

He walked over to greet them, and his usual less-than-effusive comment was, "You two look nice." He knew it was an understatement, but in his unprepared state it was the best he could manage, and as he escorted the group over to their table and set about ordering drinks, he found it difficult to take his eyes off Sally. She had looked very smart on the day they had gone to Hull, and she had looked more than presentable at Pru's cocktail party, but this was something else. Even to Clive's untrained eye, it was obvious that she had done something with her hair. He had come to realise over the weeks that she was an attractive woman, but now he could see what she could achieve if she really put her mind to it. Perhaps this was one of those painted women his mother had warned him about? But what did his mother know anyway? All the extra effort that Sally had put into her appearance didn't so much hide as enhance those very qualities that Clive found so attractive; that wonderful natural smile and those eyes that effortlessly expressed such sincerity and a genuine empathy for the feelings of others.

Clive looked at the family sitting around the table. He had been arranging these regular events with the pub for years, and he still found it most enjoyable and loved to watch the reactions of the family to the evening. The meal was duly delivered, crackers pulled, and weak riddles and jokes exchanged. Poppers were popped and toasts made. Eventually the meal was finished, and the group sat around the table chatting and laughing together and joining in with some of the carols that were being sung by the assembled crowd. It never failed to impress Clive how the collected voices around the bar, some of whom had indulged in a glass or two of cheer, could still sound so moving as they sang some of the songs of his childhood Christmases. He looked around the table at his friends. Conrad's sartorial elegance was now topped with a miniature bowler hat on an elastic string, Len was enjoying a glass of whisky and his usual banter with Minnie, who was also busying herself helping to clear the remnants of the meal.

"That was lovely, Clive. Thanks for setting it up," said June., "So when is your famous raffle?"

Clive looked around the room, which was quite full now. The plan to eat early had been a good one. "A few more minutes and then it's all go," he answered.

"Aren't you a bit hot in that tie?" asked Sally, pointing at the dated Christmas adornment that he had chosen to wear.

"A little," he confessed. "Would you ladies mind if I took it off?"

"Not at all," replied Sally, glad that her ruse to dispense with the offending article had worked, "After all, I have seen you in less formal attire. Do they serve Bull's Bitter here, by the way?"

"Oh, how I wish I could be a Bull's babe," sighed June, who had obviously heard more of the hotel incident than he would have wished.

The memory of the emergency sleepwear in Hull was hard to suppress, and Clive was sure he must be blushing. He stuffed the tie into his pocket and said, "I'd best be getting on with the raffle. I shouldn't be too long."

Clive made his way to the microphone and got the proceedings underway.

"Good evening, ladies, gentlemen, and assorted Bills. And now for the main event of the night; the Prince William raffle."

There was a mixture of applause and good-hearted jeers from the customers.

"Before we start, I would like to wish you all good luck except Jock. I have been asked by mine host Beer Bill to tell Jock that if he dares to win as many prizes as last year, then he won't leave the pub in one piece."

There was a cry of "English racists!" in a Welsh accent from near the bar.

And now, getting straight on with the business," continued Clive, "our first winner of the evening is number 96."

There was a pause while Sheila checked the list to find who had chosen the winning number before relaying the name to Clive, who announced, "Number 96, the winner of a rather splendid bottle of whisky is Duck Bill."

The winner's name was written next to the appropriate prize on the winner's sheet, and the proceedings continued with Clive keeping up a running commentary, cracking a few jokes along the way and generally keeping the crowd entertained. When half the prizes had been allocated, Clive announced, "Now for our special draw, ladies and gentlemen."

Clive rummaged around in the raffle drum and pretended to draw out a ticket.

"Number 237."

Sheila looked at her list, which she knew only went up to 200, and pretended to whisper a name for Clive.

"And this one is going to," Clive paused for dramatic effect, "someone on the top table tonight. Our own Yorkshire Len."

The assembled crowd applauded as Len came forward to receive his surprise. He took a parcel from Sheila and kissed her before taking the microphone from Clive. Len stood for a couple of seconds before making his comment.

"Eh by gum, this must be t'best bloody pub in town; I don't even recall putting up the brass for the ticket. Tha's all grand pals. Thank thee, and ha' thisens a merry Christmas."

As Len returned to his seat, Clive 'drew out' number 206, and after a few words from the landlady, he announced, "A very special winner again, our very own Minnie. Minnie looked round the dinner table in disbelief and had to be encouraged to go up for her prize. She took the wrapped present from Clive, who lowered the microphone so that she might be able to say a few words and an expectant hush fell on the crowd.

"Thank you all so much for this lovely evening. It's so nice to spend time with friends and family at this time of year, and when you don't have a lot of family like me," she said, barely holding back a tear, "then friends are extra important. Merry Christmas to you all, and thank you again."

Minnie returned to her table to the accompaniment of warm applause, and Clive quickly said, "Number 212."

After Sheila once more pretended to check her list, she whispered something to him, and he proclaimed, "And this special prize goes to…" Clive paused before looking over to his table of friends and announcing, "Conrad."

There was a cheer from the entire pub as Conrad briskly got to his feet and bustled to the prize draw area to receive a small, brightly wrapped gift. He was obviously delighted at his good luck, and leaning over to the microphone, he gave his gracious acceptance speech, "I'd love a cup of tea," before returning to his seat to the accompaniment of warm applause and good-humoured cheers.

"If I could crave your indulgence for a few more moments, ladies and gentlemen," continued Clive, "we have two other people who mean a great deal to me. Two beautiful young women who in their different ways have made my life a lot easier over the past few weeks. June, there. You wouldn't tell from her sweet and lovely appearance, but with her scheming, devious ways, she has helped us to thwart a certain local councillor's plans to sell off the house where Len, Minnie and Conrad live. She has been our mole, forewarning us of the intentions of Sleaze Ball Hodge." Clive waited for the booing to subside before continuing. "And I love her for it. So the winner of prize number 630 is June."

June was obviously surprised, but Conrad and Len pushed her gently in the direction of Clive, where she was further surprised as he kissed and hugged her affectionately while the crowd applauded. She was still dazed when she got back to her seat with her prize just in time to hear Clive announce, "And now we come to the woman who has become known to one and all as 'my attractive young girlfriend'." There was a cheer from the collected Bills.

"That reporter who found us in our famous 'love nest' in Hull could have had no idea how much trouble he would cause. I can see why people could have had their suspicions. As I look at her there now, stunningly beautiful, and I reflect on the kindness and warmth she has in abundance for those around her, I think, had the circumstances been different, it wouldn't have been difficult to fall for her. She has stood by me over the last few weeks when things have been, to say the least, a bit complicated in my life, and I thank her for it. So, ticket number 812, Sally."

Clive held out her prize, and Sally was encouraged to go up and collect it. He kissed her gently and whispered, "Thank you," in her ear. Sally returned to her seat, and Clive continued announcing the winners of the remaining raffle prizes. Shortly after calling out the last winner, Clive concluded by saying, "Congratulations to all our winners tonight. I'm sure the others will forgive you. To make sure there are no losers, I have put a few pounds behind the bar, and I would like you all to take a drink with me."

With the cheers still ringing out, Clive made his way back to his table. Conrad was already showing off his new cufflinks, and Minnie was delighted with her brooch. Len was sitting with his new flat cap on and expressing his appreciation of it to anyone who would listen.

"Well!" exclaimed June, "I wasn't expecting that, but thank you so much, this is gorgeous."

She held out her arm to show off the silver bracelet she had been given.

"Yes, they are beautiful," added Sally, showing off the similar bracelet she was wearing. She was very quiet for a moment before asking, "So, who was that with the microphone? You were a different person. What happened to the tongue-tied, quiet, lacking-in-confidence Clive?"

"Yes," said June. "Who was that charmer?"

"It's different when I have to put on a show like that. It's still me, but I am just playing a part; it's rehearsed, and I can control it. I've got all the lines. I even rehearse my ad-libs because I can generally predict how people are going to react. I don't have to respond to things others have to say or to decide what they mean. It's like acting."

"So, were you just saying the words? Was it all a show, make-believe?" asked Sally.

"No. It's all true, but it's rather like getting someone else to say the words for me."

"The 'two beautiful young women' bit was genuine then?" asked June with a knowing look at Sally.

"And the 'stunningly beautiful'?" asked Sally.

Clive felt he was getting out of his depth. Clive the showman would have prepared something to say, but not Clive the socially challenged, so he was pleased to note that Conrad was looking a little tired.

"It looks like Conrad needs to be getting to his bed soon or he'll be asleep in the pub," he commented.

"You're right," said June. "I think I'd better be getting these three home."

"I'll come along and give you a hand," offered Sally.

"Thanks, but no thanks, I can manage fine. Anyway, I think you two deserve a bit of extra time here, and I'm sure that you have a lot to talk about." With this, she stood up and leaned over to kiss Clive, taking the opportunity to whisper, "Don't mess it up, Clive."

June gathered her group together, and with many cries of seasonal goodwill they left the pub.

Clive and Sally sat for a few minutes in silence, watching the crowd enjoying themselves, while Clive tried to work out the exact meaning of June's cryptic message.

"You were very different tonight," observed Sally. "But it was just a sort of act?"

"After this last month, I don't know when life is real or when I'm in some sort of tragi-comic pantomime. I find I was part of a marriage that was a charade, and I seem to be the only one who wasn't aware of it. People are putting on a show all the time and I don't realise it. We had an innocent drink with that reporter, and then he screwed my life up further with his article. Why doesn't life come with an instruction manual? Why aren't the bad guys made to wear black hats? Why does life have to be so complicated?"

"It's the same for all of us, Clive. People are complicated; they do unpredictable things, and so we have to muddle through. There's no script; we may learn to get it right more often than we get it wrong, but we all make mistakes."

"I'd just like to get it right once in a while."

"Come on, Clive; don't start feeling sorry for yourself. I think you've done very well over the last few weeks, so give yourself some credit. You've sorted out your marriage and your wife's business and saved Kitchener House. And at the same time, you have coped with the pressures of inheriting a lot of money. That's not bad going!"

"I couldn't have managed any of that without friends like you," declared Clive in an unusual display of candour. "And then I find that friendship threatened because well-intentioned relatives upset you by trying to match us up."

"Upset! Who said I was upset? As I said at the time, I think it is very sweet that they are concerned for your happiness. I know I said I got a bit fed up with the constant attempts to find me a man, but that was just a general observation."

"You weren't offended by Nicky and Pru trying to get us together?"

"Not at all. I looked upon my friends' attempts to find me a partner as being akin to the infinite number of monkeys on typewriters. If they worked at it long enough, there was a chance that they'd produce a good result, my own complete works of Shakespeare, but the final decision would be mine and his. I like Nicky and Pru a lot; I value their judgement and appreciate their efforts on my behalf. Not to put too fine a point on it, I think you are probably the nearest thing to my complete works in years. So no, I am not upset."

Clive tried his very best to tease out exactly what was being said. He daren't hope that this meant Sally really liked him, this lovely woman who made him feel good just by being around. The one whose giggle he adored. As ever, he couldn't think of anything to say; the moment was too important to mess it up. He didn't know what to say, but he knew a man who did.

"Shall I compare thee to a summer's day? Thou art more lovely and more temperate," he said. He waited for a response.

"That's lovely," she said, leaning forward and kissing him. "So was that Clive speaking or someone else?"

"That was definitely me, but I had one hell of a scriptwriter." He leaned forward and kissed her.

"Have you got a secret supply of bottled Hull air? You're full of surprises tonight," she remarked before adding," Very nice surprises, though. So, what now?"

"Well, I am a man of my word, and I did say, only a few weeks ago, that if I did come into a lot of money, I would whisk you off for a romantic stay in Withernsea, and I am very pleased to confirm that the offer still stands."

"Ah! The promised delights of Withernsea. No seaside resort has ever sounded so attractive."

"Yes. But not now. Tonight, I think I should take you home to see if they approve of you, and who knows, maybe Nicky will try to persuade you to stay over? And this time, I don't feel inclined to object to the idea."

ABOUT THE AUTHOR

Born in Hull in 1949, I went to Beverley Grammar School and then drifted into a teaching career. My first post was at a comprehensive school in Grimsby, where I ultimately became head of religious education, despite being an atheist and the only member of staff who was excused attendance at the morning assembly. I then took a complete change of direction by moving to a school based in what was then a long-stay hospital for people with learning difficulties. Set on the edge of the moors above Todmorden, this dark, forbidding institution had been the old workhouse, and there were still a few elderly residents who had been there since it was still operating as such. Shortly after my arrival at the hospital, I saw the early attempts to close such large institutions and to promote a policy of Care in the Community. I witnessed how the initiative was implemented, with variable degrees of success. Three of the major characters in this book, while only loosely based on individuals, have their literary origins in those days. Now living near Winchester, I took early retirement after over 30 years teaching in special education. I still regard this as the best career move I ever made.

Milton Keynes UK
Ingram Content Group UK Ltd.
UKHW010301010624
443378UK00001B/25

9 781803 819044